SLOW DANCE

ON THE FAULT LINE

donald rawley

Slow dance on the fault line

Flamingo
An Imprint of HarperCollins*Publishers*

This collection is entirely a work of fiction.
The names, characters and incidents portrayed in it
are the work of the author's imagination. Any resemblance to
actual persons, living or dead, events or localities is
entirely coincidental.

Flamingo
An Imprint of HarperCollins*Publishers*
77–85 Fulham Palace Road,
Hammersmith, London W6 8JB

Published by Flamingo 1997
1 3 5 7 9 8 6 4 2

A catalogue record for this book
is available from the British Library

ISBN 0 00 225624 X

Set in Fairfield Light by
Rowland Phototypesetting Ltd, Bury St Edmunds, Suffolk

Printed and bound by
Caledonian International Book Manufacturing Ltd, Glasgow

Perhaps there are more haunted houses in Los Angeles than in any other city in the world. They are haunted by the fears of their former owners. They smell of divorce, broken contracts, studio politics, bad debts, false friend-ship, adultery, extravagance, whiskey and lies. Every closet hides the poor little ghost of a stillborn reputation. 'Go away,' it whispers, 'go back to where you came from. There is no room here. I was vain and greedy. They flattered me. I failed. You will fail. Go away.'

CHRISTOPHER ISHERWOOD

Certain of these stories have been previously published:

'DeMarco's Jazz' in *Rain City Review*, Spring 1993, Volume 1, Number 2

'A Thief in August' in *Buzz*, June/July 1993

'Rattlesnake Season' in *Tales from the Heart*, Summer 1994

'Nirvana Drive' in *Buzz*, September 1995

'Samba' in *Buzz*, December 1994

'Scheherazade in Hollywood' in *New Yorker*, November 1994

'The Black Cadillac' in *Moon*, January 1996, Volume 2, Number 1

'Slow Dance on the Fault Line' in *Yellow Silk*, Winter 1993

'Honey Carter' in *Genre*, February 1996

'The Secret Names of Whores' in *Press*, Summer 1996

'Shalimar' in *Mindscapes*, Spring 1992, Volume 2, Number 1

'The Fire of Bells' in *The Hawk*, Winter/Spring 1996, Volume 1, Number 3

For John, Ginger, Samantha,
Amy Jo and Renee,
who kept me afloat during rough seas.

contents

demarco's jazz

IT WAS AS THOUGH the trees around the house had been planted by fire. Their branches were twisted with crippled black arms and tropical berries that looked poisonous under waxed flowers. Italian cypress, so easy to grow in Los Angeles, stuck out in neat rows, wind bent at vulgar angles and hiding things that flew. Its hedges were voluptuous as an old French bed, pulsing with fat roses that spilled over a short front lawn of pink and white gravel.

Catherine saw that nothing had changed. Except the silence of the street. Apartment buildings hovered on both sides of the house and signs everywhere were in Korean. But through her taxicab window she could see the LA sun, barren as a discount yellow light bulb, still hit the house at an angle that kept most of it in shade. It was in this shade she had last known her mother, and throughout her adult years would try to remember its essence; how it caught her in half light and no light turning away from Catherine into a life Catherine would never know.

The house had been home to a fine first family of Italians whose address was Adams Boulevard and would never change until a third generation decided San Francisco was a safer place; they had been in the same hotel as the Black Dahlia the night she was murdered and there was talk at church of a second one to come. Suddenly the house was divorced and alone. It was a solid dark wood house somewhere between

3

stone and brick, Roman and French; it was Los Angeles baroque and meant to fall into ruin.

After World War II it was converted to a better apartment house for people who were in pictures, studying real estate or betting at the track. Slowly the house began to unravel like Christmas ribbon stored too long, calmly baking an invisible face. But inside there was jazz and perfume, primitive televisions and radio prayer programs, Scotch bottles with cork tops and the understood menace of too quiet nights and vacant rooms whose furniture never changed.

Catherine had lived here in 1950 in her thirteenth year and now she was fifty-three, as plump and well-heeled as only widows can be. She had come back to the house to see DeMarco's room, if the hall still smelled the same, the wood a mixture of lemon and stale oil, the red and gold wallpaper stained by a roof leak, the attic hall and the one apartment door. She paid the cabby and soon stood on the front porch, covered now in brick linoleum and counted the room numbers to see if they had been cut up further in forty years. They had not. The third floor attic flat with a hidden skylight was still number fifteen. Mr DeMarco's room.

Her mother was a black actress who worked as an extra and in bits in *Cabin In The Sky* and *New Orleans*; as a maid in countless Bs at Republic, comedy shorts at Hal Roach and later as a Nubian slave in ten years of biblical epics at MGM. Her name was Clarisse, and she kept autographed pictures from all the directors, never the stars, of every picture she worked on. Even the directors who weren't famous. Their obscurity was a sanctity in her mother's eyes as it meant they too had a story much like hers and each story was memorized for telling again when mornings were too bright and the check hadn't come in the mail.

Clarisse wore only yellow, chain-smoked English Ovals and daily denounced the church as a waste of time, religion holding black people back, keeping them docile and believing in miracles that wouldn't come. She wore French perfume, 'My Sin' by Lanvin, and after two marriages, both to Catherine's father, dated only white men. Clarisse explained to Catherine they were good for her career but they would never marry her. But the gifts rolled in on a regular basis and there was always a small bar cart with English gin, cigars and cards that would be rolled out as Catherine would be sent to the movies downtown.

Catherine never went to the movies because she worked on so many when the money got tight. It was a pattern most of her childhood; Clarisse would call in sick for her at school and sometimes for a week Catherine would be walking through sets from pictures that lasted a day in the theatres, avoiding other extras with their wide ties and backgammon games. Catherine would look at her sudden breasts in ornate plaster of Paris mirrors on rollers in between sets or try on high heels heaped in wood boxes. She knew how the magic was made. When Clarisse dressed up with her girlfriends to go see one of her pictures, pointing to her bit and smiling, Catherine would take the bus to Venice Beach and walk, letting the wind blow her dress around. Men had begun to look and she had begun to look back.

It seemed to her they existed to build and sweat. Their necks were beautiful and tough, like an animal when its fur bristles. And their smell was both a warning and a hand of many colors. But for Catherine the colors were still gray matter and she did not believe in romance. Love perhaps, but not romance. Such things were best left to women like her mother who never land a lead.

It seemed the year Catherine spent here was on the set or resting in the first floor apartment of the house. It had been the library, mahogany paneled and possessing a coffered ceiling of inlaid woods and strips of actual onyx stone, it was rumored, by the same craftsmen who made the Babylonian city of D.W. Griffith's *Intolerance*. Bits of wood were always falling on the floor and Catherine saved them in a waffle box to make into a necklace someday. Everything though was a someday, except for her escapes to the Pacific and the evidence that she was already taller than her mother. Her breasts were already twice her mother's size and sometimes they hurt. Clarisse would not allow her to shave under her arms yet, saying it was all too much for a girl of thirteen. Catherine loved her legs. They were long and well-formed, according to the magazines she read. They looked best when arched to a high high heel. Clarisse had tiny titties and skinny legs that made any shoe she wore look like swim fins. She was only five foot and her head was too big for her body. But her face was always perfectly made up, the hair Marcelled and her nails long and painted pink or jungle red. Clarisse explained everything as an act of the camera.

'It absorbs the face, honey, and that's all that matters. Remember, Catherine, you go through life and it's all above the table interest. Men and cameras look at your face first, your lips. How you smoke a cigarette.' She stubbed her cigarettes out on anything except wood.

'You see, I'm made for pictures. You'll be a nice looking girl, but not for the movies like me. Look at your chest. You

6

look like every other colored chick out there. Ready for kids and laundry.' Clarisse put her false eyelashes on first thing, before coffee. Her voice, short of a squeal and soft, would then get almost guttural.

'As long as you don't get caught with a man anything like your father.'

It was a rehearsed early morning way of getting through the day. Then calling for work on the hall phone, in her actress voice of what Clarisse thought was an English accent, with lots of great, baby, and absolutelys, and, of course, I'll be theres. It was a cycle as deliberate to Catherine as how flowers die.

It was on Tuesday June 11, the day of Catherine's birthday, that she first saw Mr DeMarco in the hall. She was slouched by her door waiting to hear if they would work that day or if she would go to school. There had been a rain the night before and it was very hot. Clarisse was complaining on the phone it was hot as summer in Miami. Everything was always Miami. That's where Catherine was born. Someplace hot and uncomfortable.

He had walked through the door with the landlady, Thelma Jane, who sometimes worked with Clarisse when they needed a very old black woman for a shot, because that's what Thelma Jane was; very old and not much else. Thelma Jane thought very highly of Clarisse, seeing her as glamorous and the right sort of actress who dressed well and paid her rent with no fuss. Catherine knew to pay her respects to Thelma Jane because she needed what her mother called 'bread and butter treatment'. But today Catherine just stared at this man who paid her no attention at all, as if he had descended from a plane and she was a wall at an airport.

He had blue eyes and black hair that was shiny and smelled like lavender 'Jockey Club'; that smell at the pharmacy that signified the men's section where young girls were seldom seen and generally asked to leave. Catherine had seen many white men, but never like this; pretty and mysterious and taking up a whole room when they walked in . . . Clarisse was still on the phone and Thelma Jane walked him slowly up the stairs, explaining it got real hot at the top but there were windows and a skylight. His pants were very tight and Catherine studied his legs and his behind as he moved up the stairs, careful not to tax the old woman. She had seen tomcats walk that way before they hit on a mouse. She could still smell him up the stairs, and she opened the front door to breathe in and take in the difference. She couldn't remember if he had smiled or not, but his lips were very full, the upper parts sculpted to points and his nose was quite broad.

Catherine could hear her mother behind her.

'We got work tomorrow at MGM. But on Thursday you might as well go to school. Who went up with Thelma Jane?'

'A white guy.' Clarisse struck a match on the wall and lit an English Oval. She put the match in her purse, careful not to throw it on the floor where Thelma Jane could see it.

'Oh, that's right. DeMarco. Thelma Jane's renting him the studio.' Her mother could never call it the attic. It had to be glamorous; a studio. Maybe he's an artist, thought Catherine, and is starving. As if on cue, Clarisse looked at her daughter and blew smoke across her thoughts.

'He's a waiter at the Coconut Grove. From what I hear he used to be in the rackets. And I also hear he's lavender.'

Catherine stared at her mother. Clarisse seemed amused.

'Oh, come on, Catherine, you must have heard it a million times on the set. You know, he doesn't like women. Queer.' Clarisse stood quietly looking up the stairs as the air became still and her cigarette smoke made curls above her head. 'But then again, maybe he's not.'

Catherine realized they were both standing at the bottom of the stairs suspended in the eight a.m. heat. And she wondered why. Why her mother liked white men and always wore yellow. Why she pretended to be so English. The door was still open to the front and the outside, where a group of pigeons had descended on some of Thelma Jane's breadcrumbs. It was still silver outside and the roses on the hedges were soaked and pointing face down. Her mother turned to her and rapped her nails on the bannister.

'You know, I almost forgot. Happy Birthday, sweetheart. What would you like to do today?'

Another week passed; school, which Catherine got through for another year, let out. Clarisse had started working as a stand-in for Lena Horne and was never home. Money and fast notes were left on the kitchen table for Catherine. One week Clarisse stayed away altogether with a whispered call that she had met a friend of the director and this could be their big ticket and that Catherine was old enough to take care of herself. Mother just kept saying keep it cool, Catherine, keep it cool.

Catherine slept till the late afternoon when she could hear jazz coming from DeMarco's attic. Her dreams were touched by the shadows of vines that covered the library's French doors, sometimes shooting under into the room in the corner where her makeshift bed was kept. She would hear Dizzy

Gillespie and Sarah Vaughan as she opened her eyes in the wet shade of the house, knowing DeMarco went to work at seven and didn't come home till dawn. There were no friends from school as Clarisse didn't want her to know a lot of black kids and white kids weren't interested, so Catherine slept and resolved to study the immediate world around her. She walked through the upstairs hall and heard an old Jewish couple fighting over their children in two languages at least, and the afternoon rattle of a Chinese woman who sewed ladies' hats at home for Bullock's Wilshire. And the summer silences, like an oven preheated and waiting for food.

There were the steps to DeMarco's attic; small and curved with his mail left on the first step. And the jazz, muted inside but clear and full outside. His phonograph was probably kept near a window by the tops of the eucalyptus. Catherine wondered if his room smelled like menthol and what his view was like. One day she picked up his mail and decided to bring it to his front door. Her hands were shaking when she picked up the mail and looked at it. There were magazines and letters from New York and Sicily and bills from barbers and clothing stores. This, obviously, was the kind of mail men get. Catherine was careful to be quiet but quick as she went up the stairs. At the top was a long hall with red and gold wallpaper and no doors. It seemed strange to her there would be a tunnel like this at the top of the house. But not frightening. At the end of the hall was DeMarco's door which was half open and it seemed to illuminate the whole hall. DeMarco was inside; she could hear him change the record and put on a big band record with a lot of drums and saxophones. As Catherine slowly walked to the door the music seemed to get frantic and uncontrolled. Something told her not to knock, but to peer inside and see if it was OK to leave the mail there and maybe even say hello to him.

As she looked in, she saw the skylight in his ceiling and how hot and airless the room was. DeMarco was standing naked with his back to her, smoking a cigarette and staring out the window. Catherine had never seen a man naked; their rears were so beautiful. DeMarco's legs were tanned and muscled, full of veins that slid around his calves. His behind was totally white and hairless, whereas his legs were very hairy; his back had an arch that hers didn't, and there was a thin film of hair on his shoulders. He swayed slightly to the music, thrusting his hips gently against the base of the window and began to turn around. Catherine shrank into the shadows of the hall and trembled. She could still see him, but she didn't know if he could see her.

Catherine suddenly felt a pain in her pelvis that reached out and shook her chest, but she could not move. She wanted to know. Now she would understand what men on the Santa Monica pier and at Venice Beach thought about when they watched her; what voice spoke to them that did not speak to her. As DeMarco turned around she breathed in, held her breath, and did not blink. His penis, the first she'd seen, was rigid and bobbing from a mat of curly black hair that seemed softer than hers and it rose up to his belly, spreading over his chest like a black tree. He had a lot of muscles and they looked frightening, but the expression on his face was sad. He rubbed his crotch and ran his hands through his hair as though he was trying to push something out of his head, then traced his lips with his fingers. DeMarco turned back to his phonograph and flipped on a new record, this time Peggy Lee, and put his arms against the window and continued to sway his hips, only now he seemed to thrust against the wall harder, as if he was trying to push it away. Catherine thought she heard him crying.

She didn't put the mail down. She ran with DeMarco's music, pinching her flushed arms, until she was back in her room of falling wooden roses, where she suddenly sat on the floor and felt wet between her legs. She pulled off her cotton skirt and saw blood over her thighs.

She knew what this was and she had started it in the same air as DeMarco. Her mother, if nothing else, had explained to her this was coming up and it was a pain in the ass and all women had it, so don't come crying to her about it. Catherine washed some handkerchiefs in the sink and slowly wiped the blood from her vagina. She then took her mother's bottle of 'My Sin' and rubbed it all over herself. She realized she was crying for no reason at all. Catherine still felt wet but put on her mother's best pair of yellow satin high heels, open-toed with a white lace bow. She lay down on her back and pushed her legs high above her. They weren't just black at that precise moment, but sepia. Sepia, the tone of Whitman's Cream Chocolates and ranch mink coats. There was orange smoke outside the window and the sound of Billie Holiday singing 'Our Love Is Here To Stay' coming from DeMarco's, from the roof it seemed, or the sky. She rubbed her pubis, which was still imperfect and grown in patches, her fingers covered with menses, and realized that someday a man would be on top of her like this, that they knew the smell of blood, as all men did, and this was their first stab.

The summer only got hotter. Catherine opened the French windows when she woke and peered through the second wall

of white and green ivy that seemed like the room's skin. It
kept out the flies that would literally cluster on sidewalks
and car roofs. DeMarco was playing 'Satin Doll' by the
Duke Ellington Orchestra and Catherine felt this music was
hers alone, uninterrupted by Clarisse and her blindfolded
urgencies. Catherine could walk around in a T-shirt left by
one of Clarisse's balding friends in gray silk suits and feel
how much more flesh a man possessed. She shaved under
her arms for the first time and dusted them with 'Evening In
Paris' powder and painted her finger and toe nails light pink,
but was alarmed at how long they took to dry. Clarisse had
kept Catherine's hair straightened ever since she was a little
girl and Catherine pulled what was there into a bun and
dressed it with pop pearls and studied herself in the mirror
for signs of vice and magic.

There had once been a formal garden outside the library
doors with a narrow rectangular reflecting pool and a small,
scalloped shell fountain, full of still water, dense with algae
and punctured with eucalyptus leaves. The yard was rife
with orioles and mockingbirds hopping through oleanders
that Catherine loved to smell but couldn't bring in the
house; purple hibiscus and morning glories were webbed
along the wall like a carnival wheel. Catherine had never
been in the garden and she surmised no one else had either.
It was 1950 after all, and people had no time for ruins.
DeMarco's jazz seemed to float down and cover the jungle
like a postcard.

A breeze lightly shook the ivy when Catherine, standing
still in the drug of a young summer, heard the sound of a
woman's voice from the attic. There was a laugh and then an
angry, hoarse whisper and the sound of the needle sliding

off the record. Catherine suddenly felt the same rush and intoxication she had two days before in the hall outside DeMarco's door. She wanted to see again but knew Clarisse could be home today and the spell would be stubbed out like an English Oval and she would be back on a set, dressed to play no one except a shadow.

Catherine quietly closed her apartment door and ran barefoot up the stairs two steps at a time, her T-shirt fluttering around her. She dangerously didn't pause at the foot of the attic stairs, but bolted up and then stood rigid at the entrance of the hall. DeMarco's door was open half-way as before and she could smell perfume and hairspray. With her back against the wall, she slid over to the same position as before and bit her lip.

There were bottles of beer all over the room and DeMarco was sitting in his underwear on a chair next to his phonograph. A well-built blonde woman in a black slip with tight bleached curls covering her head was staring out the window and shaking her glass idly so the ice rattled. Every time she breathed it was like she was breathing for the last time and wanted to confess or take absolution. When she turned to face DeMarco, Catherine could see her eyes, small and green and rampant, smudged with shaved and penciled eyebrows.

'God, it's hot in this place. You want another beer, honey?'

DeMarco shook his head and looked up at her blankly. He was beautiful just sitting, his legs spread with his boxer shorts and his hands not knowing what to do. His head was leaned back against the back of the chair and his hair didn't have any brilliantine on it. Catherine saw it was curly and stuck out at angles. He hadn't shaved and the base of his beard started down almost at the beginning of his neck. It looked like it would itch a lot. Catherine wondered how it would feel against her skin.

'Why don't you put on "Blue Moon"? I like Mel Tormé. It's soft. It's too fucking early in the afternoon.' DeMarco rose and Catherine watched each tendon work itself as he bent over, shifting through his record collection. Catherine knew somehow this woman wanted to talk and would no matter what, she would because that's why she was here. It was the way she stood on one leg with her hip jutted out. Whenever Clarisse had something to say she stood on that same leg.

Catherine had never heard 'Blue Moon' before and she thought it was beautiful and sad. DeMarco went back and sat down, putting his arms behind his head, and Catherine could only stare at his armpits; how even there, under the curls of black hair, was muscle and skin that moved on its own. He had a cigarette in his lips and slowly blew smoke out through the corner of his mouth and then through his nose.

'We used to be quite an item. Remember?' The woman narrowed her glance at the room. 'I don't know why in hell you wanna live here with the niggers. I told you before, Lenny isn't mad at you. And I'm not either. You can make up the cash. No sweat. You're part of the family and it's not like we don't know you like the boys sometimes. Hell, I've known a lot of guys like that. So what. We'll get married, you make it up to Lenny and no one has to know, right?' DeMarco put his cigarette out and stared at her. He started crying. Catherine had never seen a man cry and she felt a flush move over the back of her neck.

'Stop the fucking crying, DeMarco. I hate when a guy cries. Guys aren't suppose to cry.' The blonde knelt down on her knees and rubbed her hands over his chest. She kissed his shoulder and took a wet cocktail napkin and pressed it under his eyes.

'Men are just little boys. They never grow up. You need me to take good care of you. And you know I will.' She gradually tried to kiss him, but DeMarco turned his face away.

'Don't you ever do that to me.' She didn't seem upset but excited. Catherine watched DeMarco look up through the skylight as the blonde woman peeled down his shorts and began to play with him. Was DeMarco watching the clouds? Catherine saw him become hard and the woman put her lips on him until she had swallowed him up. 'Blue Moon' had finished and DeMarco bolted up to change the song, leaving the blonde woman on her knees with the meanest face Catherine had ever seen.

'Goddamn you then and all your fairies.' DeMarco walked into another part of the room and out of Catherine's sight. She suddenly felt lost and wondered if she should run, but watched the woman get up on her feet and dust her slip off. The blonde walked over to the window and took a gulp of Scotch out of the bottle, swished it around in her mouth and spit it out into the air. Catherine could hear DeMarco sobbing as the blonde shook herself into a black cotton dress. Her face was set and her mouth curved down like an old woman's. She pinned on a hat with a white gardenia and took her compact out of her purse and powdered her cheeks, then smeared some dark red lipstick over a vicious smile. Catherine knew she had to get out of there, but her legs didn't want to. The woman snapped her bag shut and smacked her lips on a tissue.

'I'll tell Lenny you said hi. You'll be in touch, right?'

There was silence and the sobbing had stopped. Under her breath the woman chewed the words 'cock sucker' and headed towards the door.

Catherine ran without thinking, ran faster than she ever had.

The next day Clarisse was back.

'That son of a bitch was married. He never told me.' Clarisse was changing into a yellow striped dress with black lace trim. It was only eight a.m. and she was on her fourth cup of coffee.

'I lost one goddamn week's worth of work on that . . . ass. They say Swanson's going to get the Oscar for *Sunset Boulevard* and I could have worked the party scene. They would have seen me for sure.' The 'they' Clarisse referred to was an invisible knowledge to Catherine; a ripple of wind floating through empty sets that spoke to Clarisse and the murmur of extras' lips when the lights were off and the scramble was on for tomorrow. Catherine saw how the delusions would take form. There would be a chance to be put in front of a camera, whose eye was dead as something washed up on a beach. Klieg lights would make years of apprehension suddenly disappear. Someone would see her when the wrinkles were covered with base and the costume actually shined. There would be a chance to register and stay alive forever, be special, be known. Clarisse was always right at the edge of the set, smiling and nodding her head. Clarisse was always ready and was never picked.

Catherine didn't want to work any more. She wanted to absorb the house and DeMarco's life; understand who men were and what would make them cry. Why her father would make Clarisse turn white and glassy-eyed. Why there was force around each man like an inconstant turn that drew barriers, making women like her mother hop around and say things they didn't mean. Catherine knew from an imprisoned instinct that this was her summer and the klieg lights were on; she would remember all overgrown gardens and tunnels leading to men who never spoke, how silence and heat became color when the being trapped between her legs afforded her none.

'So how's your new man friend?' Clarisse walked around the room, circling Catherine methodically, the way she did before a fight. Catherine froze.

'What do you mean?' Clarisse just nodded to herself and smirked. She lit an English Oval and studied Catherine before she flicked the used match to the floor.

'What I mean is my nail polish on your hands. And my pearls put back in the wrong place. I know where I leave things, honey. Hopefully you'll learn too.'

Catherine studied the blackened match on the rug. There were black matches all over the rug.

'You were gone.'

'Don't bullshit me. You've got some dumb buck hanging around. All I'm going to say is this. You get pregnant and you live somewhere else. With your father or your aunt, but not with me. I'm trying to get somewhere.' The preciseness of Clarisse's attack left Catherine breathless. Catherine hadn't even the time to realize she still hadn't had the sex that would warrant such anger. This must be what happened. Flesh and misery. Is this why DeMarco cried, because he knew how a Clarisse, or any woman, used such politics?

'Honest, Mama, I've been sleeping a lot. I just wanted to try it. It sure takes a long time to dry.'

'Just remember what I said. You wanna work tomorrow? Get rid of the nail polish.'

'But I don't want to work tomorrow. It's summer.'

'Don't you understand this is the only way women like us are ever going to get anything? No, I suppose you don't.' Clarisse turned to go into the bathroom. 'And you don't care either.'

It was the first time she had been called a woman. By Clarisse or anyone else. Not because her body was ripe and she knew from touching it she would become warm. It was all about money, being a woman. It was the secret that gave beauty and made them laugh. The blonde in DeMarco's room talked about cash and Lenny and the air became stale. Clarisse mentioned money and electrified the smoke which hung over her like lace. Catherine knew that DeMarco's room held more answers than her mother had, and she saw how precise and uncaring a moment can be. Her mother was right. She didn't care. And there would be no apologies.

She continued to work with her mother, but now woke up before her, at four a.m. to watch for DeMarco when he came home from work. He would pull up in a cab, not the checkered ones but long black ones, dressed in a tux with his tie taken off. Catherine could watch him easily from the furthest window to the front, which had the only view on the yard and was half-hidden by a large jade tree with a squat, bubbly trunk. DeMarco always tipped the cabby and smiled but never said anything. She had watched him every morning for a week when she noticed something different. He started looking around him, as though he was expecting a surprise. Then he would look at the house and smile and walk to the front door slowly, looking at the roses and the mysterious jasmine that bloomed only at night and that Catherine couldn't find.

She wondered what living at night must be like. If the jazz he played on still afternoons was made at night and bottled like so much milk. Who his friends were. If, like a bird, DeMarco sang and spoke, but only at night. When shadows turned into objects when the lights were off.

It was before the Fourth of July that Catherine saw DeMarco get out of the taxi with a man who looked like an army officer. He had gray hair and a fat stomach and over his suit there were about five medals with ribbons. When they got out it was a dance. As the taxi pulled away DeMarco stood with his legs apart and pretended not to notice the army man, who was staring at DeMarco's pants with bloodshot eyes, chewing his cigarette. DeMarco was lit by a cloud that kept the dawn out of reach. Everything was still blue and phosphorescent. The silence was mangled by a morning wind that shook dead palm fronds that sounded like bacon sizzle. Catherine could hear locust and water rushing through pipes. And her mother talking in her sleep. DeMarco scratched his crotch as if something were caught and the army man did the same. DeMarco turned to the house and the army man followed him, pulling up his low hanging pants and letting his cigarette drop off his lip on to the gravel. His polished shoes scraped the yard in a blind stagger. The army man didn't even look to see what the address was.

Catherine's lips were dry and her breathing made too much noise. She began to turn away when she saw the blonde woman from the attic slowly pull up in a convertible. The top was down and she was drunk enough to hit the curb but the quiet of the morning was a shawl. No one heard her. There was a man in the front seat in a black turtleneck sweater who studied the house. Catherine shrank back but kept them in view with one eye from the corner of the window where the plastic slats of the venetian blinds ended.

The blonde was wearing ostrich feathers wrapped around her head which rolled around and bobbed lazily on her shoulders. Bits of feathers would fly above her and the light wind carried them up and above. Her face seemed pale and dead. One eye looked swollen and Catherine watched her put on a pair of sunglasses, like Lana Turner's. She started to get out of the car but the man grabbed her. She didn't struggle but slumped in her seat, running her gloved hands along the oversized steering wheel.

'So what do we do now, Lenny? He's got the money. I don't want to see him kissing some creep.'

'Let's wait around a minute, OK? The guy looks like a trick.' Lenny touched her face. The blonde woman didn't shrink away. She stared straight ahead, like she was used to men touching her face. Playing with it like a pretty ring.

'Lenny, I don't wanna be here.'

'We're getting the money this morning. And DeMarco won't tell no one.'

'Jesus, Lenny, you don't have to kill the poor fairy. You already cut out his tongue. Leave him the hell alone.' The blonde brought out a tiny box and sniffed something, letting her head roll back.

'I don't wanna be here.'

Catherine ran her hands over her lips and let herself sob. She had to be quiet. If there were silences to be understood, Catherine had gathered them like flowers meant to be dried and absorb dust. She suddenly understood how wild animals

21

survive; how the more dangerous, when put into a cage survive the wild and the cage, eating what is given and still ready to bite. Clarisse would bite until she died. DeMarco didn't know how to bite and would run in circles, thinking there was a way out through the center, a hole that could be dug. And in this dawn of misplacement, of night-born women and bird-eyed men who painted their faces on a perimeter of haze and the unspoken, she saw why Clarisse wore yellow and stood at the edge of the set, waiting.

'If you gotta do it, Lenny, then for Chrissakes wait till DeMarco's asleep. He don't go beddiebye until about six then he's up at noon. And for Chrissakes, don't be sloppy. Make it quick on him.'

'You wanna go to Hawaii. You wanna fur coat. You wanna lotta things. And I'm getting this done this morning. Then we're outta here. Period.' Lenny reached over and took a briefcase from the rumble seat and opened it on his lap. Catherine couldn't see what he was doing, but her heart started to beat like a big band. She knew Clarisse would not be awake for at least one more hour. She knew where the house creaked and where it didn't. The halls were dark with the smell of hotplate cooking and late night showers to ward off the summer. She could hear her bare feet spring on the carpeting. By the time she got to DeMarco's hall the door was wide open and a dim light from his toilet lit the room. She realized they could see her if she stepped any further. She couldn't see DeMarco but the army man was there, old and blotched in boxer shorts, lying on the Murphy bed wiggling his toes in his socks.

'No wonder you leave the door open. It's hot as Jordan in here, buddy.' DeMarco stepped into the room. He was covered in baby oil and was rubbing his chest thoughtfully. The army man leered at him.

'That one is sure a beauty. I sure would love to see it in action. Ya know, my wife would like a young pup like you. But we couldn't tell her. Maybe a hotel room where I could see ya through the drapes. Ya know what I mean? But she couldn't know. Or there'd be hell to pay. What do ya think, huh? Feeling good?' The army man patted the bed next to him and began to close his eyes.

'Hell, we're just guys and I'm kinda randy. It's sure good of ya to let me stay here. I was pretty blotto. My wife woulda killed me. Say, maybe I could let you drop me off. That's how you could meet her. Yeh, that's a good idea.' DeMarco slowly walked over to him. The army man was pretending to go to sleep. Catherine did not understand the game. She felt suddenly sick to think she played the same game as this tired old man, and how it excited her. He would give him money. Clarisse played this game with her white men, when Catherine stood on the Santa Monica Pier and watched the waves slither under the gaps in the boards. Everyone knew this way of playing their odds into unknown hands that seared skin, common as her bus route when Clarisse would sit in the back and say loudly her car had broken down.

Catherine had to break this magic. DeMarco would be killed and would not be able to cry out. The jazz would be turned up and the trees would brush against the sideboards of the attic. Clarisse would stub her cigarette out and curse, waiting for the hall phone to ring. The front door would open and close without announcing who was there.

DeMarco studied the army man, who had fallen asleep. He lit a cigarette and went through the pockets of the military suit, finding a small roll of bills. He carefully took out a cigar box and shoved them in, putting the cigar box behind a stack of records. He put a record on very low, Billie Holiday again, singing 'Do Nothing Till You Hear From Me', and looked at the sun shimmering on the tops of the eucalpytus.

'Mr DeMarco.' Catherine could not believe she had said his name. DeMarco turned around and looked through the shadows at Catherine. He made no effort to hide his nakedness. Catherine took a small step towards the half light. Her nipples had become hard and her hands twitched. When she walked her knees rubbed together and she did not understand why she was walking on tiptoe. When she saw his eyes she felt naked as well. The silence made her sick.

'Mr DeMarco, the blonde lady is outside with Lenny and they are gonna get you. You better go out the back.' DeMarco just stared at her and a smile began to form. She had never seen him smile. Some of his teeth were knocked out. She looked at him slowly, then looked down at the floor.

'I know cause I've been watching you and I listen to your records.' There was a long pause and Catherine averted her eyes to the red and gold wallpaper.

'I'm sorry I've been watching you but you . . .' Catherine caught her throat and couldn't say any more. DeMarco pushed his eyebrows together and watched Catherine. She realized the shadow was dissolving around her as sunlight came through the window. Everything was a dull orange. DeMarco made a sound with his throat and Catherine looked up to see him open his mouth and then shake his head. Like thank you. Suddenly he turned away from her and quietly put his clothes on. The army man was snoring as Catherine ran down the steps to the first floor. Clarisse was up, putting on her false eyelashes.

'Where the hell were you?'

Catherine studied her mother. Her face etched in shade.

'I heard a cat in the hall. The one from next door. I let it out.'

That morning was louder than Catherine imagined. The army man ran out the door in his full suit. After he left the blonde woman came down the stairs with Lenny. It was already nine o'clock and they had no secrets from the tenants now. Nothing had been done. There was a crowd of pigeons outside that decided to fly all at once. Catherine could hear their wings beating like a mop against a wall.

'That wop son of a bitch. He blew smoke up your ass, didn't he, Lenny?' She had a spoiled, satisfied smile on her face. Catherine was watching from the pay telephone where Clarisse was coughing and setting up work. Clarisse said nothing, but watched the two as Lenny pushed the blonde woman out the door. She hung up the phone and muttered to herself.

'White trash.'

DeMarco was gone and hadn't paid the rent. Catherine went upstairs and found the phonograph thrown against the wall. The mattress was turned over and it looked like Lenny had swept the dishes off the cupboard onto the sink and floor. DeMarco's clothes were turned inside out and some had been shredded with a knife. Everything was left except the records. Catherine took the phonograph and said nothing. It didn't work, but had a beautiful wood trim. She took her bits of ceiling ormolu and wooden roses and put them in the hi-fi, and threw the waffle box away.

That November Clarisse left for good, leaving a note to Catherine that she was old enough to do whatever the hell she wanted. Catherine knew Clarisse would never call her. She was a woman in Clarisse's eyes and Clarisse would never live with another woman. She wouldn't pay good money for the humiliation of five more years in a damp library with a hot little colored chick who wanted other things; not the light and the work she fled to. It was a world of halves, living in a white world of men who would pay for her ability to play that game and speak their language. And waiting to enter it with her best yellow dress on.

Some people are misplaced in life, Catherine reasoned to herself. Just lost in a film can and never found, even when they're good. Many years later Catherine would catch glimpses of Clarisse late at night on television when her own children had gone to bed, behind Dorothy Dandridge in *Porgy and Bess*, or walking with bare feet, head bowed, carrying a tray of fruit to a Roman Emperor, then slowly backing away.

Catherine moved that November to stay with an aunt named Eugenia in Rochester, New York. In her eighteenth year she married a contractor named Tom, who gave her a large house in a grove of walnut trees, three children and one miscarriage. After thirty-five years he dropped dead at a banquet in Miami Beach. In that time Catherine had not gone back to Los Angeles. Or discussed it.

Now in her fifty-third year, she opened the same door as DeMarco and knew the same things he did. How the earth became silk under her thighs when Tom came inside her, how the night could be electric with jazz and possibilities, incandescent and irritating. How she would take her music with her, sprung from gardens and half open doors, and play it in a caress of silence.

The hall had been painted white and the dark wood seemed smothered. A little oriental girl was playing with a set of jacks in front of her apartment door. The pay phone had been replaced with a fire extinguisher. The attic stairs now had a plywood door with a deadbolt on it. In red figures scrawled with chalk was the number fifteen. Catherine knocked on the door. A young black girl with paint smudged on her face opened it.

'Yeh?' She was quite pretty and had two tiny gold rings in her nose.

'I used to live here a long time ago.'

'So?'

'I just wanted to see it again.'

'Is this for real?' A beautiful young man with long blonde hair came up from behind her. He was wearing a bathrobe, loosely tied.

'Yes, as a matter of fact. It is for real.' Catherine waited.

The blonde man looked at Catherine for a long time. Catherine could smell marijuana and something else; menthol.

'OK. What the hell.' He opened the door further and Catherine stepped inside, remembering to check the tops of the eucalyptus outside the window for birds' nests and to see if there was still a rhythm to the sky.

a thief in august

PEARL RECOGNIZES A SOUND coming from behind her. Squalid and uncontained, it is a cold brush of air, a scent of night-blooming jasmine out of season, a distinct exhale. She has heard and felt this sound for months, every night at one-thirty a.m., when she descends the back stairs from her apartment to her restaurant below. Something is sighing.

It is not the wind. This stiff, preposterous Los Angeles August is dulled by a sugary heat that keeps Pearl standing still longer than she needs to, or wants.

At first she reasoned this echo, squeal, whatever it was, came from the pine tree she had planted in the parking lot on their first Christmas. That was 1932. Johnny turned on the elegant neon sign that read ORIGINAL SPANISH KITCHEN and opened the restaurant's doors for the first time wearing a white tuxedo, like George Raft – his black, thick Italian hair slicked down with Jockey Club pomade. Johnny never stopped smiling at her that perfumed night. Pearl was twenty-one, a dancer with slim, tight hips, huge blue eyes, and nearly red hair. She was dressed in a gold lamé flamenco gown. The scent of orange blossoms hovered like fog from the surrounding groves. She could still remember all those big black cars out front with Negro drivers and platinum blonds in pale blue fox.

The pine tree grew like a child's arms, reaching up for the sky, incongruous in the tiny lot that she tried to make into a

31

yard, but failed. Now, in 1961, the pine is taller than any trees around, lush and almost tropical. But the limbs do not brush against the glass, and they are too thick to shake in a breeze.

Pearl knows there are no drafts in her upstairs apartment. Or open doors that should be closed. Above the blue-lit parking lot, she listens for the sound again. It's gone, but she knows it will come again.

She remembers the first time she was able to decipher this cold whisper. Johnny had an attack, and she was terrified, afraid he'd had a stroke. He convulsed. She picked him up, and her hands were wet with the saliva running down his neck. He didn't recognize her or speak. No one was around to help her. Their children were grown and living in Arizona. In the hospital, the doctor told Pearl that Johnny had Parkinson's disease, that it was irreversible, and she couldn't make him well.

She returned home for something inconsequential, just to get out of that horrid green room, away from the doctor's words: 'He won't know you some days; it's a slow process, good days and bad.' And that was when the sound first came to her. She looked up into the streetlights on Beverly Boulevard, directly into their cagey, electric eyes, and pretended there was a sun on her face, one that didn't age, burn, or dismiss. The sound was a full room behind her, floating on the ceiling, like a fly on a brisk crawl. The hair on her arms stood, and tears crowded her eyes. It was the sound of a cripple, a blind thing, abandoned and young, not able to understand. Then nothing.

Now the sound is something Pearl lives with, a companion of predictions and unease. She shudders in the heavy lace of this moist summer evening. Tonight the sound is loud. It makes indescribable words; she knows them but cannot decipher them, like the contents of dreams that pass upon waking.

She can smell enchiladas and spilled beer wafting up from below. Their Mexican cook, Frank Acuna, has his radio on as he always does just before closing. Pearl can hear Walter Cronkite saying the same words he did earlier on television: that Russia will continue to test their atom bombs, that this Cold War is real and Americans must be prepared for an emergency. Pearl has been through a war. She knows where words lead.

Pearl hears the hiss of cleanser hitting the hot black metal of the grill. She clutches the railing of her wrought-iron stairs and closes her eyes, breathing in every familiar scent and repeating to herself like a mantra: Johnny's fine tonight. I have to do the books. I have to help close. Frank needs more salt. I must remember the salt at my market and I must remember his wife's birthday tomorrow. I must take Johnny to the doctor at noon, and I must remember to make it seem natural, like a checkup, so he's not frightened.

Pearl runs her hands through her hair and descends the rest of the stairs slowly. The air under her feet is wrong. It is alone, incandescent, trembling. There are bells tonight, Pearl thinks, there are signals, and I still do not know what they mean.

'Johnny's having another spell, Pearl,' Frank says. His eyes do not look at her. Chubby Checker is singing 'Let's Twist Again' on the radio, and Frank won't turn around. He has been crying. He aims the sink hose at a pot like a weapon and scrubs harder than he has to.

'Turn the radio off, Frank. It's too much right now,' Pearl says with a sigh. She cannot think. The restaurant's two rooms are full of lavender smoke. The fresh red carnations she bought yesterday are already brown from cigarettes and heat. Pearl can see customers sitting alone, waiting for closing. Don't they want to go home? she wonders.

'Strange crowd tonight,' Frank says without emotion. Pearl knows he is worried about Johnny, but he won't let her see.

Her red glass candles glow like votives in a deep church, discreet as stars. Pearl can make out a murmur, not unlike the sound that comes to her upstairs, and she steps back, putting her hand over her heart. It is an unconscious gesture and it startles her. The only other time she's made this movement was when her mother died. She remembers stepping back into her bedroom upstairs away from Johnny, her hand over her heart, receding into the indigo of her room.

'Where is he?' Pearl turns her gaze back to Frank. He shrugs, keeping away. The kitchen is full of steam. He has let the hot water run too long.

Pearl walks into the restaurant, feeling that something is unbalanced. Her skin contracts and shivers. She searches for normalities, and they are all there; water pitchers are still half full on serving tables, toothpicks and tortilla chips are set on the bar. Checks in leather folders lie on tables, waiting to be paid.

She glances into an ornate gold mirror smothered with cherubs and flowers that they bought in 1939 on holiday in Guadalajara. For years she has checked herself in this mirror to make sure she is presentable. Johnny called it her beauty box. But tonight she sees nothing, just an outline.

Pearl is furious. She steps closer to the mirror, oblivious to the room. Her face gradually comes into view, and she looks, only for a moment, relieved. I am still a young woman, Pearl declares to herself. I am only fifty years old, and I am still the woman Johnny married. I am still beautiful, and very much loved. I am not a blur yet.

The sound comes back to her and she pauses, her eyes scanning the room to see if others have heard it. It has never come to her here, downstairs, and this time she is aware of chords struck like a zither, or mariachi guitars. Then a sound of hand cymbals, but muted, as though heard through a thick wall.

Pearl shakes herself and puts on a smile. There is no sound. She stares briefly at a Mexican painting next to her mirror. Its paint has begun to chip. She has memorized its palms and ruffled blue mountains, and she suddenly wishes that tonight, finally, she and Johnny could disappear into that picture – into its innocence of crude trees and Mexican men with straw hats, pushing carts. They would be that naive brushstroke, that unmixed, straight-from-the-tube color, and things would remain exact and pure.

Pearl suddenly knows where Johnny is. She does not have to turn around. She can feel him in the corner booth by the front door – Mary Pickford's table, where Johnny always sat with friends. He loved it there, under the streetlights, right off the sidewalk, where he could see people but they couldn't see him.

'Look at him,' Johnny would say, pointing to some harried man walking past. 'He's lonely. Can you see that, Pearl? He needs a good woman like you.'

*   *   *

35

Pearl makes her way through the tables. People do not seem to notice her. She realizes she is not hearing voices, but that sound again; it is an abomination, she knows it is. When she looks directly at the customers, their faces turn away from her, and she sees only neck, the shine of parted hair, an earring dangling.

Johnny is sitting in his favorite booth. There is spittle at the corner of his mouth, and Pearl reaches down, wiping it away with a red napkin. Then she sits down next to him, watching to see if he even knows she's there. His left hand is twitching, and his fingers jitter with disease. She checks herself to make sure she doesn't cry.

'You want a glass of water, Johnny honey?'

His slicked gray hair has fallen into strands across his face, and his brown eyes look up at Pearl like a young boy's. Johnny shakes and nods his head.

I fell in love with your eyes, Johnny Caretto, Pearl thinks. Show them to me tonight. Please.

She hands him a glass of water and realizes he cannot bring it up to his mouth. His lips are dry, infirm gray. Gently, Pearl helps her husband take a sip of water, but his mouth slackens, letting liquid spill on his shirt. Pearl knows this is bad, that he is leaving her. She thinks of prayers that can be recited tonight before she sleeps. 'Jesus our Saviour,' she recites under her breath, the same words she uses at Sunday services when she lights candles to the Virgin and the Apostles.

'Johnny, no, don't scare me.' Silence. Pearl realizes tears are forming, and she pretends to rub her eyes. Johnny is smiling at something in the room, nodding his head in agreement. He laughs, gurgles like a child, then laughs again. Pearl doesn't even know if he sees her.

'Johnny, look at me.' Johnny Caretto rolls his eyes upward, then focuses on the room. His arm has fallen limp. His head sways, not looking at Pearl. In a weak gesture, he tries to move one of his arms up, as if to shake a hand, and speaks.

'Good to see you, Mary.'

Pearl recoils, staring at her husband. He's talking to Mary Pickford, but she hasn't been here for ten years. She recollects a night in the forties, when Mary sat in this booth, bejeweled and drunk and cruel, speaking to Pearl in a half-whisper.

'You know, Pearl, you keep your religion and you keep your man. There's nothing worse than being alone. And don't let them feed on you.'

'Who?' Pearl asked, looking into Mary's eyes. They were faded, puffy, and hard. She still penciled her eyebrows in the style of the twenties and thirties, but her vision was weak and the pencil had become thick, a smear, making her face grotesque and irretrievable.

'People without love. They're here, everywhere. Can't you see them?' Mary lit a cigarette in a ruby-and-platinum holder and continued.

'When Doug died . . . I began to know them by name. You see, there are things in Los Angeles people don't discuss, or understand. Take a look around. You'll see.'

The light that evening had a quality that Pearl can still remember clearly: an orange tint, like a whore's hair, like a fire illuminating a small room. And that night she was aware of shadows, of desolation, and Mary's powdered, shifting face.

Pearl tries once more.

'Tell me my name, Johnny.' She can barely speak. Her voice is hoarse, and she knows it will break. 'Tell me the color of my eyes. You love my eyes. Look at me.' Pearl pauses. 'You have to, Johnny.'

Silence. He is with Mary Pickford and Linda Darnell and all the movie stars who knew him by name, shook his hand, and ate his food. Pearl can imagine what he is seeing. He is standing at the front door right now, Pearl thinks, and winces.

She remembers herself back then, young and watching this beautiful man from the back of the restaurant. She remembers thinking, He will give me daughters and a happy life, remain faithful, never stop loving me, even as I grow old. Our life is beginning at this moment.

'My eyes are blue.' Her voice trails. There is nothing to say.

She is caressing Johnny with one hand, looking for recognition, a geography where they can meet. Even one word. But there are no words on this August morning, when rats scurry up palms to their nests, and Pearl knows she is being watched.

She can see Frank in the kitchen, his face in his hands, the faucets still running. He has turned the radio back on to a late news bulletin: missiles have been deployed around the globe, and the Russians have their nuclear arsenal on alert. Then static. Then rock 'n' roll.

Pearl's eyes widen. She looks out to make sure the streetlights still work, then shrieks. It comes out unexplained. She has never heard herself shriek.

The customers are staring at her with blank, hideous expressions. Their eyes are caught in shadows, the same shadows she remembers around Mary, the same leer, orange and full of recriminations.

This dread pulls at her until she has to urinate, and she stands up, frozen. She begins to talk to herself, and she's not

38

sure if she is speaking or thinking, and she doesn't care.

Johnny and I have been here twenty-nine years. Something has let itself in, and it wants our love. It's walked behind me for months and I didn't know. It's in the walls, in the bright murals and red velvet curtains and it won't leave. It has found us, bringing everything that aches with distrust, everything unloved, and it has attached itself like moths to the streetlights outside.

The people in this room are not whole, she realizes. Something is missing from their faces. They are watching Johnny and me for warmth. They have nothing else.

'Go away,' Pearl says to them, trying to hide the nausea that rattles through her. 'Please. We're closed.'

The sound that has plagued her becomes a fugue of something misplaced, longing to be set right, forgiven, cleansed. She senses it is trying to form words, weeping like the dripping faucet in the kitchen.

Then it is gone. The room is empty. Pearl lets out a breath that has been pushing against her heart, and she feels dizzy. Frank has left for the night and the kitchen is dark. Faces are outside the restaurant's window. A hand taps on the glass. Pearl hurriedly takes a 'Closed' sign from behind the bar that they have used when they've gone on vacations, and she tapes it to the window.

She refuses to look out at these faces. She knows what she will see. Instinctively, she keeps her eyes on the floor, waiting for them to vanish into the lurid hues of August.

These faces will find somewhere else. They will visit playgrounds for the very young and sit on benches, out of sight, absorbing. They will stand on the front lawns of safe houses and inhale. They will touch unmade hotel beds and read the creases in the sheets. They are the sound, the murmur.

The noise is leaving us, like a thief who's been discovered, Pearl thinks. It cannot have us. We will never come in here again. Quietly, she puts the place in order as Johnny closes his eyes. Each tablecloth she lightly recreases along the folds so they look pressed. She sweeps the floor of ash and puts chairs on top of the tables. She makes sure dishes are stacked and her silverware is set.

It is now, when everything is as perfect as a photograph, that Pearl acts upon a distant faith. A clarity envelops her, like the breath of a young child reaching for its mother, stuttering, 'I love you, Mama.' That child has Johnny's voice and Johnny's eyes, and Pearl knows Johnny is calling her with those August words, crushed by the end of summer like any seasonal conceit. Johnny understands where I am, she thinks, even when he is far away. He loves me and he will be next to me upstairs. The thief will wait for someone else.

Like every other night, Pearl wets her fingers and puts out the candles, one by one. As she shuts the back kitchen door, Johnny, who is gently propped against her shoulder, breaks away and walks up the stairs. Pearl knows she can make him well.

There are bluebirds and crows sleeping in the pine. There are stars in a hot, crystalline sky. There are cars on boulevards, returning their owners to those they love. There is music coming from a bar down the street that should be closed at this hour.

It is a prayer, Pearl thinks. Someone is alive. It is a reason, and that, she concedes, is enough.

rattlesnake season

IT WAS RATTLESNAKE season on Mulholland Drive. The air was hoarse with a Santa Ana condition and the constant wail of fire trucks in the flat sparkle of the San Fernando Valley. Drought had eaten away the yellow green hills, once covered in mustard weed and a battalion of Chinese elms. Mountain-top pools were drying up; pool men were making a fortune repairing burned out filters and cleaning up dead birds and date palm fronds floating in the wind-scratched water.

Baby rattlers were found coiled on front doorsteps and slithering around septic tanks and burst water lines. Mexican maids suddenly had refused to walk up Beverly Glen and Goldwater Canyon Drive to the houses at the top. The pavement was burning their shoes and they complained of people being crazy with the heat; of taking corners too fast where there were no sidewalks. It was the end of August and 105 degrees in the shade. Anyone with sense was in Hawaii or Oregon.

Mulholland Drive had turned into a small town of gardeners, pool men and housekeepers on empty estates. Their owners were generally too important or just too rich to live there year round, and in this invisible city of electric gates and automatic lights, spectacular views and sudden curves, there were others who lived in the heat and crisp wind. The poor relations and struggling writers who house-sat through an agency; their address a post office box, always ready to

43

move at the slightest notice. They were people who lived in the solace of someone else's luxury. Capable of not being seen, yet invited to stay.

The house-sitters would collect the mail, monitor the utilities and sleep in any bed they chose; keep the pools filled to the correct level and swim in them when mornings were still mild, before the half hour, ten degree climb. Sometimes they were paid but often it was just free rent, for a month, maybe a year. It was a chance to score big and save some money, get that one big commercial or the first screenplay sold. They could call their families in the midwest and say, 'You'll never guess whose house I'm staying in. It's two doors down from Jack Nicholson's.' It was their first big omen in a city built on omens and predicted steps. The polish would rub off on them and soon they wouldn't have to worry.

Tony and Marsha had been house-sitting for six months with another year to go; the owner, a titled English lady married to a publisher on both continents, had four other houses to maintain and despised Los Angeles, comparing it to a pigsty with electricity. They had never met the owner and doubted they would. Their monthly check was handled through a law firm and personal correspondence of any kind was forbidden.

The house was huge and sat on top of its own discreet hill, with silk upholstered walls and marble parquet floors. Designed by an architect who had committed suicide in the late seventies, it was all curves and statements that made no sense. Its pool was designed to end at the edge of a cemented cliff, with a waterfall spilling over the side into a retaining gutter, so when they swam in it they got the feeling of swimming over the edge right out into the city. Instead of gardens, their decks jutted out into space. The house sat like a mono-lith, its bones becoming brittle and glazed in the sun. Like a whale that had eaten a ship.

Tony disliked the Santa Anas more with each passing week. They rattled the two-storey picture windows and covered everything with a thin coat of beige grit. He couldn't get any writing done with all the noise, and would take to swimming for hours, staying submerged for as long as he could hold out, then emerging to a blast of sauna and white sun, made, it seemed to him, to keep mountain-tops bald and polished. By the time he reached the sliding glass doors he was already dry. Marsha stayed out of the sun altogether, and would never sit outside, as the house had no shade. Sometimes he would see her staring at him from the immense windows, a silhouette still and focused as the house itself.

He never bothered with trunks and liked the feeling of his own nakedness with the city beneath him, often wondering what Marsha thought as she watched him. If she still loved him, or was assessing his body by what other men could offer her. In the past six months on this bulldozed hilltop of swaying cypress and birds of prey, Marsha had become silent, almost menacing, a fact Tony attributed to her pregnancy and her sobriety. She was six months pregnant but they hadn't told anyone as they didn't want to lose the house and the small salary that came with it. They had come from Boston a year ago after six years of marriage and no children. The move to California was to fulfill dreams they found distanced and abandoned with each winter snow. There would be no more walk-ups with utility meters in the closet that cost a quarter for twenty minutes. Or temp secretarial jobs that took an hour to get to and lasted a week. Tony would write his screenplays and get a good agent. And Marsha would have her child and work in flower design, which she loved; maybe even have her own shop.

But it was more than that. They had lost their sense of touch and smell for each other; the narcotic of each other's arms that guided them through their life. Tony could remember three days in Boston when they formed one certain circle of flesh, and he never stopped being inside her, on top of her, wrapped in her skin; when they were drunk and rubbing their chests together so hard there were bruises on his nipples, and Marsha would slowly sip another Scotch and wait for him to become hard again, staring like a whore at him until he did.

They had tried for so many years and it finally took. And then, with her pregnancy there seemed like nothing more to discuss. Marsha became unresponsive to Tony in small ways at first, things so menial and unspoken they became part of the season, or lack of, that terrified Tony. He turned his attention to his writing. Marsha took a small portion of their monthly check and went to the flower market downtown, buying up already old flowers for almost nothing and creating incredible floral arrangements all over the house, using the crystal vases and ikebana bronzes scattered through the end-less entertainment areas. They were perfect. Too perfect. No one saw them. They weren't allowed guests. That was part of the contract. They didn't know anybody to invite. She liked to use very sharp scissors, and cut her hand but didn't tell him. He found out when he saw half her hand bandaged. By this sixth month, the silence had become so thick he didn't need to ask.

In Boston he had loved his wife. And still did. She was oxygen and musk, calculating and frail. She had natural auburn hair that seemed to mirror each season they sped through. Her white skin could powder him with heat and pornographic oaths that he never thought he knew; her arms were the only safe place left. Here in Los Angeles, in this house of riptide balconies and spiraling air, she was trapped by a sun that would burn her Irish skin, by a poverty they had tried to escape. There wasn't a day when Marsha wouldn't remind him this house wasn't theirs, when she even chose to speak at all.

Tony considered himself a patient man. This silence would change. Pregnant women get into crazy moods. They were living in real style for a change, and pursuing exactly what they had dreamed of. He found an agent who seemed more impressed by his address than his scripts, but didn't tell him anything more than he needed to know. Nothing had been sold yet, but there was a chance of an option for one of them. Then he and Marsha could get a nice condo somewhere that would be theirs. It was all a maybe. But he didn't care. They still had another year to go taking care of the house. That was pretty good insurance.

They had overcome a lot just to get to this point. In Boston there was the booze. They had both loved to drink and had met in a bar, fell in love in a fuzzy sort of way and got married on a very drunk night. At first everything was cool. Even though there wasn't a whole bag of money sitting around, they found ways to party and get their minds off things. But it began to erode when Marsha wanted a child. Tony would come from work as a copywriter and Marsha would be on the bed, drunk and crying, sometimes masturbating in front of him. There was no talking to her then. She yelled he couldn't do it the way she wanted anymore and that she wanted a child. He had suddenly become the big failure. He woke up to too many mornings of Marsha on top of him, pumping away at his sleeping groin and making promises to herself with her eyes closed.

One day Marsha was found drunk in the supermarket and the manager called Tony to take her home. That night she started Alcoholics Anonymous. Tony wouldn't go. It was three months later they made a pact. They would both stop drinking or split up. They would move to California somehow. They would have a baby.

Once in Hollywood they found themselves a nomadic class who hovered around, lived in single apartments for very short periods of time. Things could never be as bad as Boston. Instead, things got worse. They found an apartment in the Valley next to a rock and roll band. Twelve small boxes around a kidney-shaped pool and broken aluminum furniture. They hated it.

On Sundays they would look at homes that cost a half million dollars, Tony in his coat and tie and Marsha in her one good secretary suit, walking through the empty rooms, deciding on wallpaper and what style furniture, chatting with the real estate agents in a disappointed tone. It was all they had left. They couldn't pay their rent.

Tony was forty, Marsha thirty-five. He had begun to gray at the temples and on his chest. He was still muscular and his dark blue eyes didn't need glasses. He figured that was because he wasn't writing enough. They both knew they could squeeze another month of rent out or go home to their families and become another casualty of Los Angeles.

It was on a desperate Sunday, when a marine layer made even the Valley smell like the beach, that they drove aimlessly in silence, indecisive and detached. They stopped at a house for sale in the Sherman Oaks hills. They figured it must at least cost a million, and stared at each other numbly. Marsha breathed in very deep when she got out of the car. She turned to Tony with a half smile on her face.

'You know, I like it up here. You can't hear the cars.' She hugged herself and stared at the house, knowing this would be the last one they would look at. Tony could see it in her. The way she still wanted to walk into the dream. At least one more time.

A plump blonde woman answered the door. She was flushed and wearing a dirty pink sweatsuit. They could hear the sound of children. The house was empty, except for some sleeping bags and clothes bunched together like a bed. Four little children ran down the curved ebony staircase, giggling. The woman turned to them with a frightened, pinched face and asked them if they wanted to see the kitchen, which was beautiful, with German appliances and granite counters. Tony and Marsha had seen quite a few of them. There were boxes from McDonald's and Taco Bell scattered over the counters. There wasn't a table or chairs. On the stove a beat-up soup pot was simmering with what smelled like chili. Marsha turned and stared at Tony. Then turned back to the woman.

Tony said nothing. At that moment he knew this woman was homeless, that she was staying here for a reason he couldn't quite figure. For the kids? Marsha stood with her fists clenched swaying by the window and its view of the world. He knew she was ready to cry. He had lived with her for long enough to always know. And then, in the stripes of hazy light cutting through the room, he watched her ask the woman if she lived there. Her tone was kind but had a dressed-up desperation. The woman explained she was house-sitting through an agency, that times had been tough. Then Marsha began to lie. It was the first time he had ever heard her lie. She said how they had a lovely home for sale that was vacant. Was there an agency for house-sitters? It seemed like such a good idea with all the crime and vandalism today. Tony realized they must be desperate in Marsha's eyes; he had a tendency to let things ride, and didn't see a real problem with their situation. Things would work themselves out. He never thought to ask Marsha how she felt.

She got the agency's card from the woman and looked straight through him, as if he were an object near a convenient exit. It annoyed him and excited him at the same time. Her eyes were focused past the front door and up the hill. As they left, the automatic sprinklers from the house next door left the narrow mountain road slick and shiny with spots of sun. They got in the car and Marsha spoke soft and slow, staring at a house being built further down, a hulk of wood and cement.

'I'm pregnant. And I don't want to be on the streets, which is where we're headed. I want to live in a nice house. And if you can't get it done, then I will. Just don't talk to me right now.'

'I love you, Marsha.'

Marsha sighed.

'I know you do.' For a moment their eyes met. Tony had never seen her eyes so cold. It made him want to possess her. Hit her. Make her cry and pant. He felt helpless again. It was not the first time.

He geared the car up and they drove to the top of the hill,

past Spanish villas and houses crammed together on stilts. The paved road dead-ended and there was a dirt road with a chain across it. Tony got out of the car, with Marsha watching him, and let the chain fall to the ground. They drove up the dirt road until they could see the Valley on one side and Los Angeles on the other, then they made love, hurriedly, angrily, both cities beneath them murmuring like a broadcast turned down.

The first few months in the house were fine. They added a little to their bank account, took in quite a few films, enjoyed the little luxuries; the European linens, the modern kitchen, the pool, the view and the overwhelming quiet. There were certain things that frightened Tony, although he wouldn't admit it to himself or Marsha. The house had no art on the walls; not even a little painting of flowers. Instead, there were mirrors everywhere. Huge gilt-framed mirrors in the main room, hallways that sparkled with bevel-cut wall mirrors and chandeliers of free-form crystal. It would catch him off-guard, suddenly seeing himself when he didn't want to, his image trapped and multiplied. As the sunlight would pass over the skylights, the mirrors could blind.

And the doors. The front door was solid bronze, the interior doors copper, all of them detailed in an Aztec pattern and heavy. When he shut one the room felt sealed, quiet as a full leech. These doors belonged in a mausoleum. He avoided them and tried to stay in rooms with regular doors and sliding glass doors that opened outside. At least these he understood. Half the time he never knew if Marsha was in the kitchen, where she seemed to spend an increasing amount of time, or out at the free clinic. He didn't want to learn how to use the intercom system or any other elaborate schemes that would interfere with his work. He was here to write.

By Marsha's third month she began to change and become withdrawn. The only times Tony saw her, besides in bed, were at dinner and when he happened to find her in the kitchen. The last time they had made love was in the car that day on the dirt road, and in bed Marsha wouldn't let him touch her. He focused on his writing, refusing to even masturbate, and one day drove aimlessly through the Valley, circling parks where Mexican couples were screwing in the back of scratched Cadillacs and homosexuals hung around restrooms. He never stopped, only wanting to breathe the sex in the air, the possibilities and the increasing heat.

One night he found her at three a.m. standing on the terrace, her bathrobe fluttering around her and her hair covered in palm tree pollen. She was so beautiful. He touched her shoulder and she didn't respond. He stood there for at least five minutes, staring at her, waiting for her to acknowledge him. She never did, and he went back to bed.

In her fourth month he began to worry about her. She loved to take long showers, and one morning, on a 100 degree day he found her in a bathroom dense with steam, her skin bright red from a scalding shower, sitting on the toilet and sweating, rubbing her breasts with oil. He turned off the shower and touched her nipple. She moved away.

One day, she had returned home from the free clinic and had ten bottles of nail polish on the dining room table. She had painted each nail on her hands a different color and put her hands in front of her flower arrangements, studying the colors and twisting her hands to resemble the blossoms. The flowers were everywhere; Marsha would go to a wholesale market and find twenty-four roses for a dollar, buy five bunches and bring them home. Buds that had not opened would be put in geometric patterns in shallow dishes, sitting in a thin, filmy water, then open overnight. Marsha would run her fingers through the water, watching the petals break and float. In her arrangements, any flower that showed a trace of brown was replaced.

She was ravenous, and not just for the usual pregnant things Tony remembered his mother going through with his little sister, like hamburgers, milk and ice cream. Marsha bought bags full of guavas, melons and bananas. She would walk along Mulholland and pick other people's lemons, oranges and grapefruits, sort through their trash and find half-full jars of marmalade and sauerkraut. She brought home magazines she found in the garbage and kept them in neat stacks on the kitchen counter. Tony assumed it was for the flowers.

He knew she was behaving strangely but his script was more important to him than Marsha's craziness. It was all just a phase. They always seemed to meet for dinner in the big dining room, never in the kitchen, and things seemed civilized enough. Marsha used the house's finest crystal and china, which worried Tony, but she never broke anything. Candle-light every night. As she entered her fifth month, dinner was always on the table at seven, the candles would be lit, and they would eat in silence. One night Tony found her sitting at the table with a jar of red caviar she must have found in the pantry; the expensive kind with the big red eggs from the Caspian Sea. She ate it out of the jar, with her hands, letting it trickle in orange streaks down her chin. He had enough.

'Am I supposed to be impressed by that?'

Marsha continued licking her hands.

'Marsha, talk to me, please.'

'It's delicious. You can taste each egg.'

'Use a spoon.'

'Caviar eats away good silver. Didn't you know? I read it in the silver book in the drawer. It's not our silver, Tony. I have to be careful.'

'I see.' Tony studied Marsha. She had gained about fifteen pounds. Her breasts were stretching her T-shirt. He wondered if they were full of milk yet, if he could place his lips on them and see if the milk was sweet. If she would let him.

The Santa Anas had started the end of that July, and from the two-story dining room window they could see a row of young cypress trees bending painfully in the wind. Crows and blackbirds, normally perched on their tops, had lined themselves on a wall, scavenging the ground. He stared at his wife, multiplied in the mirrored wall, taking huge bites of sliced melon, her nails ten different colors. And then it hit him. Her food was the same color as her nails. He started laughing. Marsha put down the melon.

'What are you laughing at?'

'I was just thinking. Your nails are the same color as the food you eat.'

'Of course they are.' She stared at him and smirked.

'Don't you know anything, Tony?' With that she got up and cleared the table, and they didn't speak for three days.

They slept in the same bed but didn't touch. He could feel her moving about at night, getting up from the bed then returning an hour later. One very hot July morning, he found her hand clutching his penis, which was painfully hard. She was fast asleep, and around her neck was a lei she must have made in the middle of the night from the Hibiscus that ran along the driveway. They were crushed and he could see tiny bugs hopping around the bed, but he didn't move. He could feel his balls constrict and without breathing he came, watching her breasts rise and fall, almost slapping against her belly. His semen was warm and as it trickled down on her hand she woke up, staring at it, then wiped her hand on the sheets. Never acknowledging him, she rose and walked towards the bath, then turned and smiled.

'You see, there's a religion to the jungle.'

After a particularly rough day working on a scene that wasn't working Tony asked Marsha if she wanted to see a movie. Get out of the house. They were having eggplant, rice and chicken with mangoes. Marsha just shook her head.

'I've got everything I want right here.' She continued chewing.

'My home and my baby.'

'And where do I fit in?' Tony put down his fork.

'You don't.' She bit into another orange and smiled.

Tony was not good at resolving things; this he knew was a weakness, knowing what his father had always said – let time heal. So he poured everything he had into his scripts. He began to hate a lot of things, including his weaknesses. He found Marsha the next afternoon in the kitchen with the open doors blowing in the dust and summer, with three large pots of water boiling away, a half dozen chickens hacked in quarters lying on the center island, their blood running off onto the floor, where broken packages of spaghetti and chopped vegetables had spilled. All he could smell in the room, which was steaming up, was Marsha, that innate smell he recognized as hers. She was dancing slowly to a jazz station on the radio in her bathrobe and wearing a pair of high heels in jungle red he had bought her in Boston as a gag. When he asked her what the hell was going on she smiled sweetly.

'Chicken soup for dinner, darling. We have to save our money.'

She continued to dance as Tony swept up the spaghetti and vegetables and went into the bedroom and took a nap. When he woke up for dinner the air was purple and he reasoned it must be hitting nine or ten o'clock. His soup was on the table, still hot, but Marsha had eaten hers and disappeared. Maybe she had gone for a night appointment at the free clinic. She had mentioned they were open at night. Tony ate his soup and cleared the table, listening to the wind. He then went on his nightly rounds, checking the doors and outside lights. He found Marsha in the garage, touching the angel hood ornament on the owner's Rolls-Royce, fingering it as if by the act of touching, it would become hers. For the first time in months, she looked at him without a trace of hate, and took his hand.

It was hot enough to work only in the morning; then sleep on dreary, scalded afternoons when even the television seemed too loud. Tony had moved his typewriter out onto a small patio off the pool where the wind couldn't touch him. He usually sat naked in the seven a.m. sun, smoking cigarettes and drinking ice tea. His third screenplay was almost done; a science fiction fantasy involving two women who have affairs with aliens that they find are brothers, which makes them sisters-in-law. It was a comedy, a good one. He wanted to show it to Marsha but she didn't seem interested. He knew selling it would make her happy. Anything to make her happy.

Things seemed to be another day of silences. Their detachment was worse. Tony ate on the terrace and Marsha seldom left the kitchen. She slept in another room, which angered him. He did not see why her hate had become virulent and unrealistic. He had never slapped her around. Or even yelled at her. He was not a big provider, that he knew, but he was working his ass off to see if he could become one, and in Hollywood, no less. That must account for something. He had always been taught to let things take their course.

And he had been faithful to her for six years. There were times he wanted to screw around, and there were propositions to him. He never took them up. He was excited by Marsha and felt he understood her needs, even in Boston, when things turned bad. As he thought about it, he realized most of it was bad. There was a new problem with Marsha every other month. Her nightmares and her sudden sexual heats, which was all he could describe them as, because that's what they were.

The prospect of a child made him happy but frightened. What if he didn't become a success? Her silences reminded him they were really nothing more than servants, even with the luxury at their feet. It was cold, sterile and almost a sin, staring at his tanned body in the mirror. Perhaps he was undeserving, and Marsha was. Under the rapid light of eastern clouds, sometimes shadowing the pages as he typed, Tony thought about what it could be like for them with real money. Hollywood money that just keeps rolling in. If his child would be beautiful. A little girl. With Marsha's white skin and the curve of her lips when she smiles.

He thought of this house and how it feels to be rich. How if they ever had money their house would be warm and inviting and full of people. Not like this house, where color evaporates into pulse, with only the grate of wind and low-flying planes. Its furniture chosen from fear. To Tony the house was a high dive, weightless with spread arms, its altitude was suffocating and settled nowhere. It had the hard enamel of a heaven bought. There were times, when Marsha was in her silent kitchen making the first round of coffee, that he would wake up with vertigo, shaking the sweats out in the shower. Remembering snow and the first Scotch of the evening. And Marsha's laughter as she took his clothes off by the heater.

That particular morning the winds were so high he had to work inside, then his IBM electric stopped. The power lines must be knocked out, he thought to himself. The phone was out too. He made a mental note to make sure all the glass doors were locked and fastened at the ceiling to avoid any wind damage. As he walked down the skylight lit hall he could hear Marsha chopping something in the kitchen. That, and the sound of the wind, were the only sounds he had heard in six months.

Marsha had an enormous bunch of birds of paradise and their large pointed leaves on the center island. On the floor were dozens of banana tree fronds and huge Magnolias. The room reeked of Magnolia and sap.

'Power's out. Honey, where in hell did you get all of that?'

Marsha was chopping off the lower stems of the birds of paradise with a meat cleaver, the pungent jelly dripping on the kitchen floor. She didn't answer.

'I asked you, sweetheart, where did you get all that . . . all those flowers?' Marsha kept on chopping.

'I took them out of an empty house's yard. No one knows. These cost a lot of money at the market you know.'

Tony always felt like an idiot about flowers.

'Why are you using a meat cleaver?' It seemed like a perfectly sensible question. He wasn't sure a pregnant woman should be handling a meat cleaver. He hated the sight of one; it always reminded him of a slaughterhouse. His father had worked in a meat packing plant in Boston. Tony never forgot seeing the carcasses whisked along on hooks. And how in the summer they had to wear treated cotton masks to keep from fainting.

'It makes the cut smoother and the plant lives longer. Tropical plants get stringy.' When it came to flowers Marsha took herself pretty seriously.

'I'm sure they'll look real pretty, honey.'

'Don't condescend to me.' It was as though she knew what he was saying. Was he that predictable? She put the birds of paradise in a giant Japanese porcelain vase, spreading them out at different angles and heights until they looked to Tony like an amusement park ride. What was it? The 'Octopus'. Only these didn't light up at night. And they weren't black metal, although Marsha's voice was.

'All I said was that they look nice.'

Marsha turned away from him and began to pick up the vase. Tony could see it was too heavy for her.

'I'll do that. Here, Marsha, come on.' Reluctantly she let him put the vase on the front hall table.

'Thanks.' He saw her eyes study him coolly and he realized he still hadn't put any clothes on. He had gotten used to being naked in the dry heat. He liked working this way.

'Shouldn't you put some clothes on?' Tony was tired of feeling like a buffoon around her.

'No I shouldn't. It's hot. And who's going to see? There was a time you liked me walking around naked.' Marsha pursed her lips.

'Even if this was our house you shouldn't walk around naked, period.' She walked back to the kitchen. Tony followed her in.

'What have I done to you? What have I done to make you so –'

'Go ahead Tony. Tell me the facts of life.' Marsha went back to the center island and started chopping the banana leaves, arranging them with the Magnolias. Her disregard was beginning to anger him. For six months he endured the silent treatment, tried to reason it out and let things pass.

'It's not worth trying to even fight with you right now, Marsha. I can appreciate you're pregnant. You probably feel lousy. So let's just leave it at that. OK?'

'As a matter of fact, I feel great.' The silence between them was plugged in, electric with revulsion. Tony stood with his arms crossed, knowing she would continue.

'I feel fucking great.'

Marsha stood staring at Tony with true contempt. He had never seen her face this way. Or he had never looked for it in her.

'You know, Marsha, I liked you better when you were drunk.'

'That's really funny, Tony. I liked you better when I was drunk, too.'

Tony reeled. She was just another woman. Marsha was only a name he married drunk. She had his child in her, which he never got to touch, or feel it kick. There were no moments to recall.

'Bitch.' Marsha started chopping again.

'Tony, you're a failure. I was a fool. You can't write. I read one of your scripts and you can't even spell. You're just jacking off. You couldn't even get us a decent place to live.'

Marsha wiped the meat cleaver with her apron. She ran her hands, covered with sap, through her hair. Tony realized there was something seriously wrong with her. She was ill. That was it. Mentally ill. Her hair was wet with sap and stank. He could smell it across the room. She laughed to herself and arranged the flowers again, then turned on him, hissing.

'All I wanted was a child. Did you know most female animals don't really need the male? Once they have their babies their cycle is complete. And I don't need you anymore.' Tony knew she needed help. He knew she loved her husband. He shouldn't have turned on her like that.

'I don't believe we're having this fight. I love you Marsha. Please forgive me. Let's forget this, OK?' She stood still as the vases in front of her. The wind heaved and settled. It was only ten a.m. He would call her doctor. Then he realized he had no idea of who her doctor was. She said she was going to the free clinic to save money. And he had just accepted it, never bothered to ask, figuring she knew what she was doing. He realized he didn't know a lot of things.

'I'm going to check the circuit breakers. I have a hunch it's an outside line, though. You take it easy, honey.' It was a stupid way to leave the room, but a convenient one.

The circuit breakers were in the garage, a climate controlled, robbery-proof room with a Bentley and a cream Rolls-Royce. Part of his job was to start them up and run the engines to keep the batteries alive, which he did on a regular basis. The garage was temperature controlled from a ground vent and the keys were kept in a small box under the cars. Tony got in the Bentley and revved up the engine. He realized this whole scene was nuts. He was sitting naked in a Bentley in a four million dollar house he didn't own with his wife going crazy in the kitchen. He turned the engine off, resolving nothing, checked the circuit breakers, which had nothing to do with anything in his life anymore. He walked back into the bedroom and put on a pair of jeans and a T-shirt, then went down into the Valley in his beat-up Ford to try to find a doctor.

When he came home later that morning Marsha was sitting in the living room in a big French chair facing the window. The house was hushed and perfect, with Marsha's tropical flowers everywhere; on tables and on chairs with hard seats, lined along the hall, on steps and in front of doors. She was singing to herself and didn't seem to notice he had come in.

'Marsha?' She stopped singing.

'Yes, lover?' Her voice made him cringe. It was soft and breathy; a bad imitation of a sexpot.

'I've found us a good doctor. I don't want you to do any of this free clinic stuff. I want you to come down with me right now, OK?'

'Why?' He had never heard her voice so suddenly deep.

'Because I want to make sure you're OK.'

'I'm fucking great. I already told you.'

'I don't think you are.'

'Then fuck off.' She giggled slightly, staying absolutely still in her chair. He realized she was staring at something else besides the view.

'What are you going to do, Tony, put a bag over my head like a snake?' He suddenly felt frightened.

'Stop talking like that, Marsha.'

'I'll say whatever I damn well please, buddy.'

As he slowly walked over to Marsha's chair he heard a rattle. In front of the window, about five feet from Marsha, was a large rattlesnake, coiled and studying them. Tony could only manage a whisper.

'Jesus Christ.'

'Perhaps.' Marsha remained still, her eyes focused on the snake.

'Marsha, honey, you got to move away real slow. Do as I say.'

'Why? He's been here for over a week. That's how much you know, you stupid little fuck. He's very comfortable here. Happy. You know that word, don't you? Only the stupid are ever happy, Tony.'

The rattlesnake continued to rattle. Tony thought it would strike with any wrong move. Its eyes seemed dead.

'Did you know that coyotes mate for life? They're all over these rotted hills. On the road I've watched them dig up trash cans. That's when I know there's something good in the can.'

Tony felt numb. He wanted to get her out of that chair. Cumulus clouds bearing a summer rain hovered on tips of the mountains at the northern rim of the Valley.

'You see, that's how hungry I am.'

Marsha's words made him choke on his saliva.

'At night, when you're dreaming about all the good things, Tony, things that will never happen for us, at night I come in here, sit in this chair and talk to him.'

'Marsha, we have an appointment with the doctor.' Tony tried to make his voice natural, normal. Marsha would not take her eyes off the snake.

'Faggot. You're a faggot.'

'Marsha, please, let's go. Now.'

'He doesn't bother me and I don't bother him. He's been here over a week, right there. That's how much you know, you stupid, miserable fuck.'

Tony watched the snake. It hadn't moved and the rattle had stopped. Then he saw why. It was lying dead on the air conditioner vent which came up through the floor. When the air conditioning was on, the air blew its rattle.

'I want my child to be perfect. In the jungle they eat their young if they are not perfect. Everything must be perfect.'

Tony suddenly saw himself from a mirror across the room; his wife covered in sap on the French chair, the dead rattler, the wind blowing the water in the pool, spilling over the edge into the city, the trees twisted and shaking, the sweat running down his armpits and spreading across his T-shirt, his script chopped up and scattered on the floor, the flowers everywhere like bees, the light on the rugs changing with each passing cloud, and Marsha smiling, holding a knife in her lap.

nirvana drive

EITHER SIN IS or it isn't, and it cannot be put to reason. This is what Hope is thinking as she pulls the trigger. Her gun is a metal boy that jumps in her hand, making a nearby vase of carefully arranged irises throb and shift slightly on its table. This room has condensed into a cage she has made only moments before, and the afternoon is suddenly bright as a signed deed. She is aware of every detail. The room is hers.

The first shot she takes at her husband, Frank, is in the groin. He squeals and clutches himself, all jagged and startled. The fluid from one testicle pouch is slowly running down his leg. His pants began to blossom with blood, like clouds soaking sunlight at dusk.

Frank can only stare at Hope. He sees her left eye squint, icy with detachment. Her other eye is a zero, a far-away target – black, calm, ready. He curses in Japanese, his gold glasses fall off his nose. Hope is amused. Frank's glasses were always falling off, annoying him constantly, and now, in his last moments, they are falling off again.

She laughs and shoots at his heart, the way she has rehearsed it for a year, living in her tiny condominium in Brentwood. Alone every night, she has examined her locked elbow in the brash pink light of her bathroom. And learned how to squint, point, carry the jolt.

They have been divorced exactly one year. Hope made her plans when the papers were signed and she was thrown out of her own house. She knew she would have to kill her husband, that was the only way to complete this squalid cycle, and it would have to be done in the summer, when no one is alert, when Los Angeles turns brown and hot.

Hope now knows that treachery is only another form of modern communication. During this past year she made Frank feel comfortable as she executed her moves. They lunched together, made small talk even though it was strained – murmurs about financial concerns, their grown daughter, Louise, their separate plans for the future. Frank seemed to have no plans, except, of course, to spend her money. When he politely asked her plans, she lied. Nothing they said was of even vague interest to either of them. Lunch once a month. Someplace nice. With a booth.

The gunshot is precise in its sound but she misses, hitting his shoulder blade. She hears the bullet splinter the bone and come out through the back, grazing the rug with a tiny bit of flesh that looks like live bait.

Frank falls, a popped spring toy, clumsy and suddenly fat. He begins writhing in circles on the persimmon oriental rug, speechless. Hope assumes the pain is great. That just about now Frank is feeling it, really feeling it, and the surprise of being shot is wearing off.

She seriously hopes that he will beg. But he seems to be beyond such calculations. No more manipulations from Frank, no more curtains drawn in the middle of the day, different dialects, whispers, sour deals. She realizes that this should be, and must be, a point of enjoyment for her; it should be savored.

Hope is amazed at how quiet a room becomes after a gun-shot. The air collects itself and waits. Mirrors magnify, blood pumps, thoughts assemble. Breath is a cautious, strangled language. In this open-windowed room, perched above the city and reeking of the deepest part of August, this simple murder takes on an unparalleled muteness, like a church cloister in the middle of the city. This is so easy it's serene.

The French doors open out to a flagstone patio and a pool. She realizes she will never be allowed to see this pool again. Below it, Los Angeles is drifting away from her, into a past tense, along with Frank and the last twenty-five years.

The carpet is becoming wet with blood and Frank is still turning in circles, gulping air. Hope decides she has time, she'll go ahead and aim anywhere, and shoots at his thigh, which stops the frantic writhing. She walks around Frank, thinking he might look up at her, but his eyes stay on the floor, and she suddenly realizes he might be dead.

Hope knows this dance is a last psalm. Killer and victim have only seconds to share. The killer says Pay attention to me, I've got you all to myself, and I'm the last person you'll ever see. I'm giving you a gift of white light and silence. Thank me. This is as intimate as it gets, baby, and makes sex nothing, a big thud of flesh. And I'm going to shoot you again.

Keeping the gun in one hand, Hope searches in her purse for her make-up mirror and strolls over to Frank. Bending over, she puts the mirror to his open mouth. His hands and eyelids are shaking in a palsy. She sees breath on the mirror and is satisfied, returning it to her purse.

Her change of clothes is at her condo. Her plane ticket, medication, passport, make-up, money, credit cards, prescription sunglasses, and cigarettes are all neatly stacked in her bag. The gun she will throw in a trash bin somewhere in the Valley, in a nice middle-class neighborhood.

Returning her attention to Frank, she slowly prods his face with the toe of her taupe suede high heel, careful not to stain it, and shoots at his teeth. Blood shimmers in the air like a lemon squirted over fish and she quickly withdraws her leg.

The bullet comes out of his chin and grazes his chest. Finally she hears Frank whimper. But it is not coming from him, only his nerve endings, which are tightening, forcing sound out of his larynx.

Bits of teeth are going down his throat. Hope notices this is definitely where the most blood flows, and tips Frank's head back against the rug so he doesn't choke, not just yet, then steps back and lights a cigarette. She has made sure this would be the first cigarette of the day, the one that tastes the best. She inhales deeply.

'I know I'm not supposed to smoke, Frank, but what the hell.'

Her own voice surprises her. It is deeper than she imagined. Like those women Frank would smile at in bars. Women Hope has always been a bit envious of.

'Frank, I have Louise all taken care of. Everything goes to her. Your debts will be absolved, but as usual I have to pay for them.'

The afternoon is still and Hope's cigarette smoke twirls around her.

'You are rotten, Frank.'

Hope finishes her cigarette, making sure she smokes it down to the filter, something she never does, but for this last discussion with Frank she feels one complete cigarette is appropriate; a signal of respect. She extinguishes it with spit between her fingers and puts it in her purse. Hope checks herself for blood. By keeping a measured distance from Frank, she's avoided any mess.

She decides to take a shot at his left hand, the one he used to thrust inside her with his childish contempt. Frank's body flaps and Hope takes one more shot for the road, this time at his forehead, and she doesn't miss.

Silence. Then the sound of crows and echoing sirens somewhere in the canyon. She turns and looks out the French doors and sees a helicopter from Channel 2 circling over the junction of the Hollywood and Ventura freeways. Death enters this room and puts a hand on her shoulder, saying Good work, Hope. Clean. Hope smiles.

Hope is back at her condominium in Brentwood. She has exactly one and a half hours to get to the airport, the little one in Orange County named after John Wayne. She has turned all her utilities off, defrosted her refrigerator, and made sure everything is vacuumed and clean. These are meaningless, feminine gestures, and Hope almost laughs.

Hope changes clothes, packing her killing ensemble in the suitcase, then puts on an outfit, the only one hanging in her closet, which consists of lipstick-red slacks, a gaucho jacket, a black hat she bought in Madrid, a lace blouse, and fine black alligator heels. She does not want to slip out of Los Angeles unnoticed, but rather wants someone to say later to the papers, Ah yes, that's the woman at the airport . . . she looked like a stoplight, you could see her a mile away. No, I didn't know she was a killer. She looked so beautiful. Very mysterious, like someone out of an Almodóvar film. One of those crazy women. She took a plane to New Orleans. That's all I know.

As she slips on her slacks she tries to remember if everything is correct. She has left her condominium in trust to her daughter. Frank's family can't break it. Hope decides she will use her credit cards until someone catches on. She has taken all her cash, almost thirty thousand dollars. There was a time when that was spending money for Christmas. She wonders if Louise will sell this little box and use it as her very own bail-out money when life is almost over and things are not worth staying for. Hope knows she has been a spoiled woman all her life, that her money will run out fast, and she doesn't care.

Her child is taken care of. Her little box is shut down. All she has to do is lock the doors, walk down the gold wallpapered halls, and light another cigarette, the second on this well-planned day.

She was foolish to buy this place after the divorce. All divorced women move to these little concentration camps with a view of an alley and a neighboring building, deadbolt locks, and fake fireplaces. They spend their years staring into the windows of buildings that hide the sun, hoping to catch other people's lives like a voyeur. But it never happens; never the romance of windows and silences. Curtains are drawn, and they only hear voices of other women alone, widows and recluses, bitches and cripples, all of them with a telephone.

Hope is only waiting for land and sky. The jump and growl of the plane as it heads up and the sky before her saying, Look at me, Hope. If you look hard enough you can disappear. My air is clean, full of color and wind. Come to me.

Hope unhooks her brassiere and takes out her pliable foam

breasts that look like the real thing. She runs her hands over the two precise scars that singe her chest and tries to remember what her exquisite breasts were like. She remembers the first lump. Hope ruined two mattresses from her kicking, particularly during the chemotherapy, and her hair never came back.

Now is the last time she will be looking at herself in this closed pink bathroom and Hope tries to smile. She smiled when Frank died. She knows she can do it now. From now on her breasts will look different. She will sit on a deserted beach in the Caribbean and let the sun heal her scars. No one will see her, or know that she is not in remission, that her cancer is still opening inside her like a poisonous flower. She will drink in local bars, put on crisp cotton clothes, and dance. She will let the few strands of hair on her head turn gold from the sun, maybe even use the juice of lemons and tangerines to help it along. Like a bronzed witch. She will wear straw hats with fresh flowers. She will become sexual, alive, ripe. She feels it is possible. Hope knows if you stare too long in your own reflection you will see the devil. She takes her gaze away from her wounds and changes her wig from the stiff matronly bouffant to an auburn short shag that is hanging with her last change of clothes. Hope realizes today she is exactly fifty years old. She wanted to kill Frank on her birthday.

Hope repeats the word *fifty* over like a chant until it is inside her. It is what she used to do when she found the cancer. She chanted lump . . . lump, took the medication, and tried to die.

Now for new lipstick. A blue-red from Revlon, a vibrant, insincere color that matches her slacks. She sprays herself heavily with perfume. She wants everyone on her way out to remember what she smells like. She is ready.

It is approximately four p.m. One hour ago she tried to call her daughter but couldn't find words. She called from Frank's library, his little world, and when she heard her daughter's voice come on the service she stared at Frank's body and found herself mute. She was not upset, only detached. She had already left Los Angeles when she made the call to her daughter, but her body was still here, moving about, killing, tidying up, exterminating. She had worn gloves the whole time, and they made her hands itch. She took them off in the car. Driving home, that's all she could think about. How her hands itched.

Standing in the shadows of this afternoon, Hope checks off a mental list. No one saw her go into the house on Nirvana Drive. She always hated the street name. Frank named it. It's just the private drive to her family's house. It's like naming a house Happy Hill. Ridiculous.

Nirvana Drive, the house she bought, the house her daughter grew up in, huge and tiled and deep. The house her husband of twenty-six years gradually bought out from under her, then threw her out of.

No one saw her car as she parked farther down Mulholland and pretended to be taking a stroll. At the top of the hill people are left alone.

No servants today. They stay as far away from Frank as possible on their days off. She'd entered Frank's study from the terrace, an always-open garden door. It was extremely simple. She had to wait only ten minutes for him to come into the room.

She could tell he saw through her, that he was suspicious.
She had that planned as well. She began to cry. She knew
that Frank, like most Japanese men, believed all women must
be taken care of. She knew he would let down his guard. He
walked over to her. She pulled the gun out of her purse and
shot him.

She disposed of the gun in a Dumpster in Van Nuys, then
drove over the hill, up Beverly Glen and down, listening to
harpsichord music on a classical station. She learned that
death is a rather clumsy sound and doesn't mean much. But
music can soothe. Hope thought about her action. She talked
to herself in the car, saying over and over, This is premeditated
murder, Hope, you're going to fry. And she didn't care. She
realized then, in the car, she was made of cold blood; people
who kill are capable of everything and nothing; they are
infantile, ignorant.

Hope adjusts her wig and puts the finishing touches on
her face. She knows there are places in the world she must
see, places that no one visits, full of bad religion, heat and
waves. She is going to walk into those waves, and smell the
salt.

Hope decides to leave one window open for Louise, so
when she walks into her mother's condominium the air is
fresh. She wonders if Louise will hate her. If her only daughter
will feel relief that her mother has disappeared and is not in
prison. Or if Hope's only gift, this beautiful, bright Eurasian
girl, will remember her at all. She dreads Louise finding out
about her cancer, which she probably will, from Hope's doctor.
Hope is Irish. Louise is half Irish. She will be strong.

Hope whispers a prayer as she opens the door. Please God,
forgive me for what I am about to do. Please forgive my sin.

Please do not let me die someplace that is not beautiful. And let me die alone, simply, like an animal in the woods.

It is approximately six p.m., and as Hope boards a plane to New Orleans under her own name, Frank's body stares at the ceiling with eyes the color of milk. A light wind is being born, and the simple gauze curtains framing the open French doors are rippling with a gray summer Pacific steam. Within minutes the view is obliterated, as happens at the end of August when dense fogs wrap the hills like mink.

Frank's blood has drained into an island on the persimmon oriental rug, leaving his skin almost translucent. The rug itself is sticky as honey. Flies have begun to cluster. The face staring up into nothingness does not look surprised or horrified or desperate as some murder victims do, eyes open, the mouth twisted into a belch, saying no, not me, no, it can't be. Rather, what's left of Frank's face has the look of a small creature that has been stepped on without care. The only completely tranquil features are Frank's open eyes, which are still in place. The lower part of his face is cracked open like an oyster, and the majority of his upper forehead and skull are in several pieces around him, not unlike angels around the head of a Mexican icon, the kind painted on tin.

Fog is beginning to fill the room. This old Spanish house on Nirvana Drive has been rewired so that various lights come on automatically at a certain time of day. As the desk lamp in Frank's study switches on, it seems treacherous, sinister as an approaching car, its headlights glowing in mist.

The police will not arrive for another day because the help, a Nicaraguan couple in their early seventies who have cared for the house on Nirvana Drive since the 1960s, are visiting their children in Palm Desert and will not be back until the following midmorning. By then the room will have begun to smell, even with the doors open. This leads Rosa, who knows every smell in the house, to motion to her husband, Hector, toward the study. When they discover Frank's body, they will stand motionless for several minutes, transfixed by it, knowing it will be the only scene like it that they will ever be privy to. They will call the police, then Bel Air Patrol, and in exceedingly good English report a murder. No hysteria.

Hope is certain she has left no fresh fingerprints, though her prints are bound to be in this room, and every other room of Nirvana Drive, simply from the years she lived there. Traces of her perfume, Je Reviens by Worth, will have been extinguished by the fog. Only a menace in this room will be felt, a menace fueled by exhaustion and silence.

And silent it is. Only three real sounds occur in the hours that await Frank's discovery. The wind knocks over a small crystal vase full of lopsided flowers that was an accident waiting to happen. The crystal shatters on the dark wood floor, and water from the vase slowly seeps into a loose groove. There is the sound of coyotes near the pool and veranda. They smell blood but do not venture inside, as the house is lit. And the automatic sprinklers go on and off at regular intervals. The only other sound is Frank's answering machine. A deep Japanese voice leaves an angry, threatening call at about one in the morning. No name is given, and the caller abruptly hangs up. Obviously Frank was meant to receive this call at exactly this time, and pick up. Several days later, through a translator, the police decipher the message:

Frank Kano, you there? I know you are. Pick up. Maybe you think you're too good. We know where you live, Frank. We will pick you up in Tokyo on Friday. Have everything for business.

Hope kills Frank on a Tuesday; by Friday, police have contacted Interpol and the Tokyo police, giving them Frank's flight information. Plainclothes officers are stationed at the airport. No one is picked up. No one shows.

As Frank's body begins its surprisingly fast process of rigor mortis, a letter, sealed and addressed to his daughter Louise, quietly falls on the floor catercorner from Frank's ebony-and-zebra wood desk. The police will open and read it, and contact Louise immediately. It is written half in Japanese, then in English. Also, judging from the quality of penmanship, Frank was not just drunk but under the influence of a strong narcotic when he wrote the letter, which has no date.

> *Dear Louise;*
> *Please take care of your mother. I will be going to Japan on a business trip. This will be extended, maybe several years. I will have my secretary send you all information. When I go please pay Hector and Rosa out of money I leave in envelope in study. I love you. Be good girl.*
> *Love, Dad*

It will take only four days to find out certain things about Frank Kano. That his house on Nirvana Drive is mortgaged for more than its current value. That Frank Kano is deeply in debt, to the amount of over a million dollars, most of it involving an operation of speculators in Tokyo and Beverly Hills.

That his daughter Louise is sole heir and beneficiary, and that his ex-wife has left town on a trip to New Orleans. It is found out that their divorce was due to her infidelities, not his, and that she has recently survived a radical double mastectomy and is not in remission, but has, in the doctor's opinion, two to three months to live. The police do not consider Frank Kano's ex-wife a suspect because of the nature of her illness, the conversations with her daughter who flies down from school at Berkeley, and most important, because the murder is one of the finest examples of assassination-style killing they have seen in quite some time, and generally it takes an expert to do it.

Autopsy will reveal Frank Kano ingested enormous amounts of barbiturates, including Seconal, mixing them with cocaine, alcohol, and aspirin. He would have died within a period of three to five hours anyway. When his stomach is cut open the pills remain undigested, glinting like fool's gold under the morgue lights. Frank Kano was ready to die. He just had no idea how he would die.

It is carnival in Martinique and Hope can hear flutes and drums, a pulse she has listened to for five days. The tin drums clang through banana trees and willows. Hope thinks tonight she will dance again, as she has for the past two nights, until her feet bleed from the rough streets. She will drink the rum Vieux Acajou from bottles anonymously passed to her, and she will let its deep mahogany water warm her cancers. The hands passing the rum are blue-black and shaking under white teeth and masks from parrot feathers and tinfoil; crow feathers, dove feathers, and white silk; starfish painted gold with tiny diamantés sitting high on royal, wrapped heads.

At dusk the sky fills with violet ash from bonfires and mari-juana. The farther she goes into the Carnival crowd the more chance of hashish smoke blowing backwards into her face and nose, the more loud French sighs that fall into air like snow.

Hope is past disease. She does not care anymore. She does not care if she has many men tonight, or just one, or none at all. Whatever happens is part of the end of her life. She does not care if she passes out in the street and wakes up to a morning strewn with glitter and feathers tumbling in the Caribbean wind.

Her body is tanned and alert. A new, painless lump has formed on her upper rib cage, under her arm, and she pays no attention to it. Others will form, deliberate and demanding, she knows they will, but they will not get her consent. There are too many other things right now.

The air is fragrant with French roses, pineapple, and live-stock. It is a low tide. She can smell cinnamon in the coffee a black woman named Beatrice has left on her glass patio table. She has bought in Fort de France a violet silk-and-cotton gown, slit to her privates and down to the floor. She will go out tonight and dance. She will wear a new wig, a curly blue-black raven's mop of hair that she will dress up with pearls.

Hope has checked the American papers when she can find them. Nothing has been written about Frank. She seriously believed, in her first week here, someone would be watching her. But nothing. Hope wonders if they realize it is her doing. When she does think of it, she laughs. At first, she didn't. But the sun cured her, disguised her. Hope has tasted the nothingness of the Caribbean. It is alive and purer than any geography, finer than a diamond, marriage, or a house on a hill. This vacancy, this sleep in the tropics, is even finer than death.

Hope turns to Beatrice, who has entered the room with fresh linens.

'You going dancing tonight, Beatrice?'

Beatrice shakes her head and clicks her tongue. 'Too many bad men. Only one thing on their mind.' Beatrice has a mouthful of gold teeth. Her accent is clipped, a stern French.

Beyond the hotel room drums continue to play. Beatrice rearranges a vase full of huge pink and yellow flowers. Hope coughs up some blood, casually wiping her mouth with her hand. Her nails are painted violet.

'You ever kill a man, Beatrice?' Hope's voice is hoarse, somewhat weak. Beatrice smooths out her dress.

'Twice, Miss Hope. Once with a knife. Once with poison.'

'Ah. I never thought of poison,' Hope thinks aloud.

'They tell me in church even the best-laid plans can go wrong,' Beatrice ponders, 'but if you know how to keep quiet, you can solve all your problems.'

Hope smiles. She is having pain in her left foot, probably from all the dancing. She can smell jerk chicken and freshly caught fish in the air. The perfume of honeysuckle and coconut. The drums are increasing their frenzy. Hope can hear a choir, sexual and distant. She will close her eyes for only a moment. In the next room, she can hear the flapping of sheets as Beatrice unravels them. Like the flapping of birds' wings, Hope thinks. Every kind of bird she's known.

samba

EVERY MORNING MONICA woke to a new color. The operation, which she had saved for over the past five years, was coming in two weeks. Her plane ticket to Mexico City, the clinic confirmation, the conversion of her savings into pesos – everything had been planned. She saw violets and pinks that she had never seen before. Her new life as a woman would be full of flowers, trips to different plazas for fresh fruits and vegetables, maybe even a smile at the distinguished men who happen to appraise her.

The girls at the club were so excited they whispered about Monica even when she was in the room. She felt suddenly important, feminine, and brave. She would be the first at the Pink Lantern to really go through with it. Not spending her life with siliconed breasts, estrogen, and a penis that has to be taped up every morning.

No one would know she was the original Miss Santa Monica Boulevard, hence her name, Monica. She would become another Dolores del Rio, a woman of the river, but it would be Monique del Rio: mysterious, French and Spanish, retired from Hollywood – from a glamorous career. She would even marry and adopt if the chance came.

She had promised herself to do it correctly; her doctor in Los Angeles put her through psychological tests before he referred her for the operation. She had heard the tales of drag queens who weren't sure but went through with the surgery anyway; they wound up suicides or eunuchs in a dress, hustling the streets, shunned by their families. Monica would not have it. She was meant for the change.

Her best friend, Theda, as in Theda Bara, explained everything to her one night after the show. Monica had Mexican shawls over all the lamps in her apartment, and Theda, way past fifty, was in her stage drag – a silvery puffed-shoulder number. She wore a diamond ring on every finger. Her summer diamonds: some are, some aren't, she explained. In the dim red light, she seemed tired, grotesque as she puffed on her black cigarettes and spoke in her vacant, she-male voice cluttered with hormones and years of practice.

'You see, dear, you are one of the lucky ones,' Theda said. 'God just made a small mistake with you, and she does not – I repeat, *does not* – mind if you correct it. You were meant to be a woman. Don't let the fools out there tell you different. We know, don't we?'

Theda had spent years on the strip circuit because she was fat and her tits, which were her own, looked like they belonged to a woman. And her penis was so small she could easily hide it under a G-string. She'd made a fortune stripping in Alaska in the sixties. No one ever knew she was a man. If someone got too rambunctious, she would beg off with female problems. The only obstacle was avoiding the theater managers who wanted a taste of the talent. If they had known she was a fat boy in drag she would have been killed. Fairbanks, Theda pointed out, was a boom town for a smart girl.

'Today there are no restrictions, Monica,' Theda would tell her. 'I'm the kind of drag queen that's going out of style, I suppose. Now people line up to see the tits, knowing the cock is still there.'

Monica had heard it before. She would stir another pitcher of martinis and the two would talk until three or four in the morning about the best drags, the Charles Pierces who played big halls and were real stars. Theda would reminisce about how, in the fifties, men couldn't dress in drag in public without facing arrest. In clubs they wore a tux and a wig, lipstick, maybe a pair of earrings, and conjured it up, the bitchy glamour.

The only reason Monica had started in drag was because there was no other way to get through her life on a reasonable basis. She was thirty-five, and wanting to be the woman she was, and needed to be, was like a honey that covered her heart, making her gasp for air during the early-morning hours when she tried to sleep.

Her world was self-created; it shimmered every night at the Pink Lantern. Here she discovered there were many women like her, beauties all of them, waiting for the colors only women know, the magic and the white light. It was all around them, in the eyes of their audience, the mirrored ball in the center of the room, and in the pink, hushed back bar where the girls greeted people after the show and dreamed.

Monica had worked her way up to three spots in the show – all glamour drags – lip-syncing to Latin songs. She dyed her hair jet black and wore green contacts, and her breasts, as large and soft as the doctor in Palm Springs could make them, were always displayed proudly. Electrolysis had taken care of her beard, and collagen and estrogen had made her flesh soft and rounded. Monica was lucky; hardly an Adam's apple, and tiny hands and feet. She was thin, a size six, and now went almost everywhere as a woman, even to the market.

Monica never thought about men. She could have made money advertising in *TV Epic* or *She-Male* magazine and possibly even found a lover, but disease terrified her. When she saw herself naked in her mirror, she would study her penis. It was not hers; only a mistake that belonged to someone else. The idea of men would take years of living as a woman to understand. And there was no time now.

She remembered when there was time, when she was sixteen and still living with her mother, who found her wasted on speed, wearing her old wedding dress and crying at the attic window, repeating over and over, 'I'll never get married like you, don't you see, Mama? I'll never get married like you.' Her mother stood there at the sight of her son who she knew was her daughter and spat, walking away. Monica took her mother's trunk of old clothes from the fifties and never came back.

There was Laddy, an Armenian hustler, who found Monica, Miss Santa Monica, three weeks later in front of the Formosa Café wearing high heels and a black eye. It was a dazed, hustled-out night in Los Angeles, full of shirtless kids giving head on front lawns, and alleys of night-blooming jasmine. Such nights were fast and painless except when a john found out she wasn't a woman; hence her black eye. But she was proud that she had gotten that good. Laddy told her he was straight, that he didn't like queers. But it was fast money when he needed it. He was sixteen too.

'You're a pretty woman. You know that?' he asked. Monica was startled. She had seen Laddy enough on the streets to know that he knew she wasn't a real woman. Why the act? She liked him, though. He was small and muscular, with curls of black hair on his chest that smelled like aftershave.

'Thank you. I like to think so.'

They wound up back at Laddy's place, a garage conversion. It belonged to a leather queen who let him come and go as he pleased, as long as he brought a couple of guys over every Sunday. There were books everywhere. Monica picked up a few.

'Where did you get these?' They were all about movie stars. Greta Garbo and Clark Gable. Judy Garland.

'I steal 'em from Pickwick's. It's easy. You go in with a newspaper and you come out with a book. I like to get stoned and read during the day.'

'They're great.'

'I knew you'd like them. I got them for you.'

'That's nice, Laddy.' She heard her voice become very small. He must have been watching her all this time. Waiting for the right move. He slowly reached over and kissed her. This was the first time a man had kissed her in that way, a thing she always imagined and pretended in front of her mother's mirror; how she would look up into his eyes, her neck arched, her hair falling behind her.

She lived with Laddy for six months, almost never going out. He brought her everything: books, magazines, dope, food, and candy. Laddy would find old wedding dresses in trash cans or steal them from thrift stores, and Monica would dye them midnight blue, black, and coral. They listened to Brazilian music, always the samba.

The old leather queen in the front house grew fond of Monica, calling her 'Your Grace.' Once he took her and Laddy to a club called the Bull Pen where Mexican drag queens had a Thursday night show. Everyone got smashed and Laddy pushed Monica up on the stage, grinning. There was a disco song playing and she started dancing to it. The audience applauded. Monica still remembers Laddy's face that night with his stupid, doped-up grin, so alive, keeping an eye out for johns and whistling at her.

The Bull Pen gave her a job, and three days later Laddy was gone. She woke up with the old leather queen standing over her, telling her Laddy was dead; it was the drumbeat of young men who disappear in parks. Monica took her books and dresses and left, deciding then she would become a woman.

There were more men who were roommates and occasional lovers, but they saw Monica as something else, an amusement, a party gag. She saved her money, worked hard, and said nothing. She went to a clinic and began the estrogen. By her early thirties, she'd performed in Reno and El Paso and had a secure job at the Pink Lantern. Five nights a week. After the show she often watched herself in the dark, her silhouette in the mirror. Every minute gesture took hours to perfect. She decided Mexico, with its warm winds, would be the place of her rebirth.

But there was still a vacancy she did not understand; a room she had to find, perhaps painted yellow and open to the morning sun, where she would know, finally, she was a woman. Something still didn't feel right. Until two weeks before the trip to Mexico City, when Monica met Jack.

It was the last show of the evening and the Pink Lantern was half full, mostly drunk married couples. Dee Dee, the manager, had given Monica a new number, 'The Look of Love,' by Dusty Springfield. Monica wore a black velvet strapless dress and put pearls and a strand of rhinestones through her hair. She liked the number because she could just stand and emote. No dance steps. Her feet were tired and she wanted a martini.

He was staring at her with his arm around a woman who was probably his wife. Married couples always sat rather indifferently with each other, while lovers were still thick with excitement. She played the number to him, not getting off the stage for the tip. He stood up at the end of the song and clapped and whistled. His wife, a nice-looking woman, maybe forty with upswept blond hair, smiled. Monica bowed and looked past the curtains for Theda, who was on next with her monologue of dirty jokes. Instead, she saw Dee Dee gesturing with her hands, saying Keep going, keep going.

The silence was strange to Monica, but she kept her head bowed dramatically until another song started playing; she'd know by the first few chords whether it was a lip-sync or a dance routine. She could feel the overhead lights go off and the Rita Hayworth backlights go on; she loved the way they lit her from behind, a silhouette. When the song started she was startled; it was Brazilian – a samba – her favorite, but she didn't have a routine for it. It was too slow for a regular drag queen march across the stage.

She looked back at Dee Dee again, who signaled for her to strip. She had never stripped. Why now? In two weeks she would be a woman. A woman who would never strip for anyone. A woman who would lead a gracious life. Someone quiet and dignified. Monica thought about walking off stage, but she needed this last paycheck. Dee Dee was making I'm-going-to-cut-your-throat signals.

Monica breathed in the shadows of glistening mauve and took off a glove, then another, her hips rotating very slowly.

She pushed her hair out of its bun and let the pearls and rhinestone chain fall on the stage. She could see the light hit them; they sparkled like coiled snakes. There was a chair at the far end of the stage. She walked over to it, dancing lightly to the music, and sat à la Dietrich, with legs crossed. Monica knew she had plenty of time with this song, and she smiled at the audience. She ran her hand up and down her leg, which thrust out beautifully from a five-inch heel. Then, timing herself, she began unsnapping the quick-change buttons at the back of her dress as gracefully as possible. She wasn't wearing a bra because her dress had built-in boning to push her breasts out. The only thing she had on was a thin black-lace G-string. Her penis was bound with soft black tape and would never show. She let the dress fall to the stage as she stood up, cupping her breasts. The audience seemed very still. That man was whispering something to his wife. He should be watching her! Monica walked off the stage into the audience, letting her hands drop to her sides and shaking her titties lightly. The audience was thrilled. Most of the strippers never left the stage.

Monica figured she might as well finish off with a bang, so she sauntered over to the man and bent over the table to touch his hair. Her breasts rubbed the top of his cocktail glass. His wife turned very red and averted her eyes. Monica could feel the ice steam on her nipples as she smiled at the man, looking directly into his blue eyes. Monica danced back to the stage, picked up her dress, and took a bow. The audience clapped, but lightly. They were tired, and she felt like she'd made a fool of herself.

Backstage, Dee Dee looked panicked. Dee Dee never looked panicked. 'Why the hell did you put me in a strip?'

Monica demanded. 'I never strip.' She waited for one of Dee Dee's smart-ass replies.

'Miss Theda wasn't here and you know she's always here . . . Monica, Miss Theda had a stroke and died.'

Monica studied Dee Dee's face with its beard and acne showing through white pancake make-up. The last song kept playing over in her mind: the slow *shh* of the drums, the saxophone, her naked breasts, the man's blue eyes, the smoke in the club. She studied the racks of sequined dresses in flame yellows and hot oranges that would be taken apart and resewn next week for a new show, the turkey feather trims and fake fur headdresses, the collars of paste rubies and sapphires. Theda was there, hidden in the colors and reflecting the light.

Monica started to sob.

'I'm sorry, Miss Monica, but the DJ left 'cause it's late and took all the songs. Said he wants more money. It's all we had in the bin. I put it on 'cause you like that song. Least you say you do.'

'But it's a strip song.'

'I'm sorry. I really am.'

Monica held Dee Dee's hand. She didn't know what else to do, and Dee Dee was crying too, like a boy. The same pitch. 'Has everybody else gone already? Do they know?'

Dee Dee nodded her head. 'Candy is calling everybody. She's even set up the service. It's gonna be tomorrow. Real fast. It's what Miss Theda wanted.'

That night Monica went to bed at dawn, drinking martinis and thinking of Theda. How she had wanted Monica to be a woman, living in Mexico City, speaking many languages, seeing all the colors.

*   *   *

93

Theda was laid out in a big beige coffin, wearing a white-and-red silk organza dress. All the queens from the club were there, some in smart Christian Dior black skirts and jackets bought at secondhand stores, the older drag queens in red sequin gowns, holding clusters of balloons. A jazz band played 'Climb Ev'ry Mountain' and 'Cow-Cow Boogie.' The musicians had been instructed to end with 'My Funny Valentine.'

Many of the glamour queens stayed aloof, studying each other's hair, make-up, and dresses. Others blew their noses and cried. Everyone whispered that Theda's passing was the end of an era. Monica watched the service from the back of the room. She memorized the fluttering hats, the shrieks and whispers, the music. She'd given Dee Dee her notice that morning and she was already packing for Mexico in her mind – only what a real woman would wear, not the exaggerated outfits of men hidden as women. As the service lurched on with old show tunes and recordings of Theda's act, Monica imagined what it must feel like to wear white Mexican cotton on sunburnt skin.

The reception was loaded with food: quick casseroles, store-bought quiches and cakes, Jell-O, deli turkey, cubed cheese. Candy, who'd had too much wine, got up and sang 'You Made Me Love You' and cried. Everyone began to fade. The queens started remembering their afternoon beauty naps, the slow application of make-up before the cocktail show. The top of Theda's coffin was put down in the adjoining room. Monica left quietly, not saying good-bye.

Monica stopped by the Pink Lantern to retrieve her make-up. As she was leaving, she saw the man from the night before parked outside in a silver Mercedes, watching for her. She walked past with her head bowed. He honked the horn. She pretended not to notice even though she knew it was idiotic; there was no one else around. Then he got out of his car.

Monica froze. Why was he here? Slowly she turned and looked at him. He was younger than her, with sandy blond hair and a deep tan. He was short when she had thought of him as tall. She wondered how she must look to him. Like a woman in the sun, sad and doubtful? Or a drag queen who was making the jump because everything was getting old?

He seemed out of breath when he finally spoke to her. 'You performed last night, right?'

Monica stared at him and managed a smile. 'That was me, yes.'

'You were very good.'

'Thank you.' Monica started walking to her car.

He followed her. 'My name is Jack. I'm a photographer. I would like to take some pictures of you.' Monica was almost at her car. She looked for her keys in her bag as she tried to think of the perfect thing to say to get rid of the bastard.

'Pictures? What about your wife, Jack?'

He stopped, confused. 'How did you know that was my wife?'

'Experience.'

'She thinks it's a great idea. I'm a serious photographer. Here's my card.'

Monica took it without looking at it. He was as real as any come-on, she thought, and she was leaving the come-ons behind. Monica got in her car and looked up at Jack. 'I don't think so.'

'It's for a series I'm doing for *American Photographer*. They're nudes in natural light. Without make-up or props. Nothing sexual.' Jack let his shoulders drop.

Monica appraised this man with his silver Mercedes and his tennis shoes. 'Did it ever occur to you that showing my body naked is not what I'm about?' She was furious.

'Yes. Precisely. I'm trying to capture an essence that no one understands.'

'You mean the best of both worlds? Please, Jack. I don't think so.' Monica started her engine and looked up at him.

'The series is about women,' he said.

Monica turned her engine off and tapped her nails on the steering wheel. 'Listen, I'm a preoperative transsexual. In two weeks, I fly to Mexico City to complete what I have waited a long time for. I'm not a woman yet, so buzz off. It won't work.'

'But you are a woman.' Jack looked at her and blinked his eyes nervously. 'I saw that last night. That's why I'm here.'

Monica's head began to throb as though driven by doves. Sometimes when she was frightened or confused her knees would shake, and they were shaking now. Jack smiled at her and lit a cigarette. He offered her one, which she took and inhaled deeply.

Monica still didn't understand why she was in Jack's big studio at six a.m., looking at his photographs on the rough brick wall. Jack was in the darkroom, and his wife, Sue, the lady with the upswept hair, was making pancakes in the adjoining kitchen.

'You know, Monica,' she said, 'I'm so pleased you agreed to be photographed. This is an important addition to Jack's collection. It means a great deal to him.'

Monica smiled numbly. She looked at the pictures of Sue on the wall, pregnant and naked. There were photographs of old women lying on chrome chairs, some laughing and smoking cigarettes. Monica studied their vaginas and the curls that thrust up through the roundness of their bellies. There was no fantasy here. These women in shadow and morning light were not perfect. They had been marred by reality, something that had always been unnecessary for Monica. She had shaped her life by movies and magazines, forever smoothing the formula, changing the eyeshadow, a skirt, or a perfume so it would work. A perfect woman.

Jack came out of the darkroom wearing sweats, with a sleek black camera around his neck. Monica caught herself staring at it.

'It's a top-of-the-line Olympus. Best pictures you can get,' he assured her.

Monica looked around. This light would show the lines in her face. She thought about running very fast into the darkroom and not coming out. This was all wrong.

'You want to get started?' Jack asked, smiling. 'I want you to be comfortable. Don't mind Sue. Should I turn up the heat?'

'Yes.'

Jack went over to the wall and adjusted the thermostat. 'Well, how about it?'

Monica took her clothes off. First the shoes and skirt, then her blouse. She slowly peeled her panties down, then looked around, first at Sue, then Jack.

'I have to take the tape off. It takes a little while.' Her voice was pathetic and small. She slowly undid the tape while standing up, her hair hanging over her face. When her penis finally emerged it seemed like a child she had forgotten. She started to cry.

Sue walked over and handed her a cup of coffee. 'Sweetheart, don't be embarrassed. You're a very special lady, you know?' Her eyes sparkled. 'And by the way, the coffee is spiked with enough rum to set you on your ass for a week.'

'Thanks.'

'Monica, I want you here by the glass wall,' Jack said. 'See how the light is hitting it?'

She nodded.

'Stand facing me in half shadow. Just look at me the way you are now. You don't have to pose, just stand there and relax.'

Monica tried to tuck her penis farther into her legs.

'Leave your penis alone,' he said.

Monica looked at Sue, who gave her a big smile and a thumbs-up sign. As Jack's flash began to pierce her eyes, Monica realized her hair was hanging in strands over her face and her eyes were red. She could feel them.

'You're still too self-conscious, Monica, honey. All you've got to do is relax. So when do you go to Mexico?' Jack asked.

'Two weeks.'

'That's better. Now turn slightly to your right.'

'How long does the operation take?' It was Sue's voice.

'About six hours. Sometimes longer. Sometimes less, I guess.'

'Are you going to live there or come back here?'

Monica turned to look at Sue as she spoke. 'Oh, live there. I know it's supposed to be real crowded, but I hear it's wonderful, too.' She suddenly realized how innocent she must sound. Like a little girl.

'I'm so envious of you.' The frankness in Sue's voice stunned Monica. Jack stopped to reload his camera.

'What do you mean?' Monica asked.

'The idea of starting over with an identity you've decided on for yourself. Every woman wants to be able to have that freedom of choice. We get married and divorced and have children and take care of our parents, but never ourselves. You're lucky.'

Jack laughed. 'Sue wants to go in your place, Monica.'

'Well, I don't think Sue would ever want to be in *my* place.'

Sue sipped her coffee. 'You'd be surprised, honey.'

Jack positioned Monica in the middle of the room and walked around her, taking pictures. It was then that Monica saw herself for the first time as a woman like Sue, in a kitchen, running down the hall to check on a baby, breasts and hair in the light. She smiled to herself. The colors she saw were no longer artificial, only for the stage. She knew this was the start of her trip; she was moments away from Mexico City. The colors were measured and clear as bells.

Two weeks later, Mexico City belongs to Monica. It's big, screaming with life, smothered in a red dirt she sees on children's hands and women's shawls. She's had two days to wander the city and find an old apartment bathed in sun with terra-cotta walls overlooking a courtyard of tomato plants and wrought-iron cages filled with game hens and doves.

Everywhere there is the drama she'd hoped for. There are parks filled with flowers and dirty lagoons. Men who spit out coca leaves and dance shirtless, with patent-leather shoes and slick hair. Girls who run around in school uniforms and church dresses. Women who step elegantly out of taxis in white leather suits. There is the odor of foods cooked on makeshift grills, and kitchens full of dogs. There are billboards of women in black, smoking cigarettes with soldiers behind them like a firing squad, upside-down exclamation points, and the chatter of Mexican pop that rises like an aria out of the streets.

Now in her hospital room Monica looks out over a park filled with Aztec stones and unwatered grass. Medical students are having lunch outside, their white coats fluttering in the hot wind. She has written to everyone in Los Angeles, at first choosing postcards of Mexican film stars with names like Marta and Diabla, then putting them back in favor of the ones with pictures of peasant women holding flowers in their arms and smiling with blackened teeth. These, Monica realizes, are the real woman. These are the postcards that have her signature on the back.

No one here will ever know Miss Santa Monica. She will make her trips to the plazas, maybe someday buy a small car she can take to the mountains and to Acapulco even though the roads are bad. She will always stop to consider each color laid before her, and she will be free.

The doctor comes in, and Monica's heart is beating rapidly. He is a kind man with a crew cut and expensive new shoes that she can smell from her bed. He sits beside her and holds her hand. His English is perfect. 'I think we're about ready, don't you?' he asks.

She nods her head.

'Monica, you must remember there will be a great deal of pain when you wake up. And it doesn't go away until your body adjusts to its new set of rules. Can you accept this?'

'Yes, doctor.'

'The tissue from your penis will be inverted, so in the future if you choose to have relations you will experience a sense of pleasure. But remember, it is not orgasm. Those days, my dear, will be gone.'

'I understand.' She turns her head and looks at the telegram Jack and Sue sent her. She's taped it to her wall.

'BEST PICTURES YET STOP WE LOVE YOU STOP
GOOD LUCK STOP.'

A spray of orchids and Mexican wildflowers that smell like licorice are by her bed. Her pubis has been shaved, and the painkillers were injected an hour ago. She can fly now, above mountains and stages of mirrored lights open to sky. With sequined wings and drugstore perfume leaving clouds of snow behind her.

Monica watches the nurses with their teased blond hair and too much make-up. She knows they approve of what she's doing, she can see they think she'll be quite attractive as Monique del Rio. The ceiling is mint green. She thinks it should be painted with a fresco of little boys who become women in the clouds, with God's hand, a woman's hand, touching their faces.

Monica thinks back on years of nights spent singing with no voice, the pain of estrogen throbbing in her breasts, making her cry for no reason, and the first glimpse of her new chest in the clinic mirror. She remembers the gutters where she was beaten and discarded, her mother's menacing silence when she came home bruised, already knowing she was a woman.

One of the nurses puts the gas cup over Monica's nose and mouth. She can hear a samba coming through the walls – a young man's yelp and the roll of soft drums, then a woman's voice singing in Brazilian with maracas. She can hear the sea humming lazily somewhere south where the carnivals pulse nightly.

Monique del Rio laughs as she goes under, laughs with all the women whose secrets will be hers. She sits with them in a circle in the sun, dreaming with a swollen belly and the smell of men forever beyond the garden wall.

scheherazade in hollywood

THE POLO LOUNGE, 1.30 P.M.,
THE MIDDLE OF AUGUST

No one should be caught dead here in the middle of August, when the regulars are gone, and the heat freezes the green and salmon-pink walls into something desperately sweet, like old Easter candy. But it is my favorite place in the world when it is almost empty; only one other place has as much going for it, and that's the Colosseum in Rome when the cats come out at night.

Scheherazade, named by her Iranian mother and Mexican father – Sherry to her friends – has asked me out to lunch. She is always late. I chain-smoke, and the waiter knows to fill my iced tea, bring lemons, and keep an extra glass of ice at the side. It used to be Scotch, and before that, vodka with bouillon and peppercorns for breakfast. But not anymore.

I have selected a table under the center tree, because I like shade when it's as hot as this and I like the way leaves sometimes flutter down on the table. Very picturesque. I also know that Sherry, when she arrives, will study her surroundings to make sure that picturesque is exactly what they are.

Some whores marry and marry well; Sherry has married twice to great advantage, from what she has told me. Single again, she can't resist being back on the game. She says it keeps her days interesting and her nights booked. Sherry anoints our meetings with gifts and cards and laughter. The one unspoken rule is that I believe every word she says, and she is an astonishing liar.

Sherry must think I am rich. I have always lived well and never had a dime – still don't, and don't know if I ever will. My family had money, and my lover has money, but me? It doesn't matter.

That is a lie. Money matters to everyone.

Sherry walks in; a table of tourists becomes hushed, sensing that something is up, that this could be the Polaroid moment. I am the man in the corner, conveniently sweating in the shade, nondescript and satisfactory, like a telephone in a ladies' lounge.

Sherry has raven-black hair that glints with tiny sparkles of blue and violet. Her skin is not tanned so much as carefully colored by the sun. Her eyes are jungle-green; her carefully applied false eyelashes shadow glossed lips that have been outlined with a one-hair brush. She wears a shocking-pink Ungaro suit with matching heels; jewels include a ten-carat canary-yellow diamond ring that she says was a gift, of course, and a black-jade bracelet, brooch, necklace, and earrings.

No hat today – it's too hot – and her black hair is pulled back tightly into a ponytail.

This is her average luncheon ensemble. Within three seconds, Sherry has scanned the place for married men, men with money, and men without, resting her chin on Bruno's shoulder as she whispers the usual dirty lisp in his ear. This is the code, and it works. Everyone is pleasant, and nothing goes wrong. This is why lunch is a hundred dollars. Her diamond reflects the entire room like a kaleidoscope, saying, *Don't approach me unless you know how*. The tourists are speechless.

So you see why the Polo Lounge and Los Angeles exist. To render people speechless. Their eyes become heavy with avarice, chilled white wine, leaden plates of chicken salad, and waiters who know.

'You could at least say hello, Sam.'

I rise, flushed, giving her a solid kiss on the mouth. No air kisses for us. Sherry giggles like a flute.

'I swear I'll change you yet.'

'Tell it to Wayne.' I pull out her chair.

Wayne is my lover. The one with the money. He's much older than I am, and we've been together ten years. I still have to put up with the usual remarks. I don't mind. We have a sprawling house in the San Fernando Valley, four dogs, fountains, and a pool. Ten years is serious.

'And interrupt a solid marriage? Never,' Sherry says.

Like hell.

'Unless, of course –' We catch each other's eyes and laugh. This sets the tone. She has news.

'I've decided to write a book, and I want you to help me. I mean, you write poetry and screenplays and all those things. Wouldn't it be fun?'

No, it wouldn't. After a few drinks, everyone I meet wants me to write their story. I know tomorrow she will be on to something else. I inhale deeply for drama. Her eyes are assessing me.

'Well, you've certainly had a fascinating life,' I say.

She leans back in her chair and crosses her legs, triumphant. Her voice becomes low, conspiratorial, a measured smirk.

'And we both know how to tell the story, don't we?' But she is speaking to the room, not to me – as if the room could hear, or would want to. She is studying her left eye in a ruby-and-enamel compact, and then I realize she is winking at someone on the other side of the patio. Excitement is expensive, and professionals waste no time. A good whore could make it as a psychiatrist, I reason.

I like the way I am part of the 'we.' Suddenly, I am sexual, smart, mysterious. A participant in the feminine hunt. I have never been a whore, but I enjoy thinking like one.

'You look radiant,' I say.

'The jade came from Fred. Oh, but you know that.' She pauses for effect. 'What you don't know is the same man from Houston –'

'Hank. Hank in the sod biz from Houston.'

'Right. Well, the old fart blows into town, calls me *from* Fred's and says he's cancelled the sale. Of *these* pieces, which I've had for over two months. He tells me he's going to call the cops if I don't show up with the jewelry. That he was coerced. Now you know and I know that any policeman is going to take one look at a sixty-year-old man who buys a valuable jade set for a pretty woman not his wife and know he hasn't been coerced for shit. I decide to go along with it. I am not thrilled, as you can well imagine, but I am amused. So I trot over there wearing all of this' – she runs her hands over the brooch – 'and a thin silk dress that is barely legal. I put ice on my nipples so they stand straight out like horns. And *no* underwear. Little heels with bows on the toes. Anyways, I look at him and the cross-eyed saleslady –'

'She must have had quite a view, probably doubled. Or tripled,' I say in a low voice.

Sherry laughs. 'Exactly. And I give him the old Honey-why-haven't-you-called-me routine . . . you know, the I'll-return-them-but-I've-never-had-a-chance-to-wear-them bit. I say it loud enough so everyone in the store can hear me. Pouty eyes, liquid lips, the works.'

'Then what?'

'He starts to stutter and cough, looking at the outline of my bush. Turns out he wasn't going to call the cops. Or make me return anything. He was jealous. A married man with five kids and six grandchildren, jealous of me. And guess what?'

'He bought you something else?'

'You bet. A strand of South Sea pearls. Big black ones.'

A major lie, a well-planned lie. Every fine whore will tell you they don't have to sleep with anyone for anything – that they can get jewels by batting their eyelashes. She probably had to go down on him more than once, probably a whole weekend, and black South Sea pearls, which I know cost hundreds of thousands of dollars, are not gotten by wearing a thin silk dress. It is entirely possible she scored a strand of dyed cultured pearls, and will pass them off as Tahitian.

'Wow. I don't know how you do it.'

There are other stories at lunch. How a man she dates, a movie star with a cocaine problem, climbed up the fire escape at her Mid-Wilshire twelfth-floor penthouse and held her, naked, at knifepoint, when she had a black football star – no, make it two black football stars – waiting for her in the bedroom. She was too embarrassed to admit she'd forgotten his booking. Or how the staff at the hotel in Maui named the largest orange-and-silver koi fish after her, Scheherazade.

I am in a state of surrender. I feel delicious, and we slow our pace to include our dreams, exchanging all of them, letting the afternoon slide under us like a cool sheet after a swim.

10 P.M., A DINNER PARTY IN LOS FELIZ, SEPTEMBER

The Felixes, a couple from La Jolla who made their fortune in outboard motors, have invited me for dinner. Wayne won't come; he says he's too old for this kind of thing, and I know he's right. Standing in the Felixes' living room, which is crumbling and full of furniture from China, I wish I were home with him. But a part of me wants to gape and play the voyeur.

There is a strange society in Hollywood of people with ridiculous fortunes who have never worked and attend everything. Their lives are a negative not developed. Poised and curled like rattlers, they survive in the dusty French grandeur of Hancock Park, the monstrous steel-and-concrete homes high in Bel Air, bought with laundered money, and the casas in Palm Springs, with private family cemeteries and statues pricked by cacti. This is where stars who have faded go to hide, to be used for décor. They hang around until they die.

Tonight the society queens are here in droves. I know all of them, and I say hello to everyone. The queens are the kind who walk the walk of spoiled women; they think I'm pretty and nice and slightly dull, believing that I married well and that that is the only entrée needed.

Then there are the women named Eleanor and Tasha and Kelly who have passed fifty, who are covered in jewels and polyester slacks and dancing with no one in particular. Their husbands are in the television business and have grown too big for any one room. They sit outside on the columned terrace with televisions plugged into outside walls, their bourbon slowly swirling with perfect, fat ice cubes and ginger ale from

Lucky, harping into the night, like the parrots that live free in the canyons and scatter feathers into yucca and onto over-cut lawns.

I finally see Sherry. She is sitting on a sofa, surrounded by queens and some young hoods; they know they can't pimp her, because she looks way too expensive, but to be seen with her is a step up, and they hope someone is looking. The queens memorize her laughter and the way she exhales, let-ting the smoke drift out of her nostrils as though it were opium.

She wears a black-satin strapless gown, her nipples barely covered. Around her neck she is wearing that strand of black pearls, stroking them to draw attention to them as she tells stories. And the way she tells them is magnificent, lowering her voice to a whisper, her shoulders lightly powdered, her profile skull-like in the lights of the city. After a gulp of champagne, she slams the glass down on the smoked-mirror table to make a point. No one moves, and in the ensuing silence there is a collective sigh.

Sherry grimaces, looks around for a break, and sees me. She crooks one finger, motioning for me to come over, and blows me a kiss. The queens are annoyed. She crosses her legs and throws her hair gently around, leaning back into the deep cushions of the sofa. I sit down next to her and smile, saying nothing, waiting to see what will happen. Sherry slides her satined weight over to me, presses against me. It is a movement so completely natural that I flinch; like an opera singer just opening her mouth, Sherry uses silence with rehearsed force.

'Wanna do it?' she lisps in my ear.

'Sure, Sherry, but I'm expensive.'

'And so we should be, darling. Especially together. Very, very expensive.' She nudges me to look out at the city.

The September Santa Anas have made Los Angeles shimmer. It seems that tonight every light in the city below us has been turned on, every necklace taken out of the safe. And I remind myself that this is why I am here. To sit with a beautiful whore, high up sub-tropical mountains, and look at a city that survives on the invisible.

'You see that? I want that.' Sherry's voice is almost sad. She is playing with me. Below, in the perfumed, electric glitter, I can hear sirens. Sherry rests her hand on mine. I suddenly wonder if we will be friends when we are very, very old.

'It takes time,' I say quietly.

'But I can have it?' A child's voice.

'Of course you can. You can have anything you want.'

She takes her champagne glass and wets her fingers, dabbing me behind the ears. I love the smells surrounding me – liquor and Joy perfume, hairspray and English cigarettes, leather and French roses. Sherry and I are superstitious: champagne behind the ears for luck; no locked doors; wear red to win, violet to seduce.

'Why don't you relax, Sam? Have a drink on me. Just this once. I won't tell.'

'No.'

I realize I sound annoyed, and get up to leave.

'Love you, Sam.'

'Love you, too. Call me.'

It is an old house, full of old people and old furniture, soft, easy-to-digest food, and electric candles; there is a guest book in the foyer, which I don't sign when I leave, thinking how something missed in Sherry tonight, that her silhouette was old, perched against the city like a crow on a telephone pole, seasonal and searching for food.

SHERRY IS ALMOST FORTY.

I do not know that Sherry is almost forty. She has kept her age a smear, a fast introduction where the words are mumbled. She has never spoken of it, and I have never asked, but forty is a serious age in her business. Fees plummet.

I hear everything on the phone, from a bitchy boy named Julian, who seems to survive by doing anything the day provides; recently he caught up with Sherry, drawn to her stories and doing her hair, once a week, for free. She sold him her Eldorado, and he was furious because it is constantly in the shop. He is out for revenge.

'You should see the gray hair.' I hear a snip, snip on the other end. He is either doing hair or cutting coupons.

'Really,' I say. I have gray hair.

'I mean, fair is fair. She used me.'

'You let yourself be used.'

'What do you mean?'

'You know how she is. It's all business to her.' I say this cautiously, and then I listen.

'Look, I know more about her than you do.' He swallows, and I hear him over the receiver; he must keep a great deal of spittle in his mouth to swallow that hard. I am positive he doesn't know any more than I do.

'I consider Sherry a great friend,' I say. 'We know each other very well.'

'I bet you don't know she lives with a drag queen named

Ellis, and that's where she gets all those pretty clothes. They're the same size.'

'No, I didn't.'

'And that dump she tells everybody is some penthouse is a one-bedroom on Olympic, near downtown.'

I debate whether I should keep listening. I wonder if Sherry will call me tomorrow and mention Julian. Sherry has never invited me to her house. Some people do and some don't.

'How fascinating.'

He thinks I'm serious and continues. 'She worships you, you know. Whenever I see her at the mall —'

'At the *mall*?'

'Yeah, she works at Bullock's, in the costume-jewelry department. I thought you knew.'

'No, I didn't.' I am impressed.

'I was the one who introduced her to Ellis, when her dad died. She took care of him, lived with him for years.'

'But that's impossible. Sherry's mother and father live in Egypt, where his business is.' I think of Egyptian skin, of women with kohl under their eyes.

'You gotta be kidding. Sherry's from Fresno. So am I.' Julian's voice becomes giddy.

I say nothing. Julian can hear my intake of breath.

'Sherry's always been a fag hag. That girl's never had a boyfriend.'

I realize I am the most gullible of all queens. And that I am Sherry's litmus test — to see how blue turns to red and fades.

'I think she's frigid,' Julian goes on.

How kind of you, I think. Sherry ought to find herself a better hairdresser.

'She's terrified of men. Runs away from anything serious.'

'That I doubt.'

'Oh no, it's true. Frigid.'

I have to get off the phone; I'm liking it less and less. Goodbyes with Julian are not necessary, and I hang up, light a cigarette, and watch the sun pattern the garden with a vermilion lace, drying everything it touches.

POOLSIDE IN JANUARY.

I don't hear from Sherry for six months. Then the breathy voice is on the phone again. It is a surprisingly hot January morning, exotic with pine and leftover tinsel glittering on the street. The air is full of chocolate and nuts and young citrus; it is the perfect moment to re-enter someone's life.

'Hello, sweetpea. I just blew in from Vegas. And guess what? I got married.'

Liar. He owns you now. Whoever he is, he'll make you work.

'That's wonderful.' I know I sound guarded. I keep thinking she's been fired from Bullock's and lives now under a pier, telling stories under nets of seaweed, flies crawling on her arms. Beautiful women always know when men are hiding something, and Sherry feels the pause, knows what it entails.

'You don't sound too thrilled.'

'When will we see you?'

'Now. Right now.'

'Wayne's out of town.'

'Send him my best, but I'm still coming over.'

I admit to myself that I have missed her, and that I am

curious to see how long perfection can last. My voice becomes soft, feminine.

'OK.'

'I want you to meet my new hubby. He owns a casino, darling, and he's part of the Mob. Don't you just *love* it?'

'Is he really — I mean, do you know how dangerous that can be?' Is every word a lie?

'Nonsense. He's — we've got a bodyguard, an Indian named Charlie, who's a trip.'

'Oh, dear.'

'Anyways, I want you to be cool. Seymour doesn't know anything about my sordid past. He thinks I worked at Bullock's as a salesgirl. Can you imagine?'

'Seymour?'

'Seymour Stein . . . Stop laughing. It's true. All of it. So no talk, OK?'

'Fine.'

Suddenly Sherry's voice is business-like, efficient and parched. 'Seymour bought me a bikini, and we're coming swimming. He wants me to show it off.'

'It's Monday —'

'I know, but we're only here for the day. Be my friend, OK?'

Within the hour, Sherry rings at the front gate, a black wrought-iron door from the twenties, smothered in yellow hibiscus. Her black hair, once sleek and straight, is now curly and thrown on top of her head with a bandanna. She is wearing a Pucci tunic and has huge hoops in her ears. The clear January heat is liquid around her, a gauze, and I know this new Sherry will move through heat and tropical cities with their curtains and intense sun. She will gamble and win, buy jewelry that's real, and keep it in a make-up pouch. She will buy gifts for young men.

She grins when she sees me. Behind her is a cherry-red Mercedes 450SL and a beady-eyed, pale little elderly man smoking a cigarillo. Next to him is a huge Indian man, exactly as she said. His hair, which has the same coal shine as Sherry's, is in a ponytail that goes down to his hips. Then Sherry blocks my vision. She is radiant.

'Did you see the Mercedes?' Her whisper is so loud the dogs in the house start barking. Without missing a beat, she lets in the Indian, who is now carrying Seymour in his arms. I am amazed at how tiny this man is, contorted and puffing furiously on his cigarillo. 'Seymour has arthritis.'

The Indian stares at me as though I am to be hunted at a later point in my life and eaten. 'Seymour, this is my best friend, Sam.'

'*How*yado.'

'Charlie, this is Sam. Now, you be nice to him. He's one of us.' I wonder what Sherry means. Am I a hood?

'Hello, Charlie.' Silence. 'Well well *well*. Let's get a swim and a couple of drinks.' More silence. Sherry coughs.

Then, from Seymour: 'You got a nice place here, Sam. You got a comfy chair?'

I am gracious and smiling.

'Of course. Come this way.' As we walk through the house toward the pool, Seymour's ashes are everywhere – in the air and fluttering down on the dogs' faces.

'You sure got a lot of antiques. This place looks like a museum.'

'Thanks,' I say.

On the loggia, Charlie puts Seymour down in a large wicker

chair that resembles a throne. Sherry squeals and peels off to reveal a string bikini and a rash on her upper thigh which looks like cigarette burns. She is wearing five-inch-heeled open-toed gold mules that clack when she walks. Very Lolita. Seymour stubs his cigarillo out and immediately lights another one with a diamond-studded lighter. Sherry watches me, flirting with Seymour, then dives into the pool, swimming underwater with long, exact strokes. The only noise at this moment is the sprinklers hissing next door.

'She's a good girl.' Seymour turns and looks at me, then clears his throat. I nod my head yes and listen to the water lapping the edges of the pool. I think how Wayne would enjoy this.

'Would you like a drink? A Margarita?' For some reason, I don't see Seymour drinking gin or sherry.

'Sure.' Seymour smiles, then coughs. Soon I emerge from the kitchen with Margaritas, and an iced tea for me. Seymour takes one from the tray and gestures for me to sit down.

Sherry is dog-paddling in the pool, and I look for Charlie, seeing his clothes on the pavement. He is standing naked by the diving board. I can't handle it. Sherry squeals and goes underwater as Charlie dives in.

'That girl certainly has a set of lungs, doesn't she?'

'Absolutely.' As I squeeze lemon in my iced tea it squirts in my eye.

'Hope you don't mind Charlie. Kid never swims with a suit. Full Cherokee. He's my adopted son.'

'Quite a large young man.'

'You ain't just kiddin'.' Seymour rustles in his seat. I realize he is having some sort of gastric problem.

My eye is tearing, and I twist the ring around my finger so it catches the sun.

'So when were you two married?' I ask.

'Yesterday. We're on our honeymoon. Just a night, then back to the casino. It's a small place, but we do good business. There's no bad business. You queer?' No one has ever asked me this. Seymour sips his drink, studying me.

'Yes.'

'Good. The baby needs a good queer friend.'

I am not sure what to say next. Seymour is in control.

'Been to Vegas lately?'

'Actually, I've never been.' Which is true; Wayne refuses to go, calling it a scar in the desert.

'Never? You come soon as our guest, right?'

Seymour must have been a major shark in his prime. The way he throws out the word 'right' eliminates argument.

'You know her pretty well, don't ya, kid? She's a liar, isn't she? I had her checked out. She's harmless. A good, sweet kid.'

'Seymour, I –'

'There she goes again. Look at that girl swim.'

Sherry comes out of the pool, followed by Charlie, who shakes himself dry. Seymour picks up on my widening stare, and quietly speaks.

'That's the way the Indians do it, ya know, shake it off just like a hound – and they never change.' There is awe in his voice. As Sherry comes over to us she takes a Margarita. She sits next to Seymour. Charlie puts his clothes on and sits in the corner, keeping an eye on me.

'Tell Sam what we're goin' ta do, Helen.'

'Helen?' An ice cube has gone down my throat.

Seymour shoots a withering glance at me. 'Of course it's Helen. Isn't your name Helen, Helen?'

Sherry giggles and coos at Seymour, kicking my foot quickly. Seymour clicks his tongue against his false teeth. Sherry's hair has fallen in wet curls on her shoulders. She lights a cigarette and studies me.

'Seymour says I can have a house in Beverly Hills, besides the house in Vegas. And I want you to help me find it. Please, Sam. We'll have fun.'

'Sure. That's great.'

'She's worked hard all her life, ya know. Took care of a sick old man when her mother cleared out,' Seymour growls.

Sherry pats his hand. 'That's enough, darling.'

Suddenly, the lies are floating skyward, like cut balloons. Sherry is Helen, and Helen is forty, and I am rooted in the moment, watching the salt from the Margaritas spill in chunks on the tile.

the black cadillac

'It was a 1969 black Cadillac convertible. I remember it frightened me. It had an expensive paint job and highly polished black leather seats. The brights were on and the radio was turned on to an oldies station, pounding out "I'm just a lonely boy, I ain't got a home." The key was broken in the ignition, and the car was blocking the driveway of 2678 Old Topanga Road – I think, because we're at 2650, so it's three doors down. I don't know why, but I looked in the glove compartment, and the I.D. was cleared out. I looked for license plates; nothing.'

Jenna, into her tape recorder.
August 2nd, 12.30 a.m.

THERE ARE PLACES where people vanish. In the most normal of circumstances, at any time of the day. A soul is extinguished and kidnapped, causing us to shudder and not know why; readjust our car mirrors and check our hands, our shoes; perhaps even embrace each other, just to make sure everything is as it was. Suddenly, someone is gone.

Jenna felt it as Michael lay on top of her, the sweat from his chest rolling down her ribs. As he slid off, she heard it as well. An absence of something; a noise that, after six months in the canyon, she hadn't heard before. It was a car or the sound of a car running, then a gasp. Then, in a clear distinct order: something soft being tossed, the sound of insects on a summer night, Michael's breath on her eyes as he came, the

123

whir of the air-conditioner, and finally, gravel being dragged or scraped.

'Michael, did you hear it?' Jenna pulled herself up on the pillows, leaving the light off.

'Hear what?' His left leg rubbed against hers, and she could tell he was fading into sleep.

'Michael.' Michael scratched his chest.

'Baby, it was a coyote or something.'

'I heard a car. Someone and a car. Right when we finished.'

'Oh Christ.'

'Something bad has happened.'

'Nothing bad has happened. Now go to sleep.'

Jenna was up, putting a jogging suit on.

'We should know what's going on. Around us.' Michael was determined to fall asleep.

She didn't have to walk far. In the leaden August night everything had its own place, lazy and still. Then Jenna saw it, and she felt odd, sexual, strong. It was a black 1969 Cadillac convertible, empty and parked at a strange angle, its brights shining on the bearded trunk of a squat old palm. She could hear rock and roll, raunchy and deliberate as a slow fuck, coming from the car radio.

Jenna stopped and took in the picture in front of her, satisfied she had been right. It was slightly after midnight. She wished she could see better, but a Pacific fog shrouded any trace of the moon, which should have been almost full.

This was the time of year reptiles came out at night and Jenna froze, assessing her situation. It would be wonderful for her book, this scene. Quietly she walked over to the car, noticing it had no license plates. A chill grabbed her arms.

124

Something was wrong. She saw the key was broken in the ignition. She should go home now; absolutely.

Then she noticed how perfect the car was, as though no one ever drove it. Not even a candy wrapper or a cigarette butt in the open ashtray. Why was the ashtray open? She wanted to see if there was any information in the glove compartment, but she thought about fingerprints, so she put her hand into her oversized sweatshirt and quietly twisted it open. Empty.

She shut it and stepped back from the car. Palm blossoms fell in her hair and she brushed them away. She could hear field rats climbing up the trees, and at this moment she was aware of another distinct sensation. Her palms were hot, and she realized when she had touched the car, it felt like excited flesh.

Something in the brush up the drive moved. Jenna didn't pause to think, but walked, almost ran, down the quarter mile to her cottage, not looking back. Her body was convulsing with a sexual jitter she had never felt before. By the time she had taken off her clothes and spoken into the tape recorder, she stood in front of Michael, her nipples sore and her legs wet, and she spoke to him in a measured, loud rasp.

'Michael.'

'What's wrong?'

'Do it to me. Now. Fuck me.'

'What?'

'Now.'

That night she dreamed many dreams, none of which she remembered in the morning. Except they were in a black that smelled like a woman, covering her senses with grasping hands.

'The coolest car in the world is a 1969 cherry Cadillac convertible. Pink, pimp purple, gold, banana, silver, aubergine, and black. Oh yes. It's got the best of everything. It's big and squalid and luxurious as a blackjack win. It's got cruise control, make-up mirrors, and carpeting everywhere. It's like your grandmother and mother were winking at you, saying this is the only way to go, baby, and you can lie down in the back seat on a summer night and do it as much as you want. And the car is always a her, your best friend who always tells you, "You look great, baby." '

Jenna, into her tape recorder.
August 3rd, 9.00 a.m.

'That doesn't sound like you at all. I was listening.'

Michael was in the kitchen, having a cup of coffee. Jenna walked in and slumped in her chair, ignoring him.

'You know, if you typed it out instead of transcribing it, you'd be a real writer.'

Michael grinned and grabbed her and his keys, kissing her on the cheek. It was his daily, effortless, good morning gotta run kiss.

'Have fun at the studio, Michael.'

'Sure.' Jenna loved Michael in the morning. She loved the hair on his chest and his beard, his way of holding her, supporting her. He would be strong and muscular even when he was an old man. She could see it in the way he walked.

Now, in the quiet of this rustic kitchen, shoved against a dirt hill spotted with ice plants and blooming thistle, Jenna tried to recount what happened last night, but she couldn't.

The next thing she was aware of was that she was walking back down the road to see if the car was still there. The sun seared gaps of yellow and orange into the hills. Eucalyptus leaves were blowing over the faded tar of the road, hitting her knees and thighs.

The car wasn't there. Not a tire mark, or a spot of oil, or bent grass. Jenna shuddered, thinking whoever owned it must have had it towed away. If so, there would have to be traces somewhere. This stretch of road was incredibly quiet. She would have heard a tow truck.

A clear, empty wind blew her hair around. Jenna peered up the drive, this narrow little lane of palms, that the Cadillac had obscured and blocked the night before. It was summer and bad things don't happen on summer mornings.

This property and its long, curved drive had the opaque geometry of something baroque and European, with twisted leaves like shells covering tree trunks and swimming in slate and wood. This place certainly must have cost a lot of money, or certainly would cost a lot today. Its privacy held an anonymous, rich patina, drowsy and experienced and old.

'I walked up the drive and looked at the house, pretending to be interested in leasing, although no one was there and no one would give a shit in this dry awful canyon. Last night a car was here, now nothing, not a trace or remnant of anything. It blocked a driveway; the palms at the base of this driveway hide broken wrought iron gates that are worth a lot of money and tile posts that twist up, sort of, with mosaic chips. It's a long, narrow drive. The Cadillac must have been barely able to maneuver it. The house at the end is big, very pretty, with a front porch and clapboard, built in the thirties, I think. You put a swing on the front yard tree or have garden parties here. It's fully furnished and all the furniture is covered in sheets. No one does this anymore. This is very old fashioned, even for the East Coast, where people have cabins and things. Furniture today is either stolen or sold when people move. Not covered in sheets, waiting.'

Jenna, into her tape recorder.
August 4th, Noon

What Jenna loved completely was how strong she felt since she'd seen this car; how when she touched it the feeling of flesh hit her brain and didn't leave. It was this feeling of flesh and sex and power she felt all the time now, around Michael and when she was on her own. She wanted to know more.

There was more than this, more to understand. She slept through the afternoon, without dreams, her mind encased in a black that smelled of velvet and sweat and liquor. When she woke up she still had the sensation of laughter and gin. She knew it was gin, from the juniper berries and their perfume, and the smell of men after they had made love, completely different from that of a woman.

Jenna rose and looked at herself in the mirror, in the late hues of an August afternoon. She felt different and she smiled, then experienced a shock. She always had a full, beautiful smile, with perfect teeth her mother paid a lot of money for; now when she smiled it was out of the side of her mouth, like she had been hit, and could only manage a crooked leer. It made her laugh and think about cocksucking, and she laughed some more. How would she smile around Michael?

Jenna talked some more into her machine, this time about what she was feeling inside, how she was hot and ready to rub the walls with it, how Michael was going to get his when he got home. And then laughter that didn't sound like hers, but wonderful still, full of innuendo and sophistication. Whore. She repeated the word over and over again until she got it right.

It was about seven and the air had become lavender and full of barbecue smoke. Jenna had become very antsy, pacing the floors of her bedroom, looking out the window for Michael's car, until she walked out of the house and waited for him on the driveway, standing with her legs apart, like a man, hands on hips.

And then she felt it. Something coming towards her that was terrifying, reeking of black shiny cars, nights without lights, black mink coats, rooms full of ebony furniture and crows in cages. And women who inhale the black.

Then, without a pause, Jenna saw the black Cadillac. A chill dried her lips as the rock and roll came back to her, fast in its own wind. A blonde woman was driving it, with dark sunglasses and a cigarette between her lips. This was real. She could even see the fire at the end of her cigarette, but her face was a smear; she was going too fast. The blonde looked at her, and Jenna suddenly understood the black, felt the velvet and the liquor and the men. Her knees buckled, and she watched the world around her slowly slide away, as she collapsed on the pavement of the drive.

She heard Michael's car screech in front of her. She could smell engine oil and the smell of their kitchen, hearing him say something like what the hell are you doing you could have hurt yourself wake up wake up baby. At the same time there was another voice in the black, soothing and feminine, saying let's have a party. Just you and me and some guys. We'll make some cash and get fucked good and hard. What do ya say? Be a sport.

Jenna woke up, slumped in her chair in the kitchen, with Michael standing over her. Her palms were hot.

'Baby, did you hurt yourself?'

'No.' His eyes were so full of color.

'Come here, Michael.'

'What?'

'I said come here.'

'Jenna, what is going on with you?'

'Ah, go on, be a sport. Let me have it. Now, Michael, I want it now. In my mouth.'

The next morning Jenna argued with Michael, screaming at him. She told him to take a hike. She had a headache and her vagina was sore. She wanted a drink. As Jenna poured herself a gin and lime on the rocks, and lit a cigarette, she suddenly realized she had never smoked or drank, and Jenna began to scream.

> 'She's a blonde. Like white blonde ... platinum blonde, like Marilyn Monroe in 1962, ready to just float off, real thin and ethereal. I couldn't see her eyes. I saw her. I saw her driving that big black Cadillac convertible and she was real, goddamnit. And she communicated with me without saying a word. Pink, glossy lips and cigarettes. What I don't understand is: what is this girl doing in Topanga Canyon?'
>
> *Jenna, into her tape recorder.*
> *August 5th, 9.00 a.m.*

Jenna walked up the road, past where she had seen the house and the black Cadillac. Each house she saw had no cars, or signs of life. The houses were all clean and painted, but their lawns were brown and the sound of insects was deafening. This isn't where people live, thought Jenna, walking and shuddering on the dry stretch of narrow, steep road.

Then, at the end of the road, she saw gates that were so

out of place she stopped and laughed. As she turned around she realized the entire canyon, or most of it, was below her, and Jenna felt suddenly dizzy. Huge and antique and imperious, the gates looked like they were imported from Europe, and they were open, fixed in place with a small stone dog that acted as a doorstop. From there, a manicured straight drive, perfectly French, with clipped hedges, led to a white gravel motor court and a jewel-box chateau smothered in pink roses.

An elderly black maid, in a starched black and white uniform, opened the door and stood looking at Jenna, who smiled and waved. She suddenly felt like a child, that she needed permission to enter this hallucination. Black maids don't exist – and little French chateaux in the middle of Topanga Canyon? Impossible.

A tiny, elderly woman came out and peered at Jenna. She was a perfect little creature, with flame-red hair and a powder-lined face. She was dressed in a Chanel suit with a single rope of pearls, silk stockings, and a silk blouse. It was a hundred degrees outside, and the woman fanned herself with a magazine, motioning Jenna to come closer.

Soon they were facing each other, Jenna smiling and not knowing why. The old woman stubbed a cigarette out in the gravel and patted her hair.

'What do you want? Are you lost?' Her voice was like crystal.

Jenna shook her head no, thinking of exactly how to phrase what she had to say.

'No. Actually, I'm your neighbor. I live a half mile down the road.'

'You mean the cottage house with the green trim.'

'Yes, as a matter of fact.' Jenna watched the old woman smile broadly, her face cracking into a desert.

'I built that house in 1939, before the War, with my husband. We built all the houses on this road, except for that goddamn A-frame below you. Please, come in. You look rather warm.'

As she walked inside, an air enveloped her – of well-used perfume and a feminine schedule that never altered. The elderly black maid slowly limped into the kitchen and Jenna stood looking around the house. There were glittering, freshly-cleaned chandeliers, Aubusson rugs and silk damask draperies that matched fine period French furniture. French Impressionist oils hung on the walls, lit and dusted. On a Byzantine hall table, under a Venetian mirror, were photographs of the Duke and Duchess of Windsor, Cole Porter, Greta Garbo, and President Truman. She realized her mouth was open.

'It's beautiful.' The air smelled of roses and tobacco.

'Thank you. Please, sit down.' The old woman sat comfortably in an old French chair. Next to it was a TV on wheels and a lace-covered table with cigarettes and a very full ashtray. The old woman immediately lit a cigarette and stared at Jenna, flicking her peach-colored nails, breathing in her cigarette smoke with long, deliberate, and refined motion. She was aware Jenna was staring at her.

'Young lady, I am eighty-five years old. I like to smoke. It passes the time. These are the same cigarettes they give to convicts in prison. They are Pall Malls and they are excellent.' She waved her hand in the air as a final pronouncement. This was grandeur, Jenna thought.

'Just taking a walk?'

'Yes, sort of.'

'How is that old house standing up? You rent, obviously.'

'Yes.'

'There was a time that . . . What is your name, dear?'

'Jenna.'

'There was a time, Jenna, that this canyon was idyllic. We built for the Hollywood crowd, Gable and Lombard. And the English set, too. Everyone had a sense of beauty then. Style and grace. The houses were magnificent. We brought over Italian artisans. Then the hippies moved in. And all these fly-by-night developers. Jews.'

Jenna was Jewish and she didn't like the way this woman said it, but kept quiet. The maid wheeled in a tiny silver cart with the most exquisite glass of iced tea Jenna had ever seen. The old woman was handed a Bloody Mary, which she sniffed; once the maid was out, she took a small decanter of vodka from under her chair pillow and poured more in. She drank the entire cocktail in several gulps, then patted her mouth with a linen napkin.

'No one comes to visit much anymore.'

'I hope I haven't intruded.'

'Not at all.' Smoke ran through the room in slow, circular clouds.

'Several nights ago, something strange happened. I'm a writer, and I'm trying to decipher it. I wanted to ask neighbors questions, but no one ever seems to be around.'

'That is because, excepting yours, and that goddamn A-frame, all the houses I own. I keep them empty. Go on.'

'Now I see. Well, in the middle of the night, two nights ago, I saw this car, and it's disappeared, and I'm trying to make sense of it.'

'What kind of car?' The room seemed suddenly dark. The

old woman patted her hair again, staring slightly beyond Jenna, out through the French doors into her garden.

'It was a black Cadillac convertible. 1969.'

The old woman stood up and walked over to her French doors, opening them.

'Go on.'

'Last night I saw it again, and a blonde woman was driving it. Does she live here with you?'

'No.' The old woman's voice had become hard, horrifying; all nails and jagged knuckles.

'What did this woman look like?' The old woman asked the question as if she knew the answer.

'She was a platinum blonde. Very glamorous.' The old woman didn't bother to look at Jenna, but walked over to her cigarettes and lit another, then walked back to the doors.

'I know who she is.' The way she said it made Jenna's flesh wither.

'Who is she?'

'Not yet. Has anything in your life changed recently?'

'Like what?'

'Your appetites.'

'Yes.' Jenna heard herself say it but didn't know why she said it, knowing exactly what the old woman meant.

'Do you understand what it means to disappear? Vanish into another state of being, like when we die?'

'I don't understand.'

'Oh, I think you do. This woman was here, alive, and I knew of her. My husband and I traveled everywhere, knew everyone. We built Los Angeles. We brought the water and the roads into this canyon, built the house, developed Beverly Hills and Malibu when they were nothing more than hiking trails. We were happy, and then, right as we were becoming old, this woman rented a house from us down the road.' The old woman's face had turned into a scowl amidst the vases of cabbage roses and Chinese bronzes.

'It was 1967. The filthy hippies had moved into the bottom of Topanga and it was disgusting. This woman was an actress at Universal who never made a film. She was kept on the books because she was a whore. She worked on her back and she loved it. She couldn't get enough of it. I found out she was having these parties, in that house, that I rented to her, for groups of men. Sometimes ten, fifteen of them. She liked to be strapped to the bed and take them on, two, three at a time. Her appetites were . . .' The old woman took a deep drag on her cigarette, '. . . without question unimaginable.

'She met my husband. He deserted me for her and her parties. The men around her were like dogs. I never saw her face, but I know she was beautiful, and lascivious, and a demon. She was ridden with narcotics and disease, and the only thing I felt when I thought of her was an overwhelming black, like pitch, that made me ill.'

Jenna felt strapped to the chair. She had not expected this.

'I know she'd be dead by now, but no one's found her. And the men. All the men who swam in her degradation, my husband among them, disappeared. Some of these men were important, too. If you don't believe me, I'll give you their names. Look them up in newspaper files, police files – you'll see.'

'What was her name?' Jenna could feel her palms becoming hot, her legs twitching.

'I don't know. My rental contracts were lost. No one at the studio has any records. The only thing I found was that goddamn black Cadillac on the side of the road in 1970 and I had it junked.'

'No license plates?'

'Nothing. I'll tell you one thing, young lady. Don't think about the car. Don't think about the woman, or the house, or what I've told you, because people disappear for no reason.'

Jenna felt herself begin to shake and want to throw up. She bolted from her chair and ran past the old woman and her maid, past the silk tapestries and the hazy afternoon until she could breathe, on the road, where there was dirt and leaves and a place to go. Slowly, a half smile twisted out of the corner of her mouth and she cackled.

'Stupid dried up old cunt.'

What a moon tonight, Jenna thought as she peeled her clothes off in front of the mirror. The black voice had begun to sing loudly inside her and she loved it, loved the way her nipples were hardening in a blind heave of sex, making her come without thinking, dehydrating her. She was grinning out of the side of her mouth and winking at imaginary men, whispering obscenities and measuring her tongue.

She had to get out of here – this place was a dump – and look for some real men with some money who knew how to party. She put on a pair of cut-offs and a swimsuit top and a pair of high heels, then walked out the front door, leaving her bag on the kitchen table. She must have walked alone down the canyon road for over an hour, her hair blowing everywhere like fire, until she came to a stoplight.

This was easy. So easy that she laughed when a middle-aged businessman pulled up in a gray Buick from the sixties, his face white and pinched, licking his lips and rolling down the windows, telling her he was a salesman on his way to Canyon

Country and was she going that way? And she kept laughing as she got in, her eyes sparkling.

This was a rolling joke and they kept laughing on the San Diego Freeway north, past the lights of the San Fernando Valley and into the hills, where Jenna wanted to party. The road got darker and she cranked up the car radio and took off her blouse, spittle running down her cheek. She was talking oh so dirty and grinding her ass into the velour seat, her high heels on the dashboard. The businessman's arms were cold and dead and it excited her even more and she laughed whassa matter you just get up from a grave buddy and he said this is a great turnoff, it's real quiet here. Nice and dark, and I've used this place before. Jenna cackled, moaning sure baby, whatever floats your boat; she wanted to taste semen and blood, hers in his mouth and his on her skin, and it was then, when the salesman touched her breast with a hand that felt like a knife and drove down a dirt road, that Jenna saw the black Cadillac convertible next to her, the woman with platinum blonde hair and no face, and she started screaming, screaming with excitement as she was kissed with a dead man's breath, screaming because she couldn't see in the back seat what was rubbing her legs over and over, and screaming because she knew she wasn't coming back.

taylor and the mod girls

TODAY IS TAYLOR'S BIRTHDAY. He is twenty years old, and from his position on the terrace he has the Pacific spread out before him, and a clear California sun above. His mother, Sheila, faces his wheelchair to the north-west, so Taylor can see the line of mountains and cliffs stretching up the coast.

Neighbors on Carbon Beach always wave to Taylor on their late afternoon walks. Taylor waves back by pushing a button on the sides of his wheelchair. There is an oversized paper hand Sheila found at a shopping mall in Malibu. The hand, attached to a car antenna, rocks back and forth.

Taylor is retarded, and also paraplegic, with legs spindled and weary as an old parrot. His face has the down of a young boy, with gray eyes that stare intently at things his mother wishes she could comprehend. His head bobs when he smiles with his thick black glasses that make him look like Yves Saint Laurent, or so his mother says. When he speaks he sounds like a Southerner with too much to drink; 's's become 'sh's and vowels roll out like slow bowling balls. It is a man-boy voice, soft and forgiving, if Taylor has anything to forgive.

He forgives his body, with smooth, muscular little arms that end in hands, forged into claws that sit at an angle. He forgives his old father who died before he was born. Daddy is a word he does not understand and the Ds of the alphabet do not come easily. It is the lack of coordination of the tongue to the upper palate, which can only be touched spasmodically.

141

Watching Taylor push his button, Sheila looks out to the glitter of the Pacific and runs her hand through her long blonde hair, then waves to the Brilldenburgs as they jog by.

Today Sheila keeps him in the sun, making sure the radio is turned to KISS-FM. Taylor likes the taste of Diet Coke and has a cup and straw near his head. He's had a good appetite this morning and already polished off two sandwiches of Underwood's Devilled Ham by noon.

Sheila leans over the balcony, breathing in the smell of the beach. Another day in the sun. She reminds herself to be nice today to her friends. For years she tried to get other teenagers to be friends with Taylor, but there was always an excuse. Now it's just her girlfriends from the sixties, and the occasional ex-lover who pops in for a mercy fuck.

Sheila notices several batches of kelp and sandflies not far from the terrace. This is a bad sign. Taylor is terrified of kelp; can see it coming from miles out and yells to mother and bangs the arm of his wheelchair with his elbow.

In Taylor's room there are no toys. Mostly due to various apparatuses involved in his nightly ins and outs of bed, going to the bathroom and dressing. His mother actually built a special house, like a red barn, for his electric wheelchair so when Taylor sleeps his wheelchair gets to sleep too. The room has a huge picture window overlooking Carbon Beach. Life is simple. A chosen formula of light and answers whispered by the sea.

This afternoon Taylor is agitated. He knows from the paper cutouts and the white lace tablecloth on the wrought iron table by the pool that it's his birthday. He had wheeled himself into his mother's bedroom by accident and saw her wrapping a gift. Quietly he backed out and then giggled in the hall. He knows.

The mod girls are coming, Taylor thinks to himself as the waves break on the beach.

His mother, Sheila would do much more if she could. At this point in both their lives she does everything she can. She was an actress in the late sixties and early seventies who was famous. Taylor knows all her pictures in silver frames in her bedroom; that she's special. And that something happened, but doesn't know that it was him. His mother has long blonde hair that is curly and makes him laugh when it bounces on her shoulders.

There was a time when Sheila Jones had hair cut like Joan of Arc and dyed silver, walking eternally thin through a series of acid films that hit at the right time.

Before Taylor, Sheila lived in Rome and ate butterfly wings and flowers for lunch; advocated free love, and was seen wandering through the streets near the Trevi Fountain clothed in a wrap of see-through chiffon, and smoking hashish. There were fights in clubs like the 'Jackie O' where a glass of champagne was the price of a hotel room and billionaires made whores rich; Sheila was oblivious and fragile and the Romans worshipped her, calling her *la divinita*.

Sheila tries to erase the sixties but cannot. It's glued to her persona like glitter; tough and high and made for night.

She remembers amphetamines with different colors for different cities, and how life went hip. All the rich boys and girls were ready for obliteration, never captivity; their bodies would be paid for and their corpses abandoned in suites at the Pierre and the Waldorf.

'Happy birthday, Taylor-boy.'

Taylor grins, forms the word 'pres' and bends his head over to his mother. Sheila stops to wipe saliva from his chin, and kisses him on his forehead.

'We've got only a few minutes before we've got company, Taylor. The mod girls, Taylor. They're coming to see you.'

Taylor pushes his button and the giant hand rocks back and forth.

Opening the sliding glass doors to the kitchen and dining room, Sheila remembers about how last night Taylor saw her on MTV. A band named after an obscure food had blacklight portraits of Sheila with dandelions in her hair, their fur blowing around her pouting silver lips. Taylor banged on his wheelchair and gurgled, 'Mmmahmm.'

She's amused that this skinny, spaced-out doll was her. It doesn't bother her that Taylor recognizes her on TV. She likes the idea of Taylor cocooned in her image, without threats, and that Mama is everywhere for him. She wonders by what unseen process she was selected to represent an era, now sitting with a retarded son in a big house on the beach, her face a flat television icon.

She often wheels Taylor through Forest Lawns and super-markets, horror movies and Taco Bells, talking to him, making him write on pads and asking him what he thinks. Taylor can write some, and his sentence structure is up to over ten words. Sheila knows Taylor is thinking much more than he is able to write. Possibly it is a hidden agenda for something else, a shorthand only Taylor knows.

For Taylor, Sheila picks the Monday and Tuesday horror movie matinees in cool, dark theatres with carpeted ramps. She buys Milk Duds and the largest Diet Coke. Taylor loves popcorn, but it is difficult for him to handle. Sheila often brings a small cotton blanket so his pants lap won't be stained. They both love the theatres with cup holders attached to the seat.

Sheila always takes the Ventura in from Malibu and they hit the theatres in North Hollywood, like the Century 7 and the United Artists' Valley Plaza. Here they have a 'Hire the Handicapped' policy, and she is always impressed when she sees the young woman in the wheelchair at the ticket window. Taylor could do this someday. Maybe more. On Mondays and Tuesdays, a special school for the retarded brings in groups of teenage handicapped for the shows, in jogging suits and Reeboks, standing patiently in line, always excited, but not quite sure why. She thought at one time this would make Taylor comfortable and happy, but he doesn't notice anything except the movie, the popcorn and his mother.

It is here in the unevocable silence, the blue light before the curtains draw back, that Sheila takes her shoes off and watches Taylor for some sign, a physical resemblance to her or her dead husband, that will let her know she wasn't branded; her uterus psychotic and poised like a dog with bared teeth.

She finds the signs and breathes in deep. When she is here she can remember what it was all about, often not watching the films at all, but seeing the sets and the darkness that surround them. How she got to the point she didn't know what city she was in, or who the director was, or the man in her bed.

With Taylor in her Spanish house by the sea, watching television every night and waiting for nothing at all, Sheila is glad everything happened. She is glad to be fifty-two years old. She is glad for matinees and waves on the rocks, slow dusks and all-night markets. And for her son who smells like her. He is her shell to hear the sea, her young man of odds and mountains. He is her second heart, held by wire, beating and warm.

Sheila turns up KISS-FM and Taylor bobs his head. He likes techno-industrial-disco, where the beat is repetitive and goes on forever. A girl in a bikini lays down a large pink and yellow blanket. Sheila reminds herself to check Taylor's pants for semen stains before the guests arrive. Since his fifteenth year, Taylor's genitals react and work on their own.

Walking back into the house and toward the kitchen, Sheila remembers how, twenty years ago, her baby boy didn't respond. She remembers how no one called.

Then the arduous process of self-education. How to best care for Taylor. As an infant he crawled like a maimed animal and she devised a walker-like device with a back and padding that moved according to Taylor's whim. When he was old enough to understand and facilitate a wheelchair, she had a custom electric one made. She realized she was lucky to be rich. And that luck was relegated to daily events.

She stopped seeing men. After a year her house smelled of women who live alone; a distinct powder to every room, closed shades, secure bolts, unsexual arrangements of furniture predisposed to comfort.

She became an exceptional gardener, working in the sun every day, with Taylor in his chair watching the waves. Her flowers were Zinnias and colonchas, round and circus bright, and Japanese Magnolias and bonsai trees that she faithfully clipped, and planted in handpainted urns. On their trips to

Forest Lawn, where she had bought a small hilltop for her mother, Taylor and herself, she asked gardeners which flowers should be planted in which season; whether it was wise to put tropical plants by the sea in winter.

She had her pool painted black, like a lagoon, and swam religiously in the morning and in the Pacific in the afternoon when it was hot and quiet. Taylor would watch, screaming with delight when she was winded by a big wave. She collected shells when the tide went out, looking for abalone shells for Taylor, who liked to run his fingers over the mother-of-pearl center.

Sheila doesn't think about the fact that Taylor sometimes becomes violent, hurting only himself, or that he may have less than five birthdays to go, according to his doctor. Sheila thinks instead about pulling the chocolate-spice birthday cake out of the refrigerator so it will be room temperature. She thinks about Edythe and Romy and Claudia, what they will be wearing, who's got a new husband.

Sheila pulls out Taylor's present from the top cabinet over the washer and dryer. She bought Taylor an automatic keyboard that he can play on his lap. Turning around in the kitchen, she mentally checks off her party list, is satisfied, and opens the poolside doors.

'Hello, darling, I'm in from Honolulu from a marijuana *ranch*, not a farm, mind you, and I brought three smelly leis for Taylor and a great bag of dope for you, dear.'

Edythe air kisses Sheila and hands her a plastic baggie. Edythe is wearing a black Rudi Gernreich minidress against very tan skin. Her white hair is cut in a shag. She was 'Girl of the Year' in 1965.

'How do you get it through?'

'No customs, dear. We're talking Hawaii. It's not Hong Kong you know.' Edythe purses her peach lips. 'You know, Sheila, someday you really must learn to toughen up. Life's no fun *soft*.'

Sheila winces. Edythe turns Sheila around.

'Good. You lost weight. Now where is the birthday boy?'

Sheila points to the terrace and Edythe smiles.

'Oh, Sheila, while you're hiding the pot in your underwear drawer *do* fix me a double Stoly and ice, *lots* of lime juice.'

Edythe walks out to the terrace and kneels in front of Taylor. The ocean has built up a wind, and she kisses Taylor on the forehead three times.

'You are the love of my life, darling handsome boy. I love you more than life itself,' Edythe whispers in Taylor's ear, putting the three plumeria leis around Taylor's neck. Taylor is laughing when Sheila brings out Edythe's drink. Quickly Sheila takes a Diet Coke with a straw from a side table and makes Taylor sip.

'Sometimes, if he laughs too much, he gags. His gag reflex is shot,' Sheila says quietly. Sheila can hear the clink of ice in Edythe's glass. Edythe has her back turned to them.

'Refill?' Sheila asks sweetly. Edythe does not turn around, but raises her empty glass to Sheila, who gently takes it and goes to the kitchen.

'Doorbell!' Sheila hears Edythe yell from the terrace. She will let Edythe answer the door. She will be serene today, for her Taylor, for her friends. She will squeeze the lime slowly. Perfectly.

Sheila sees Claudia standing in the entrance, extravagantly embracing Edythe. Sheila knows Claudia only drinks Grasshoppers, and has a full pitcher in the refrigerator. To Sheila, Claudia has always had the most annoying habit of standing in doorways as though she were clutching an award.

Claudia made films for any Italian director with 'i' at the end of their name. Claudia is wearing a white leather motorcycle jacket.

'Ooh, a Grasshopper. Yum. Yum. You look divine, Sheila. Where is my darling Taylor?' Claudia squeezes Sheila, looking out towards the sea.

Claudia touches Taylor's shoulder and runs her hand through his hair. He cranes his neck and squints up at her through the late afternoon sun. His eyes are green.

'Mi amore, bello, bello.' Claudia reaches inside the pocket of her white leather jeans and pulls out a heavy gold and diamond ring. Gently she takes Taylor's paralyzed hand and opens it as best she can, then slips the ring on his wedding finger.

'Watch, Taylor, watch,' Claudia coos, positioning his hand in a shaft of sunlight. Sheila and Edythe are leaning against a kitchen wall, watching her.

'It sparkles in the sun, Taylor. Now, my pet, you are a married man.' Taylor rests his chin on his chest, looking at the ring. Claudia turns and smiles at Edythe and Sheila.

'Doorbell!' Edythe screams, running for the front door. Sheila decides to get through this afternoon, she will also have a double Stoly. Sheila has never particularly liked Romy, as Romy seems to be on another planet. But Romy is loyal. If that is any excuse.

In exaggerated silence, Romy walks past the girls, to the terrace and Taylor. She is barefoot, with sequined flowers woven in her electric-gray hair and a port-colored velvet dress.

'Happy birthday, Taylor.' Romy makes an imaginary box with her hands and with much fanfare places it in Taylor's lap. Taylor giggles and bangs the sides of his wheelchair.

'It'll drop,' says Romy cautiously.

'What the hell are you up to?' asks Edythe.

'I'm taking mime lessons,' Romy says cheerfully.

'That's a really cheap gift, Romy,' Edythe says, a tin rising in her voice. Romy shrugs. The mod girls retire to the kitchen, and Taylor is suddenly asleep in the sun.

'So what happened to Margo and Irene?' Sheila asks lazily, stirring the ice in her drink with her finger.

'Hysterectomy and cancer,' Edythe says dully, staring at her squeezed lime.

'I saw Roman Polanski in Paris two years ago,' says Romy. 'That new girl isn't half as pretty as Sharon.'

'Seen Linda McCartney lately?' Sheila asks. Edythe shakes her head, tapping her nails on the pine table.

'She's in frozen foods.'

'Anita Ekberg is big as a house,' Claudia says in a low voice. 'The only one who still looks good is Monica Vitti. I saw her in Switzerland four weeks ago.'

'I always liked Monica,' Sheila says idly. 'But I lead a quiet life.'

'What about Tess?' Claudia asks.

'Overdose,' Edythe snaps.

'Samantha?'

'Plane crash.'

'Maria?'

'Overdose.'

'Sylvia?'

'Breast cancer.'

'Jesus Christ,' Sheila mutters to herself, thinking of those cascades of light where she was once, shimmering, her pale face dressed in a Technicolor burn. Those beautiful, beautiful women. She was one of them. Sheila rises and holds up her drink in a toast.

'Here's to Taylor.'

The mod girls rise and clink glasses. Edythe makes a toast.

'Here's to Camilla Sparv and Catherine Spaak. God only knows whatever became of them.'

'Hear, hear,' Claudia says, and downs her fourth Grasshopper.

'Do you want to see my mime of Taylor?' Romy asks. There is sudden silence.

'Sure. Why not?' Sheila says in an exhausted voice.

Romy stands and assumes the clinches and poses of a competitive bodybuilder. She takes a beach ball in the corner of the kitchen and lifts it, finishing as Atlas holding up the earth. Sheila laughs, then looks at her watch and rises.

'We should light the candles on Taylor's cake. He's twenty today.'

The mod girls make pleasant, unintelligible sounds.

Sheila looks out towards the terrace. An early evening fog is rolling towards the house, over the silvered tips of waves.

'Claudia, would you roll the party table in from the pool? It'll be cool in about an hour,' Sheila says, her voice smooth and relaxed.

'Anything for Taylor,' Claudia says.

'Have you ever seen the fog roll in here in California?' Sheila asks Edythe.

'Of course. Not lately.'

'Well, watch.'

Claudia rolls the white laced party table inside. Romy sets Taylor's cake on it and begins to light candles. Suddenly Sheila has run out to the terrace. Taylor is screaming in horror. As the women surround him, he calms down, and Sheila looks out to the sea.

'The kelp is rolling in. He hates the kelp.' Sheila pushes Taylor into the kitchen and puts him in front of his party table with its lace and paper plates and chocolate birthday cake. She turns out the lights in the kitchen so there is a sense the candles are flickering. Taylor's eyes move over the cake and his giant hand rocks back and forth. Sudden quiet. Edythe shuts the sliding glass doors and fog hits all the windows of the house at once, like a wet sheet with tears. The girls sing 'Happy Birthday, Taylor,' and everyone helps to blow the candles out.

slow dance
on the fault line

FAITH HAS NOT SPOKEN for weeks. Not to the nurses or her husband's doctor, her mother or closest friends. Since Ted's heart attack, people knew not to call; she would pick up the phone and only listen, then quietly put the receiver down. Now when Faith walks into a room, there is the acute exhaustion of her silence. She is there to listen, nod her head, understand. There is nothing more for her to say.

She is silent with terror. She feels the succinct, flat drop of abandonment, sudden poverty, addiction and death. Faith is forty and her husband, Ted, is forty-one. She reasons she is young, that she had never foreseen or predicted anything. She is still beautiful and now deserted.

One month ago Ted had a heart attack that left him withering like lettuce left in the sun. The doctors have given him days, a week at most, to live. Faith can only remember their shoes, never raising her head to the incorrigible hospital white that has followed her now for a month like a hot ending, where light obliterates breath and water and flesh.

It happened at dinner, at a nothing little place in the Valley they had stopped at after a screening at Warner Brothers. It happens to everyone just like this, Faith had thought. You are sitting on the toilet, having dinner at a fast food restaurant, putting bleach into the washing machine and you go, or start the slow process. Blood had come out of his mouth and ears and he had slumped onto the food, his hand pushing chow mein onto the tablecloth. She had gone nuts, remembering nothing until after the sedation, when Ted was lying in bed at home, next to a nurse, the stink of his dying crawling through the long halls.

Ted was an agent at William Morris and Faith was an agent's wife. She had never worked. She was addicted to a certain amount of Valium and other prescriptions but they softened the edges. She had coped for twenty years to make sure she was everything Ted wanted her to be. Valium helped. Perfection helped. A smooth face. A smooth house.

Ted had big star clients and a big house and they were in astonishing debt. There were two mortgages and payments were late. Their matching Jaguars were bought on time and letters had come in for repossession. Out of seventeen cards, only three were not maxed out. No health insurance. No life insurance. No savings. She had paid for the hospital with a credit card. She was drawing money on the last credit cards to pay for the nurses. She had put the Jasper Johns up for sale, but the dealer explained it was a minor piece and there were no takers. She kept her jewelry. She wouldn't sell her jewelry. Now she wore as much of it as she could.

Neither had any family, children, good friends. Faith had stopped talking when she realized at his death she would be left with nothing. Maybe her clothes. The days were a game; she shut everything out, helping with Ted's catheter and bed pan, cleaning the mucus running down to his lips, under his pink upturned eyes and calcimined lids. She would touch the sponge to the pale ash of his skin, falling inward like dry rotted wood, then walk past the nurse into the bathroom.

There she would wash her hands repeatedly with liquid soap, spray herself with Chanel No. 19, re-do the make-up on her face several times. Once she masturbated with the nurse in the next room. The make-up had to be right. She tried to speak to herself in the mirror, but that's where the numbness was. Now it was three Valium a day, sometimes four, and the wait.

She only noticed the sky, began to study it each evening and tried to re-educate herself on color. She notices her face, the immediate world before her, where her feet walked, how to close a door quietly like it had never been opened. Every evening she got into her silver Jaguar and drove along Mulholland Drive, watching the sky. Certain dusks it was bewildered, questioning; other times, impatient. It made her feel like a child in her deadened flesh; it made her feel something.

She remembered as a little girl watching skies and asking things her parents couldn't answer. Then, as an adult, she hadn't paid attention for over twenty years. There were stars, and sunsets. Each moment became an aphasia and a halt. Winds would shift and stutter, smelling of other lives.

It is her birthday today, and this October in Los Angeles is over 100 degrees. There have been brush fires destroying new construction in the northern Valley mountains, and the Santa Anas have begun to light the sky with the char of oil and bundled wood. It is an arsonist's sky, Faith thinks, sore in its own skin, inflamed and livid.

Storm clouds are coming in fast, leaking wet lavender and coarse gray violets into the edge. She sees aubergine and peach light in the west; a blue she remembers on Mexican tile. She takes the curves of Mulholland slowly, staying close to the yellow line. On her car radio she hears there will be an electrical storm tonight; no chance, no percentages, the storm is already here.

157

She parks on Mulholland and lights a cigarette in her car. Her hands are numb and her left leg has fallen asleep. She will wait for the thunder and lightning. She has all the time in the world.

It begins with heavy dusty drops of rain and the sound of the elements colliding, rumbling, like an elevator dropping. Then white light in veins, like the veins of a man's arm running from the wrist to the shoulder, then nothing. If God is a man, then these are his arms; if God is a woman, then these are her lover's, Faith reasons.

She wonders if, at this moment, her husband has died. If she should be there, or here to see him rise. She wonders if the nurse is frantic and cursing her. No one knows how tired she is, and in her soothing air conditioned car she tries to cry, thinking the storm will let it out. It is dangerous sitting on the top of a mountain in a car during an electrical storm. It is dangerous not to be able to feel.

Faith massages her leg and decides to drive down into the Valley, from here a shallow pond covered with fireflies and damp air. At dusk she will drive through alleys full of pillowless couches, dead plants and stacks of magazines. She understands why pretty things get thrown away.

Faith has driven for an hour, through the poison, past tract houses and sex stores, Magnolia trees and carpets of ivy. The scent of the storm is getting stronger. Faith notices inconsequential things she normally wouldn't see when she drives; plaster elves and birdbaths, dogs turning corners, women counting money in glassed-in motel offices, the moments when streetlights turn on.

Children stand on front lawns and gape at the storm, then

squeal, running around in circles. People are driving strangely, making wide left turns and almost hitting curbs, stopping for no reason and yelling at the driver next to them. Faith is hungry, thinks she should stop for a taco, but there are too many fast food stands for her to be able to make a decision. The possibilities of taking one firm step in any direction are endless; she will keep driving tonight until the car runs out of gas. She doesn't know what else to do.

She is on Victory Boulevard headed into the flat gape of the West Valley, when, just out of Reseda, she sees a carnival on a vacant lot. It's a cheap one, with ten or twelve rides, and has been set up overnight. Each ride is lit with blinking lights and moving up and out into the sky at a different angle and rhythm. She thinks of big bands in the forties where men stand up and point their horns up and down, tapping their polished shoes, polished as Ted's doctor's shoes walking down deliberate and well understood corridors.

She puts on a tape of Harry Connick, Jr. and drives onto the dirt lot where she can park and watch the carnival. She turns the air conditioner off and rolls down the windows, letting the tropical blast of night air clean the car out, make it part of the scene. She turns the headlights off and watches people move in the dark towards the lights of the carnival.

The odor of smoke hovers in the trees like fuzz on a wash. It is the burnt oil from the giant, rocking machines. There are no families here, only some scattered Mexican couples and women she reasons are just like her, walking through the electricity, stumbling to the lights, the rock and roll, the cotton candy and chili dogs. They are alone, damaged, walking toward anything that gives light, anything that isn't home, where death and obliteration wait under hooked rugs and wallpaper.

And then there are the men. They stand by parked cars, just beyond the streetlights, combing their hair with one knee up, attentive and silent, their silhouettes dark bronze and featureless.

They are homosexual, Faith thinks; I've seen them before. Two days ago, she had been at . . . she had been at a park at dusk, driving, stopping and thinking, when she had seen them, hanging around restrooms under palms and at the edges of orange tree borders, absolutely still. Then combing their hair and checking their watches, walking in and out of the restrooms in a monotony, into other men's cars where their heads would disappear, then back into the scalding Valley sun. She had watched for hours that slow evening, falling asleep, then waking up when a bum had knocked at her window.

It was a hunt. She wondered if tonight she was hunting, if carnivals like this are made for the hunt, where people who are lost come to eat. She only wanted the numbness to last forever. She would go on every ride twice, there was enough money. Today.

This is an October of fire and children's eyes, of shuttered rooms and men she cannot see. Faith looks in her purse for Valium, cigarettes, and money. Checking, checking. Her lips must be re-painted. It's her birthday. She takes a Valium and lines her lips, runs her hands through her hair and realizes she couldn't feel her hair, lights another cigarette and slowly gets out of the car.

She does not know why she is here except she cannot sit in Ted's room anymore with a nurse she will never see again. The house will be taken away from her, put up for sale and there aren't even pictures of it, or scrapbooks. They never kept scrapbooks, considering it unsophisticated. There would be nothing by Christmas. Only a sense of something torn, drawers emptied and new cities, hotel rooms and planes.

Her high heel catches on a rock and she falls down, then gets up and steadies herself. The men in the shadows say and do nothing. She can only hear the shifting of boots, a car door quietly closing behind her. The wind of the storm pushes her beige silk dress against her body. There is no front gate, no entry to focus us; the rides are scattered and form a messy line that reaches to the back of the dirt lot.

She thinks of all the places she's never been to, of living naked in the trees, sleepwalking through gardens and beaches and trains with private rooms. At the front booth of the first ride she hands the girl ten dollars for ten dollars worth of tickets. There are no smiles, and Faith assumes they are both silent women.

The half empty carnival is full of color and movement, defying the regular flashes of lightning. God is taking pictures tonight, Faith thinks. Each ride has its own music playing, and Faith decides not to choose, but walk to the first one and keep going down the line. Until she reaches the last ride. That one she will ride until her money runs out. Then she will drive until her gas runs out. Then she will lie down and sleep.

Faith walks past revolving, empty kiddie rides; scratched teacups, tiny boats and sports cars in Day-Glo glitter under dirty pink and yellow tents. They are attached to the motor by chains. There isn't a carousel with beautifully painted horses, or anything remotely innocent here. This is a carnival for children used to chipped toys. And they are home tonight, listening to the thunder.

She gives a ticket to a freshly scrubbed man with jowls and gin blossoms, pink as a pig. He runs the Tilt-O-Whirl, and straps her carefully into the red oval chair, looking at her like she is a piece of grandmother's china. She feels secure now. Complete and ready. She will spin hard in a silence until there is no world around her. This is good.

She feels she is on the edge of the Pacific, her face the hue of cold mist. Her feet tense. She can feel something. Of becoming another element, of tasting salt and anything that gives life, controls the moon and eats away cliffs.

It is at this moment that she sees a man staring at her. Standing against the ticket booth to the Octopus, a black iron, pink lit spider ride, he is ugly and damned and he smiles. The ride heaves and sways in jagged stretches, like any animal used to crawling on ocean bottoms, drinking the life around it. The tiny cars at the end of each of the Octopus' arms spin under the electrical storm, up and down to the Rolling Stones' 'Sympathy for the Devil'. She can see there is only one couple on the ride. The woman has curly jet black hair and it is falling in her face. She is screaming, exquisitely frightened, and her boyfriend or husband or brother is laughing, his arm around her and his hand massaging her breast.

She feels like a fool sitting on the Tilt-O-Whirl, numb and dazed in her beige silk dress with her hands in her lap and her legs crossed like she is at a cocktail lounge. But this is what she wants; to be out of place, foreign, traveling in circles. She focuses her eyes so she stares past him but can watch him without effort.

He doesn't have a shirt on and his shoulders are dirty, watery from the sudden shift of rain that breaks the static in the air like urine. She wants to watch this man and knows she can. The fat man is making her sit here, strapped in, until more people show up for the ride.

He is the most muscular man she has ever seen. Not a bodybuilder, but just huge and hard, with tattoos crawling up his scarred arms. She discerns women riding dragons, skulls and hatchets and clouds covering his shoulders. There is an eagle in flight across his chest, one of its wings touching his nipple, which is pierced. She looks at the ground, then looks up again, realizing he is watching her.

She sees his eyes, sable brown and feminine, almond-shaped with thick lashes. The rest of his face is horrible, like he's been in an accident. The kind of accident men get into when they get loaded and fight each other. His nose is almost Negro, smashed up and broken and his lips are bulbous, crooked under a pencil-thin moustache. He is bald and pock-marked with oversized ears that point up at an obscene stance. His head is too small for his body and his eyes are too large for his pitiful face. His arms and hands are immense, muscu-lar, and he is swaybacked. She knows he is younger than she is. He doesn't make sense to her. She is used to men who are easy to decipher, size up, control.

He spits, stretches his arms above his head in a sudden wave of rain and lets his muscles flex, yawns and scratches his armpit, then grins at her. His two front teeth are silver. One of his eyebrows is half singed off. Then he looks down at his crotch and up at her, licking his lips. Faith is not frightened. She is surprised. She watches him from across the dirt lot and is entranced, thinking of the same fascination she experienced watching her first pornographic film, for those beginning minutes, until the repetition began to bore her. It's those beginning minutes when everything is alive, Faith thinks. She realized he has broken through. She is too tired to smile.

The Tilt-O-Whirl begins to gyrate and wheeze, spinning in half circles, undecided. The Mexican couple are in the car next to her. The ride picks up and she suddenly likes the way her back is slammed against the metal, the circles that hit hard. What is the music? Bonnie Raitt is singing something she has heard for the past two years, but only the pulse of the song comes through as the wheels of the Tilt-O-Whirl mainline and spit sparks and oil. She likes the incoherence and cacophony. She understands it. She wants everything she can understand.

When she gets off the ride her legs are weak. He is at the gate. Smiling as though they are friends.

'You are one beautiful woman. And that car blows me away. I saw you come in, you know. I watched you. You going on all the rides tonight? I can tell. Got nothing better to do, do you? I'll go on them with you.'

Faith walks by him. This silence is making her mad. Nothing will form in her mouth. Her vocal chords sting. She turns around and stares at his chest, his arms, and pockmarked cheeks. His bald head, covered with drops of rain.

'Bet you think I'm a carny, don't you? I'm not. I live around the corner. I'm easy to find, baby. In the trailer park around the corner. There's only one.'

Faith tries to breathe. Her chest is tight.

'Let's go on the Sizzler. You want to. Come on. Maybe lightning'll hit us. Maybe you'll touch me. Maybe I'll tell you poetry men tell women who are lost at night. Come on.'

His voice is soft and basso hoarse. He effortlessly puts his arm around Faith and walks her over to the Sizzler, almost lifting her off the ground. For some reason she closes her eyes. Then she knows. It is to feel another man's arms around her, record the sensation.

'You're stoned, aren't you? Bet it's some kind of rich lady's drug. You got a couple for me? Give me some later and I'll fuck all night. Dare me.'

His muscles are surprisingly soft, or it is soft skin wrapped around stone, she is not sure. The Sizzler looks like an angel food cake pan with leather straps and caged sides. Faith can see it turns around furiously and glues people to its sides. Centrifugal force. It is orange and withering black, children's Halloween colors. Candy corn and papier-mâché.

She doesn't know why this man is touching her, or his name, or if Ted is dead. She is completely disconnected, a visitor to 8.30 at night, a place that will be gone in the morning. She is not frightened. She is going on all the rides.

He grabs two tickets from the roll clutched in her hand.

'You're going to like this. You're going to like me. I want you real bad, lady, I got a hard-on right now and you're not saying a word. You let me around you and I like that. When we get on I want you to do everything I say.'

Faith stares at his giant's back, at his ass when he pushes ahead of her like a child.

'Come here. You can use the straps if you like. Nah, don't use them. I want to be able to crawl all over you. Look, we're the only people on the ride.'

He positions her next to him. Faith feels dizzy from the fourth Valium she has taken in the car. She might faint and suddenly she doesn't care. She knows she will be picked up. This unnamed man's shoulders are a foot higher than hers.

He looks down at her and smiles. He strokes her hair. She stares straight ahead.

'You're soft.'

His hands are huge and cracked; the calluses and blisters on his palms catch in her hair. He lets go and she closes her eyes again. When she opens them he is rubbing his chest with slow even strokes, pinching his nipples and then rubbing his chest again, rapidly. He doesn't look at Faith, but whispers in a music:

'Feel the eagle on my chest. Touch him. Can you feel his wings? Can you feel his feathers? He's flying. Feel him.'

He takes Faith's hand and places it on the center of his chest. She doesn't feel anything except the coarseness of tattooed flesh and his heartbeat. He takes his hand away from hers as a taunt. She quietly leaves her hand there.

'Feel my nipples. Each one. Slowly. Do it.'

The ride begins to lurch and slowly rotate. It builds its speed with a precision that takes Faith's breath into spasms; a cancer that is colorless and suffocates. She is thrown once again against the cage wall. One of her shoes has come off and has inched up towards her shoulder. The man has pinned one arm and leg over her; she can feel his erection on her hip, extravagant and moving with the same force as his limbs.

'See how it feels baby. To be pinned to a wall and not be able to move. And I'm right here on you, around you.'

The Sizzler has tilted up at a forty-five degree angle and they have lost gravity at a cut-rate carnival. Rain comes, then a white endurance, electric and brief, and they continue to spin, stuck to the wall and he keeps whispering in her ear, things she cannot understand.

She does not know where he will take her, if he will be

violent, if he is diseased and rambling. She is shaking her brains, she is having a good time, she is young.

'I can keep you this way forever if you like. I can keep you against a wall, allow you only your breath. We don't have to leave. We can stay this way all night, curled in mid air, anything you want.'

It is almost one a.m. and they have been on every ride; the Paratrooper, the Round-Up, the Tilt-O-Whirl, the Zipper, the Sizzler, the Cliffhanger and the Octopus. She doesn't remember the rest. He has whispered obscenities and hung them like doves at her neck. He has held her like a father, made her touch his genitals and touched her vagina through her briefs, rubbing her pubic hair with his immense hands until it hurt. He's licked her brassière through her silk dress until there are great spots on the front that stink of his breath. He has made her close her eyes most of the night.

On solid ground her legs give way. He buys her a beer with quarters out of her purse and she does not care. She takes another Valium, thinking soon she could be someone else. He lights a cigarette and holds it to her lips. As she smokes through his hand she smells semen and tobacco and an utterance of night that can cure, the perfume of men and chants she has suddenly heard, as if they were delivered.

Then they are dancing in the parking lot, her Jaguar door open, Harry Connick, Jr. singing on the tape deck. She does not remember putting it on. The men in the shadows are there, watching, sitting on their cars. Certain cars are rattling where they are having sex. He is holding her against him with both arms and her feet are dragging the ground. She is coherent and calm. She is listening.

'I'm the poet, baby, who's waiting for you.'

He's ugly as a tropical flower with overwaxed leaves that fight for sunlight in the steam. She wonders if there are tattoos on his penis, if he sat, drunk, in front of the tattoo artist, keeping it hard as he wiped tiny dots of blood away as the ink went in. The same ink that forms skies, blue skin and veins that constrict into the branches of bare October trees, vicious among the palms that only grow fat and brown-green.

This is what men are made of. They are veins that shoot through the ground, covering black soil with musk. They reek of come and earth and they calculate their facelessness.

'Baby, I can take you to a place where there's an earthquake every day. In the desert between the Salton Sea and the Mexican border, where rocks move and men make women shake.'

He lets his moustache brush against her earring, then along the ridge of her ear.

'I'll fuck you so hard and so often the only smell you'll know is me, the only God you'll know is me, the only food you'll want is me. I'll keep you wet all day and crying for me at night. I'll lick and clean you like a dog and I won't let you out of my sight.'

His breath smells of tequila and chocolate mints. Faith can feel it on the fine hair of her cheek. He brushes his lips against hers and she smells marijuana, motorcycle exhaust, flames. The storm has not let up, the fires have not ceased, and the carnival is still buzzing in the pitch.

'I'll teach you how to suck my beautiful big cock and lick my balls. I'll teach you over and over until you get it right. I'll save all my come for you baby. I'll fuck you in the ass and eat your pretty pussy while I'm fucking you. I'll comb your hair while you sleep and play with your titties while you dream of me, so you're wet when you wake up.'

Faith rolls her head and looks at the sky. She must look at the sky. It will have answers. It will explain to her what season it is, why she is still alive, where she is.

'I'll make you laugh. I'll feed you snakes and wild birds. I'll make you jewelry from Indian beads and quartz. I'll teach you how to slow dance on the fault line, with fire under our feet, where we could drop in if the earth shifts. I'll teach you the music of rivers and canyons. I'll drink your sweat and paint you in the sand.'

Faith almost speaks. Then closes her eyes.

'I'll take you to Mexico and South America and we'll get lost in towns with four-room hotels. We'll put on shows and teach the whores how to do it. We'll travel only on nights with no clouds so we can see the moon. I'll love you.'

Faith begins to back away from him. He becomes rapid. His voice a growl. His chest becomes tight. He squeezes his cock through his pants.

'Look at it. It's yours. I live in a trailer park. I eat out of cans and write poetry on paper towels. I need money and I need you.'

Faith watches this man, this child animal with a broken nose and pierced nipples and she knows he is a narcotic, the hesitation before the rush and she is waiting. Waiting to feel it on her skin, waiting for the blood to seep through Ted's brain and then into his lungs in the ancient language of lightning.

'So what do you do, little lady with a silk dress and a silver car? I'll give you everything. Stay with me tonight and don't go back. I'm desperate and alone. We're all alone. Forget where you came from. Let me fuck the words out of your throat.'

She can hear the gasp of two men in the shadows. A car has stopped shaking. Thunder.

'What's the matter? Can't you talk? You're not deaf. Or mute. You're just playing with your own little balls of shit.'

'My husband's dying.' Her own voice surprises her. It must belong to someone else. It sounds hollow and pinched like a Hollywood woman, an old woman who cannot be taught. She steadies herself and pulls away completely from him.

'Let him die. Kill him. Kill him for me. Put the son of a bitch out of his misery. I'll give you my address. I'm easy to find. If you want I'll kill him for you. I'll be gentle. You want me to use a pillow, a gun, a knife, just let me know. I'll fuck you after. I'll fuck you so hard you won't care. You won't be afraid anymore.'

Faith listens to the silence, staring at him. He looks like a child.

'I got nothing to lose lady and there's only one thing I want. I want a woman. I jack off all day long. I can do it for hours. I don't care what I have to do to get you. I'm lonely and I want a woman to love me. You.'

The lights of the Octopus and the Sizzler are being turned off. The storm is focused east, and the sky is still lit at intervals but it has become a warm glow, translucent yellow. Faith is aware of the streetlights, of police lights at another end of the lot, and she gets into her car. She has her keys somewhere, the ignition of course, they have to be in the ignition for the tape to play. The men in the shadows have become distant and they too are dispersing.

She could go home now. She can talk, feel the blood in her neck. The man is still standing in the middle of the parking lot.

She had expected him to grab her hair and pull her into the dark. She would float. But he didn't. He just stands there as she gets in the Jaguar and slams the door shut.

'I want a woman to love me.'

Faith turns the ignition key.

'Come back to me when he dies.'

It is her birthday. Faith checks her lips in the rearview mirror and slowly pulls out of the lot. She will have to remember where she is.

A week later Ted is dead. Two weeks after that Faith has bought two tickets to Cancun, converted her jewelry into dollars and pesos, put the house up for sale and declared bankruptcy. She now talks, only about business, facts, essentials. Los Angeles is covered with the linen of crisp winter flowers and a warm midday sun, the haze of the Pacific and the sense that things are real, if only for a matter of days.

She has bought an extra ticket for the man at the carnival. If she cannot find him she will cash it in at the airport. She has everything she owns in one bag, has bought a supply of Valium that should last a month or more. The Jaguar has been turned in and she has a rental car and she is driving through Reseda, trying to remember where the carnival was; which allotted dirt park was singed by it.

There is no trailer park. She keeps driving, looking for something that would be part of him. She is driving too fast. She rolls around a corner and suddenly finds it. It is early, and dawn comes in a henna flame. She has watched the sky every day since Ted's death and she has promised herself she will watch it in Mexico. It is now her companion.

Faith considers what will happen in Mexico. That one day she will wake up with this man, whose skin is a childhood taste, like sickness and cough syrup. That it will end. He will walk into the jungle, wait for another woman and hunt. She will start swimming in the Caribbean and not stop.

The trailer park is just as he said it was. Around the corner, but there were a hundred vacant lots. She drives slowly down the narrow trailer park drive, past Chinese lanterns and tiny fences. She stops the car and gets out and walks in the early a.m. shiver. He said he was easy to find.

She sees a sleeping blanket with a mass huddled in front of the office trailer. She walks over to it and looks down. She kicks it. She doesn't care. As the bundle moves over, she sees his face covered with blood that has dried. He has been fighting.

They will sleep in Mexico, clean and oiled. She will rub his body in the sun, watch the eagle writhe under her thumb, the woman on the dragon glittering on her palm. She will absorb his desperation until they are both without language or thought.

He opens his eyes and looks up at her. He is naked under the sleeping blanket. He has lost his clothes. He smiles.

honey carter

HONEY CARTER IS DYING. His arms are speckled with cancer, but he holds them up to me as though they are rolled sugar pirouettes, ready to be poked in a dish of ice cream. His hands flutter back to his sides under the weight of glittering, stacked bracelets. All of Honey Carter's jewelry is faux, not fake. Faux goes beyond reality. Fake just is.

He licks the top of his lips several times, then asks one of his daughters for a Kool. She lights one and gently puts it into a rhinestone cigarette holder and hands it to Honey, who will puff on it as he speaks to me, letting burning embers fall on his sheets. There are holes in his satin blanket and the pillowcases. I see a corner of his mattress has burned away. *That* must have been an interesting evening.

This woman, Francine, is about seventy and dressed in high-heels and Capri slacks. She is one of Honey Carter's daughters, and he has over ten of them. I sincerely doubt Honey conceived any of these dolls, as they aren't much younger than he. Stiff-haired, alcoholic women with social pretensions, the Carter girls had pretty shady lives in the '50s and '60s, but somehow they kept their money. Over these past few weeks they have stayed downstairs, pouring pitchers of martinis, discussing Honey in detail, and walking into walls in some of the darker rooms like the kitchen.

I know that everything of any value in Honey's house by now has disappeared and that the Carter girls have new sets of china, Venetian glass ashtrays, and the occasional jade Goddess of Mercy. Still, earlier in the day Francine called and told me to hightail it, Honey was going to give me my inheritance.

'I'm giving my emeralds to the blind, Sam. They should go to help those little blind children.' Honey's voice is weak, a pale yellow, like the walls of his always shuttered bedroom. Francine has decided to join the rest of her siblings downstairs for a new pitcher; I am quite certain she can smell the brand of gin from the second floor. She smiles benevolently as she teeters out of the room.

'That's a very fine charity, Honey,' I said quietly. Honey smiles and motions for me to look under the bed.

'The crocodile make-up bag. Bring it up.' He is coughing.

I look under Honey's bed and find the crocodile case. Beyond it are things so covered with dust they have lost their form. I shiver and sit on Honey's bed as he snaps open the latch.

'I always promised you something to take care of those writer's hands. Now it's time.' Honey opens the case with great pride. Inside are a few rhinestone rings, several gold-plated bracelets, and three dragonfly pins.

'You wear the dragonflies on your lapel. They're good luck.' His hands are translucent. As he drops the dragonflies in my palm I can see the veins and bones of his fingers. I look into his eyes and realize there are cataracts that I didn't notice before.

'Now hold out your hands. Flat out. That's right.' Shaking, Honey slips the rhinestone rings onto my fingers. There are four. I feel his hands touch mine. I don't feel flesh, only air.

'These were given to me by Harry Cohn. They're real, made

by Schiaparelli. Direct from Paris. He was mad for me you know.'

'I know, Honey. I remember when he gave you a diamond bracelet and it was hidden in a bouquet of flowers. You were mad at him and you threw it out the window, vase and all, into a canyon and it landed in John Barrymore's fountain and he called you up.'

'That's right. You remember. It was on Tower Road. I was only eighteen, but I was treated well in those days.'

Harry Cohn was never in love with Honey Carter. Harry Cohn was too busy making Rita Hayworth's life miserable and by that time John Barrymore was dead. This is not unusual for Honey. According to Honey, many famous men had been madly in love with him. I have often wondered if he ever fell in love. He says he only dates married men; that Kay Spreckels was furious when she found out her husband Clark Gable made a pass at Honey in 1963. Clark Gable died in 1960.

Honey continues to weakly attach the bracelets on my wrist.

'I'll do it,' I say.

'No. These have you written all over them. It's up to me to put them on, otherwise they'll never have any *cachet*.' He stacks these bracelets, two on each wrist. The gold plating has worn off on all except one. 'And you get to keep the case, too.' He smiles, leaning back against his pillow.

'Thank you, Honey,' I said.

'Light me a Kool, will you, darling?'

I hold up my hands to what little light illuminates the room and I think, *Well, you finally got your jewels*. Honey always said he painted his walls a butter yellow, but now I realize they are covered with nicotine. This is what death does. It makes you see the nicotine stains on the wall, the pot metal under gold. He reaches up and touches my cheek with the back of his hand and his wrinkles feel like mink.

'Such a beautiful man you are. And such ugly goddamn hands.'

I am one of those people who love decayed verandas, hotels in the off-season, tropical flowers hiding spiders. I love anything that haunts; the once grand, dishevelled, or the vaguely royal, like ice water in a silver goblet. Or the perfume of an elderly woman.

That is why I love Honey Carter.

I first meet Honey in 1990, four years before his death. He is having a New Year's Eve party at his house on Caracas Drive in the old part of Hollywood, where homes have bell towers and indoor swimming pools with frescoes on the ceiling and swim-up bars. Honey's house was built in 1939 as a replica of Tara from *Gone With the Wind,* and has six peeling pillars on a front porch covered with vines and broken wrought-iron furniture. Upon entering I find about three hundred people crammed into the downstairs rooms. A tall black woman in a violet sequined gown is standing on a chair trying to signal her friend across the room. I am told this is the party of the year, there will never be another party like this, this is *the* party *at last.*

There are enormous quantities of liquor being poured, but no food, and no host. It is almost 1.30 in the morning. When I mention this to an ex-tennis sensation he puts his arm around my lower waist and says, 'Just wait.'

I have spent most of my life waiting and tonight I decide will not be the night I will wait too much longer. The ex-tennis sensation's hand seems to drift to someone else's lower waist and I begin to absorb small details about the room. Its draperies are tattered and permanently closed. The rug has never been vacuumed or perhaps it has been vacuumed, once, several years ago, during a fit of temper. Everywhere I look there are candelabras, crystal bowls filled with peanuts and popcorn, poorly done portraits of stern women in ball dresses and furs, next to coromandel screens whose jade has fallen out.

There is no air here. Hustlers are rubbing up against ex-wives, ex-producers, and ex-cons. Someone is talking about Cinecitta in the good old days. someone else is talking about waiting for the dawn flight to Vegas. It is the fifth party I've been to tonight and all I want to do is sit down.

Everyone here is out for something. A pretty young man is snapping his fingers to Joe Williams singing from a stereo console and says, 'Man, I really like that Sinatra.' Then he announces loudly he is hot and takes off his shirt, throwing it out into the room. An anonymous hand rubs a $50 bill across the young man's bare chest, and he just keeps laughing, snapping his fingers, and moving through the crowd.

I find a small part of the staircase in the front hall and I sit down. Looking up, I suddenly see Honey Carter. He appears in a long rose satin dress at the top of the stairs. He has on a fresh gardenia corsage and a cobweb of blush across his old cheeks, with longish silver hair swept up into a thin chignon. Gloves. Earrings. Eyes vivid as a just cleaned chandelier.

He begins to descend, triumphant, in four-inch heels, stepping into a slow, calculated rhythm as this New Year's morning begins to shake with jazz and avarice. I am transfixed. I hear someone in the crowd below laugh, applaud, then go back to

his original conversation. His female companion is not listening. She walks past him up to the staircase and whispers:

'Would you get a load of her.'

The room is silent and Honey acts as if he doesn't care.

'Hello, madam,' I murmur as he glides past.

'Hello to you.' His gloved hand lightly touches my chin and
he stops, thinking the better of just walking by. He raises my
head until we make eye contact. I can see Honey is very, very
high. There is a heavy smell of marijuana around his powdered
shoulders. His lips form a fat heart. He must be seventy-five
years old.

A heavyset, middle-aged Texan, dressed in white fringed
leather, who has something to do with vitamins and pyramids,
leads Honey away. What I find out is that Honey will repeat
this particular entrance four more times during the evening,
each time in a different gown and set of colors. He will get
higher and the applause will get heavier. I will stay until dawn
and I will not mind waiting, nor will I ever find any food, or
a comfortable place to sit. And I will feel entirely alive.
Because a little part of me is Honey, and I know he is teaching
all of us below, fresh out of jail or fresh out of love, how to
descend. How to walk down a staircase in a ball gown and
smile.

Honey is cross with me. We are driving in his gold 1965
Bentley to Tijuana. The leather seats are so dry and cracked
I have the beginnings of a scar on my upper thigh. There is
no air-conditioning and Honey has rolled down the windows.
I notice several spider webs in the back seat break and dissolve
in the heat. It is the end of September and the Santa Anas
have taken over. Driving down along the Pacific coast, we

pass the San Onofre nuclear power plant and Honey mentions they look like giant cement breasts pointing up to heaven. I reply nuclear power should be abolished, that it will kill us all, and Honey *tsks* and tells me I am very young.

That is how the argument begins. I remind Honey I am a respected journalist, a poet. He takes a beret out of his hair and throws it onto the freeway. San Diego looms in the distance.

'Yes. Yes. But do they know you in Jackson Hole?'

'I beg your pardon?'

'Do they know you in Jackson Hole, Wyoming? Because, darling, if they know you in Jackson Hole, they'll know you anywhere.'

'I really have no idea.' I close my eyes and let the wind blow through my hair. I do not know why I am headed to Tijuana. I have been told Honey is fond of me. That he believes in what I do. I think he likes having someone around to listen.

I open my eyes and look at Honey. His lips are pursed and his thin hair is blowing around his face.

'You're absolutely right, Honey,' I say quietly. He seems satisfied.

'I only drive this old girl to Tijuana. Never in Los Angeles,' he says. 'All those horrid people would try to rob me with this car.'

I know the truth. Honey hates to drive, and prefers to be driven whenever possible. So he can get good and drunk without worrying about police, or inconsequential things like pedestrians and garage doors. That's how the Carter girls must have come into existence. To keep Honey in motion. Honey asked me to drive at the beginning of our journey and I declined. This was a mistake. Never decline an old beauty anything. They'll remember.

Suddenly we are at the border and I forget how filthy and remember how wonderful Mexico really is. I am aware of color again, of hot orange and gold, and the sound of Mexican pop music in the air.

'God, I love Mexico,' he screams out the window to a man holding the reins of a donkey painted like a zebra with a sombrero on its head and a sign saying: *Fotografia Uno Dollar*. 'I can breathe here!'

I am sweating profusely and beg to be taken somewhere cool.

'Do you really know why I love Mexico?' Honey asks me with one eyebrow slightly bent. I say I have no idea.

'Because in Tijuana, even the salesgirls try to look like movie stars. Lotsa makeup. Tight skirts and a look, you know. The men stand with their legs far apart, like they've got to keep it aired out. These men, they look good in white, always white, and trust me, they're lovers. The real thing. Down in Rosarito Beach they eat lobsters at noon and dance on the tables, licking their fingers. That's what I call a real man.'

At Caesar's, the maitre d' sees Honey and I walk in, claps his hands and holds them briefly, as if in prayer, then bows. 'Honey!'

This is not unusual. I find every man of a certain age and wisdom claims to have known Honey, to have danced with him while their wives watched. Sometimes these patient wives lost their bemused expressions. Sometimes oaths were uttered, doors slammed.

'Charming man, but older than God,' Honey mutters into my left ear between clenched, smiling teeth.

Caesar's is proud of the fact it is the only true home of the original Caesar Salad. The walls are colored bull's-blood red and coated with Tijuana dust. It hits my lungs like a drug, reeking of meat and chillies, drugstore hair spray, and the scent of being in a place where there is no time. I think if I were to slide into a back booth here, I would live forever.

Two blonde, older women in the booth next to us whisper in a lispy Castilian Spanish and keep tiny, battery-operated fans in their left hands, passing them in front of their faces as they eat and talk.

'So the make-up doesn't run,' Honey says in a low voice, looking at me slyly. I realize my mouth is open. I close it.

'What is that smell?' I ask.

'Vanilla. Do you know Spanish?'

'Sort of,' I answer. Honey leans to me and pretends to talk to me, but he is listening to their conversation.

'Both these ladies have just come from the hairdresser. One has just lost a husband, the other can't get one. The widow is trying to sell her house in Ensenada, memories you know, but there are no takers. The single lady wants to go to Mexico City for a vacation, doesn't want to go alone, is trying to get the widow to go with her, possibly pay for the trip as well. What better way to become close friends in Tijuana than to have your hair dyed, together? Only the bleach used was impure; see how much hair is burned on the back of the widow's neck? So they use vanilla; the smell of vanilla covers the smell of the bleach.'

'How do you know all of this?' I ask, delighted.

'Experience. The ability to listen. The bleach was a hex. These two women will wind up bitter enemies.'

Honey keeps ordering large pitchers of iced sangria. I drink soda water. I discover everyone here is very old, that the lights are dimmed as a cosmetic.

I begin to laugh. I feel like I'm drunk and I'm not. A man wearing a paisley tuxedo jacket sits down to an organ and begins to play Caesar's daily luncheon music: 'I Left My Heart In San Francisco,' sung in Spanish to a bossa nova beat. He presses several buttons on the keyboard. Jungle noises and bongos are added.

'What's so funny to you? Is it this place? It's got quite a history.' Honey does not seem amused by my laughter. I look up at the ceiling. Small crystal chandeliers, and there are a lot of them, sway and tinkle to the rhythm. Towards the bar, in front of flocked wallpaper, two waiters in white jackets with Jockey Club pomade in their hair, stand in shadows, smoking cigarettes. Above them is an enormous oil painting of Leda and the Swan, taken, Honey points out, from the finest whorehouse in Vera Cruz.

'You're a lonely soul, laughing at old people. We try our best.'

I become quiet.

'I never would laugh at you, Honey. I'm just thinking.'

Honey's voice cuts through immediately. His words are becoming slurred.

'You think too much. When you're in Mexico, you're supposed to *not* think.'

I know how nostalgia has its own colors, fragrances, and they can only be told to the young. The colors change. They are never as good as the colors before them.

Honey grabs my hands.

'I thought so,' he says cryptically.

'What?'

'You have a writer's hands. Do your palms ever sweat?'

'No,' I answer hesitantly. They don't. I have always felt they look almost withered.

'Hemingway had hands like this. Scaly. I used to see him at that horrid restaurant in Havana where I got food poisoning. The Floridita. I preferred that casino that Battista owned. He almost got me in bed, you know. Battista was a charmer.'

'Really,' I murmur. Honey never cuts his nails and they are pinching my fingers.

'It doesn't matter. You love to create. Anyone with talent has problems enough. Your hands should be covered in jewels. I will arrange it. You see, I never had talent. But I made up for it in charm.'

Honey lets go of my hand. The man at the organ begins to play a Mexican version of 'Beautiful Balloon' by the Fifth Dimension. It is one o'clock in the afternoon.

Mariachis come in after the organist has finished and they play on slow, exquisitely soft guitars. Honey begins talking about Barbara Hutton's house in Tangier, dancing with Truman Capote in a nightclub in Athens next to Tallulah Bankhead, how he used to take meat pies and melon to the Duke and Duchess of Windsor to cure their considerable hangovers.

'Where was this?' I ask darkly. I am curious.

'In Paris, darling, where else? It was the only place those two could live for a dollar a year.'

'How in the world were you able to meet them?'

Honey chirps: 'Anyone with $500 and clean fingernails could meet those two!'

Fifty years delivers a certain patina to tall tales. Honey seems vague at the right moments, but also quite clear on how his world was lived – full of a certain magic I try to understand. I want to know how the Windsors were so special that no one seemed to be able to touch them. I asked Honey how these people lived on a daily basis.

'Breakfast, lunch, and dinner, just like everyone else.'

I imagine breakfast, lunch, and dinner overlooking the Mediterranean, or from a suite at the Waldorf, or Noel Coward's house in Ocho Rios.

'I know that look,' Honey says.

'No one behaves this way anymore,' I say, shrugging.

'You could, Sam. I think you're destined. I know how you love whores and liars. You know why? Because on us, color becomes pure. Everyone else is just wearing grey.'

At that moment Honey downs the last of his sangria and begins to recite something from memory.

'I always look out for the butcher's daughter, a stout beefy girl who all week swings an axe with the ferocity of any two men, but on Sunday, coiffed and scented, careening on two-inch heels, and accompanied by her fiancé, a slender boy rising not quite to her shoulder, there is about her a romance of triumph that stalls the satiric tongues; hers is the haughtiness, the belief in oneself, that should be the spirit of a promenade.'

Honey's eyes are misting over. I know very soon he will fall asleep. And that I will drive him back to Los Angeles in a Bentley with one spark plug.

'That's beautiful. Who wrote that?'

'My dear friend Truman Capote. We were summering at his old house, *Fontana Vecchia*, old fountain, in Taormina, a horrible place, in 1951. We would sit and drink on the promenade, and it was magic, and I was actually young. Truman became excited and wrote this down. Then he made me memorize it. I still, when the world becomes too plain, too correct and dull, I say this out loud whenever and to whomever I please. It is why, when you don't have a religion, you can still have a saving grace.'

Honey Carter never wakes up before noon, at least that is what he strives for. He explains if he could become a kind of vampire he would, as he prefers the night completely over the day. We are at Trancas Beach, at noon, 'the ungodly hour' according to Honey. He is muttering under his pink and aqua rice paper umbrella.

'Goddamn sun. When you're twelve, perhaps, get burnt. But at my age, it will turn me into something that lays eggs and sheds its skin.'

It is the summer of 1994 and Honey doesn't have a whole lot of time left. This comes direct from a Carter girl, Lola Delgado, who tells me Honey can't breathe at night. That he's way too frail for eighty. That he can't remember.

'You know Honey pretty darn well.' Lola pauses for effect on the telephone the night before. 'All he does is remember. And if he can't do that, well, maybe it's time for him to kick the bucket, meet his maker.'

'I got it, Lola.' I can't explain to Lola, who still says *darn*, that Honey's maker is himself. He wasn't so much made as evolved.

Lola Delgado has invited Honey and I for breakfast, a meal Honey loves at two o'clock in the morning, not at noon. This means I pick up Honey at ten-thirty to get him in my car (the Bentley no longer runs, and is being used for storing canned goods in the garage) and drive the full hour and some up the

Pacific Coast Highway to Trancas Beach. We arrive early and sit down in a rather louche manner in Lola's dining room. There is a large picture window, under which the high tide is breaking. This picture window shakes with each new wave. A spray of sea and kelp slide down it like mucus.

Lola's formica table, marble-toned and oval, seats twelve. Around it are yellowing tufted white leather swivel chairs. I can smell bacon in the kitchen and begin to twirl around in my chair.

'Stop that. You're going on thirty-seven.' Honey's tone is fierce.

'But I always feel young when I am with you. Like I could be a little boy,' I say.

'Well, you aren't. And that's that.'

Honey is still smoking Kools and drinking gin and tonics. For breakfast he is wearing a white silk suit and ballet shoes made of crocodile. Annoyed with this entire excursion, he taps his now closed parasol on Lola's travertine marble floor.

'The woman's an alcoholic. She doesn't know how to cook breakfast.'

I can hear Lola in the kitchen opening a bottle of champagne. There are no champagne glasses on the table and it is set for three.

Lola kicks open the door holding a tray of breakfast. Excepting burnt bacon, the rest of our meal consists of apple strudel, cinnamon rolls, and strawberry shortcake. Lola is very proud of her figure. She is sixty-five and was once a starlet at Columbia, under Harry Cohn, Honey's old flame. Then her name was Lola Duprey. On the dining room walls there are pictures of her from 1949, wearing marcelled hair and liver red lipstick. She seems sultry, dissatisfied, and very beautiful. I wonder how many women on these cool, powdered beaches almost became stars. How many hope someone will still recognize them at the supermarket and announce, *You never should have left pictures. You're still looking great, baby.*

What Lola does have, apparently, is close to $50 million and she and Honey spend a great deal of time talking about the past. I know Honey isn't after her money, but he does like to sniff it once in a while.

Later, Honey and I are standing on the terrace. The waves are hitting hard, and neither of us can go to the railing, or we will get wet.

I let the Pacific breeze, with its layers of salt and ragged youth, wash over us. Honey's eyes stare directly at the high tide as if it weren't there. He is wearing some pretty severe jewelry on his hands. I realize I will have to put on my sunglasses to look at his fingers.

'Well, well. You'll be taking over soon.' Honey's voice comes from behind. I shiver.

'What are you talking about?' I ask sweetly.

'I think you know.'

A new wave breaks and the entire terrace seems to shake. Honey sighs, leaning over to me.

'I certainly hope that horrible woman comes out with our drinks shortly, if she expects me to sit outside in the middle of the afternoon . . .'

Lola Delgado lurches through her French doors out onto the terrace, holding a tray of two margaritas in stem glasses, two Cuba Libres in tall glasses with umbrellas, and a glass of soda for me. Also on this tray are a bowl of miniature candy bars and a bowl of jelly beans.

'Now we can relax.'

Lola Delgado says this in a cello voice, the wind blowing her white hair into spun glass. She has taken her shoes off and sits under a canvas awning, patting the chair next to her. 'Come here, Honey, you bad boy.'

Honey backs away from me, from the spray of the Pacific, and waves to me as if I am far away, on a buoy, or watching him from a boat. He spins his parasol with both hands, like a geisha, and turns to Lola Delgado. His smile is clean, and suddenly I see a young man in Paris and Hollywood and Biarritz, walking down the street of the hour. I hear laughter, gulls, sports cars on the Pacific Coast Highway. I hold up my hands, framing them against the sun and I think, someday, these ugly writer's hands will be covered with jewels.

the secret names of whores

DELILAH IS A GOOD Christian woman who likes the radio on twenty-four hours a day. First salsa in the morning, horns and maracas and painted guitars, then prayer radio as she cleans houses on slow afternoons. Delilah makes fifty dollars a day and she works six days a week. She's learned her English from sermons. Then in her own bedroom of lavender carpet and silk flowers, she lets Tony Bennett and Frank Sinatra hold her in the yellow-tinged dark. As the night blooms in silence and shadowed citrus, the music stays in her dreams, somnolent and exhausted.

Her face is healthy brown, innocent and fat. She is most proud of her ears, tiny things that are her one delicate feature. She keeps her hair rubine, done once a month by her cousin Maria and swept up with black plastic combs to show her ears off. She has thirty pairs of dangling, oversized costume earrings, one for each day of the month, and a filigree gold pair for special occasions.

Delilah saves everything, from glass jars and paper bags, to postcards and restaurant honey. She knows this is the way to become rich. Delilah takes everything that is free. It is a protection, and she hoards each charity in a turquoise bungalow built in the twenties, one of hundreds with the perfume of failed women who stayed trapped, the starlets and mistresses who flow through the studios like irrigation water. Now her street is a jungle where weeds become trees and pit bulls in cages snap at flies.

It is here, in this flat waste of drives and lanes with saint's names, behind Paramount Pictures and below the old Goldwyn Studios, that Delilah has made her home. The immigrant apartments and battered Mexican-style cottages have always been poor, resonating a subliminal decay. They are never lived in long, cheap to rent and never remembered. Here Armenian women and Mexican women stare from rusted screens and poinsettias bought in drugstores, that took in the ground and now cover windows. Their loins are damp with hysteria. They have been taken like a catalogue and will not give their names or speak to strangers, praying for any man who can see the questions they leave taped on walls. On mirrors and cars. The directions out.

Except for Delilah. Her lawn is neatly trimmed with patches of wildflowers and the bars on her windows have been painted glossy white. She is friendly with other women nearby, women who work at Kodak and film editing offices, in cocktail lounges and hair salons. They meet for drinks and at church; watch over each other's children and disregard the haunted faces of the other women who are just passing through. They have forgotten men, and wearing lipstick every night and tasting the sweat of a man's thighs. They paint their front doors pink and green and have names for each other, secret names of whores that they say with a wink and another beer.

Delilah is her nickname but now she uses it every day. Her friends are Jane and Iris and Dot, but their whispered names are Dixie, Coco and Princess, or Thelma who became Jinx, and Sally who is Frosty. Together they save their money in silver-red Valentine's boxes hidden in garages, tend their lemon trees on Sundays and know they will never move.

Delilah understands Jesus and his pain, how angels walk in morning sun and the heart in music. There is a wedding dress still crisp in her mother's cedar closet in Santo Domingo. She is saving it for her daughter, Angelica. There are certain things Delilah insists be perfect. One is her living room. Then, her daughter. And most important to the flow of all things is how they celebrate life. Christmas and Easter take months of planning. There are balloons and freshly baked cakes in the sun. There must always be sun.

Angelica is now five and plump as her mother, in lace dresses and tiny white buckled shoes, with ribbons pinching her scalp. She likes to squeal and chase field rats that come into their back yard through a hole caused by a tractor that backed up. Delilah hates this hole, which leads to Hollywood Memorial Cemetery, and has planted honeysuckle and pink and white ferns that won't take. The only thing covering it is a century plant, grotesque and sharp and covered with webs, with a single long stem of blossoms that have lasted most of the year.

She'd first seen the flower in January and now it is Easter and not a blossom has gone brown. Waxy and pompous, its giant stem has thrust six feet up and even the wind can't shake it. Delilah can see the brown grass of the cemetery, short and parched as the man who repairs her shoes, but chooses not to look through the hole, and becomes cross with Angelica when she tries.

Delilah explains some fields of the dead have good spirits but this place doesn't, that you must hold your breath when you pass by, or they will enter. She knows men and women go there at night to make love, and homosexuals, who frighten her. She leaves the radio on a little louder and crosses herself.

Her daughter is undamaged and it must stay that way, as virgins always fly straight to heaven if taken too soon. She has not yet explained to Angelica that her father is a criminal, that he sits in a prison in the Dominican Republic, or that they hold the same face, or that all bruises are mistakes and healing is a gift of time women allow; that all men are a danger of incongruous flesh and their shine only darkens a woman's skin.

She was pregnant with Angelica when she wound up with relatives in Hollywood, looking at signs in English that were stained by auto exhaust and graffiti. She missed rain and shallow tide pools and walking with a paper-thin parasol in the mornings. Delilah missed her church and the smell of its clay walls and spilled wine, but learned her English and walked to the buses that would take her to clean houses that all looked alike.

Now, Delilah has grown accustomed to working for women with high-heels who never look her in the eye. Her feet itch from bleach and the sidewalk heat makes her wear pads under her arms. At the end of her day, walking down Santa Monica Boulevard, she prays for the black man to be playing his bongos in front of the dry cleaners, and always gives him a full dollar before her marketing. She knows he is from the island, too. When she hears his drums in the stale, confused air, she thinks of mamees who carried fruit in their aprons, under Caribbean clouds that hung over her like a lace fan, Spanish moss and the threat of Saturday nights.

And today Delilah survives well. There will be balloons for Angelica's Easter; chocolate cake and candy rabbits and a hunt for eggs with faces painted to resemble blue-eyed, blonde-haired women with long, pasted lashes. She is throwing a little party for Angelica's friends. There will be the laughter of Coco, Dixie, Princess and Jinx, their children running through the yard, all girls and one little boy who could be a girl, white lilies and pink carnations, and votives lit to the wax eyes of female Saints who say this is right. It is the only way.

Coco is the first to arrive, at eleven, tugging Little Howie, whose father was shot and killed in New York. Little Howie is very pretty. His mulatto skin and curly blonde hair are soft as powder. His green eyes assess everything and he likes to be around the women and their daughters, where he can play with the other girls' toys without being teased. The women seem to know what is in store for Little Howie, but love him as they love Coco, an Irish girl who got a bad deal but makes a good living at the cocktail lounge where they meet each Monday for Happy Hour.

The sky is clear over baby blankets on clotheslines, pink as a movie star's lips. Coco and Delilah let the children run off into the back yard as they settle into the kitchen, listening to a gospel Easter show and giggling, pouring a little Scotch in their coffee. Soon Dixie, Frosty and Princess are there too and the bottle is empty, the children are playing and the air is smoky with cigarettes and lasagne baking. Later, when the women leave, Delilah will start the Easter Egg hunt, but for now it is a time for gossip and the steam of ice and gold liquor in coffee cups.

The radio's gospel moves over Delilah's kitchen like the shadow of leaves from the avocado tree, which they surmise is older and sweeter than they are. Cigarettes are stubbed out in glass hotel ashtrays with names like Sunset Casa and the Impromptu Inn, places that Delilah has worked and taken linens and towels from, and enough ashtrays for all the girls. Delilah has beautiful sheets and guest towels stacked in her linen closet, and the girls have always admired Delilah's way of sifting out things no one will miss.

'It's a gift, if you ask me.' Frosty announces, as she has announced every time at Delilah's. 'Delilah will wind up with a house in Beverly Hills, because someone won't want it. You know what I mean?'

The girls nod their heads, signaling each other it's time to go, to allow themselves a free Sunday with hidden men and simple passions they won't discuss with anyone. It is Easter. A holiday. As the girls sigh and stub their cigarettes out, listening to their children screaming outside, they are all caught in the same dream. A thought passes through their scrubbed wrists like fire; that somewhere there are women dancing for the first time, rubbing their legs with creme so they shine. Women of reds and glistening pinks that no one sees, and French floral dresses hung indifferently in huge closets. Women with arms full of flowers and the dark earth that makes fruit. Women who have easy births and lucky daughters, seasons nodding to the light like sugar on their tongues.

Today, they leave laughing and a little high on an Easter noon. They will go their secret ways, ready for words only men use, the numb rub when they straddle and pump, undoing the monotonies. As the girls say good-bye, Delilah notices they are looking in different directions, their eyes transfixed on something before them that only they see, their lips curling into smiles. They will be back at six, and no one will say they have been anywhere, or done anything worth talking about. Delilah knows, because she has been there, too.

Delilah is wearing a purple lace dress with white satin bows and an Easter apron. She checks herself in the mirror, then goes out into the back yard with a tray of cake and jelly beans and Coca-Cola with paper cups. The children fidget in their folding chairs, and a light wind blows the paper tablecloth inches above an old redwood table that she found in the trash. As the children begin to eat, she looks at them and sits down.

'Momma's going to tell a story!' Angelica knows, and bites her paper cup.

'That's right. I am.' Delilah is proud of her English. The sun is warm and she is happy at this moment. Later she will have a vodka with the orange juice she will squeeze fresh for los niños. And the whole afternoon will stay warm, petted by a light wind and the soul of Jesus.

'Do you believe in ghosts?' Delilah crosses her legs, wishing at this moment they were a little thinner. Angelica and Mary Francis and Little Howie begin to squeal.

'Easter celebrates the ghost of Christ, who walked this earth and was our savior. They say the only animals who know where Christ is, because his ghost still walks the earth, are the bunnies, and because they can't talk, his secret is safe. But the bunnies like to hide the hens' eggs in the bushes to tell us where he is, like a clue, and he gets very, very angry because he doesn't want us to know.'

Angelica gets up and stands on her chair, facing the other children like an actress.

'Momma says that movie star ghosts are next door and Christ won't talk to them.'

'That's enough, Angelica.'

'Momma says I can't be a movie star, but that's what I want to be.' Angela turns around on her chair, holding her dress with both hands.

'Let me finish my story. Sit down.' Delilah is annoyed.

Little Howie whispers fatty fatty and Mary Francis' cola shoots out of her nose as she laughs. Delilah continues.

'So this morning I found one of these bunnies and I realized that all his eggs are hidden, right here, and that there is a golden egg, and if you find it you get a real prize, but I can't tell you what it is till you find it. Now everyone eat their cake, because when I say so, it'll be time to look for the eggs.' Delilah pretends to look at her watch as the children finish their sweets.

The wind has begun to get a little stronger and she can hear it in the palms and the tops of the Magnolias in the cemetery. She can hear gospel singers in the kitchen and smell ham and sweet potatoes down the street, and finds herself looking at her hands to see if they are still young, then turns to the children, who have been waiting silently.

'Go.' They scream and scatter.

'Wait. Here, I forgot. Take these baskets for your eggs. Now go.' Delilah smiles.

As she walks back into her kitchen she thinks of the wind on her island, where shells and ferns spoke, when every night was summer and every day a white sheet; how she moved her hips to tin drums and high tides, how her nipples would harden when fog swallowed air at dusk, and her husband would close the shutters of their room. She remembers their garden and the squirrel monkey who slept on the roof and bit her hand. She remembers police, boys she had gone to school with, in pressed khaki uniforms and sunglasses, taking her husband away and the radio was always on, with the President's voice and a crowd cheering in the Santo Domingo.

Delilah reasons that is why her radio is always on; perhaps she will hear the President's voice again, this time speaking the language of Jesus, and tin drums will be heard down the drive. But her island is not important here. Nothing is important here, except blonde women and money and fast cars. She accepts it, except for movies, the ones on Santa Monica, with naked women and men, and the smell of urine on the sidewalk; those are the devil's movie stars. Delilah does not believe in movie stars of any kind.

She is glad they built a shopping center on the land in front of the graveyard. Now she does not have to cross herself and hold her breath when she walks by, or see the tourist buses going in and out as if they were visiting hell.

'I now quote from the Sermon on the Mount.' Delilah is squeezing oranges and she listens to the dramatic pause on the radio, broadcast from a church she has never been to, with a congregation coughing lightly and squirming in the pews. She imagines the church's stained glass is vermilion and ash, bottle blue and orchid, its light focused on the altar like a rainbow.

'Ye are the salt of the earth, but if the salt have lost his savor, wherewith shall it be salted; it is thenceforth good for nothing, but to be cast out, and to be trodden under the foot of men.' She hears amens and several chords of organ music with a tambourine. The wind seems to be building, and her avocado tree is shaking. A full pitcher of orange juice is ready and she squeezes some into her own glass, which is half-full of vodka from the cupboard. She hears the children playing, laughing, shouting. The juice is sticking and thickening in pulp between her fingers. She wipes her hands, putting three cubes in her glass and begins to sip.

'We are the light of the world. A city that is set on a hill cannot be hid. Neither do men light a candle, and put it under a bushel, but on a candlestick; and it giveth light to all that are in the house . . . Let your light so shine before men that they may see your good works, and glorify your Father which is in heaven.' The preacher's voice vibrates.

'Amen,' Delilah whispers like a kiss under her breath, seeing her husband erect in purple smoke and walking towards her through the shuttered light of their upstairs bedroom, the squirrel monkey scratching on the shutters.

'And think that today of all holy days is for the children to hear God's words as they are spoken here, to give as only a child can give; in innocence, not ignorance, running to find the light. Like all of God's little children, we will run to find the light!'

Delilah echoes the amens of the congregation who seem to be with her as she closes her eyes, the vodka running down to her toes, thinking of Coco and Jinx and where they are in Los Angeles, some place secret and held to their hearts like the men who are inside of them for an afternoon, like the husband she will never see again. Delilah remembers his hair smelled of wet ocean roads and salt, and he danced naked in a yellowed field just for her, his mouth open for prayer, his heartbeat the music of dawn.

Outside Angelica has found the most eggs but she won't admit she saw where her mother was hiding them. Still, she doesn't know where the golden egg is, and turns to Little Howie and the pack of girls and puts her basket down in a patch of crabgrass.

'Do you want to see the movie stars?' A hush falls on the girls and they turn their heads slowly, peering at the house. Gospel music is blaring; black voices and clapping hands and high-pitched shouts.

'Sure.' Little Howie is the first to step up and take her hand.

Angelica is poised like a ringleader and she lowers her voice, something she saw her mother do. This means she's important.

'I bet the golden egg is through that hole. Where the movie stars are,' Angelica says, conspiratorially.

'Your momma will be really mad.' Mary Francis twists the bottom of her skirt with her left hand and rubs her nose with her right, trying not to look at the house.

'Momma never comes outside until the music is over. We can be secret agents. And we're all famous and pretty.'

The children begin to crawl through past the century plant, then through the hole; following Angelica's lead they pretend it has doors. As each child pops through they squeal. Mary Francis is the last to go, keeping her eye on the house until the very last second, because she knows if her momma did come out she would be OK if she was still in the back yard.

On the other side of the wall the music from Delilah's kitchen is faint. Everything is very still, except for an elderly woman getting into her car. The children hide behind a palm tree. Angelica darts to another palm and whispers:

'Be careful, she's got a gun. Look for the egg!'

Angelica is floating, knowing this is part of being a movie

star, and begins to run, screaming and singing, through graves
and unkept flowers and weeds that have been placed at stone
markers. She smells things she has never smelled before, like
Magnolias that have rusted in the sun and fallen to the ground
in great open husks of scent. She can smell mounds of earth
sitting next to freshly dug holes. The other children are following her and to all of them it seems like a place that they see
in Saturday morning cartoons, with Scooby Doo and Alvin
and the Chipmunks and any friend they want, invisible, running beside them. High clouds have bleached the sun into
no color at all, and the children love the feeling of wind on
their legs and hair, and shouting across space with no one to
hear them. They do not know what mausoleums and crypts
are, thinking them little houses with columns and gates and
statues and everyone has their favorite, Angelica's being the
biggest and grandest.

'See? I'm a rich movie star. Howie, you are my sister and
also a secret agent who's gonna rescue me but we gotta find
the mountain.'

Little Howie nods his head and runs with Angelica. The
other girls are worried, they are trailing far behind them. Mary
Francis looks around and bites her lip.

'We're supposed to hold our breath, remember? If we don't
bad things will happen.' The other girls agree, and they begin
to walk slowly together, their cheeks fat with air, eyes
determined.

Little Howie and Angelica are out of breath and they have
stopped at Tyrone Power's tomb, covered with tiny graffiti
and overlooking a canal-like lagoon of water the color of mala-
chite, full of water lilies, and garbage that has collected in
the reeds at the side. Angelica decides to speak.

'This is the mountain, see? And there's the ocean. Now the golden egg is ours, but we're both naked.' Little Howie nods his head and takes off his clothes as the other girls have come up to the tomb, still holding their breath, and woozy. Angelica takes off her clothes and the other girls start laughing, letting the air escape as she and Howie, who's always wanted to be a naked girl on top of a mountain, begin to pose like they are afraid, looking for the villain, on top of Tyrone Power's tomb.

'We're naked and they're gonna get the egg. Help!' Angelica jumps down off the tomb as her clothes begin to blow away. She runs naked to the lagoon, her baby fat shaking and her hair ribbons unraveling on her shoulders. Little Howie is lost in his dreams, still pretending to be a naked girl who's a secret agent and a movie star on top of a mountain with a golden egg.

The other girls have seen little Howie's weenie before so they follow Angelica to the lagoon.

'I need to hide. They're looking for me!'

One of the girls finds a fallen palm frond and puts it in front of Angelica, but she is not sure who Angelica is hiding from. Angelica splashes some water from the lagoon on her and looks around, smiling and naked.

'This will make me a movie star for sure.'

'And God said, the children of the earth know no wrong; they see with the eyes we have lost, their innocence is our sal-va-tion!' Delilah opens her eyes.

'Amen!' she whispers. Delilah realizes she is drunk, that she has been asleep. And suddenly she remembers the children. What time is it? Two o'clock.

'Fear not death, little children, he is but a comfort when thou art tired. He is the future friend to us all.'

Delilah wipes her eyes and sets the orange juice in paper cups on a tray and walks unsteadily outside. She realizes it must be the combination of Scotch with her coffee and vodka with the orange juice that must have done it to her. It doesn't seem possible. She only had five drinks. Jinx and Frosty could drink her under the table. Princess liked champagne, and bought cases of the cheap stuff, Jacques Bonet, which she drank in tall iced tea glasses on the rocks. They were all putting on weight.

She hears the black man with his bongos and realizes he must be with his girlfriend at the triplex down the block, and thinks we all have homes today, on Easter, and none of us is lost. It is God's will.

Delilah drops the tray of fresh orange juice when she sees the back yard. The children aren't there. The paper tablecloth has blown up and is caught on her clothes-line. Pieces of chocolate cake, jelly beans and crumpled napkins are fudged on the lawn. When she begins to shout Angelica's name, she is not sure it is her own voice. She sounds like an angry, drunk man, her voice is so guttural. She sounds like her husband yelling to her on the way to prison, when he stared at her, repeating something she couldn't understand, as the doors closed on the police truck.

'Children, come back! I have to give you your prizes!' She sees the baskets half-full of eggs, some tipped over, by the century plant, and her heart begins to palpitate. She can hear her own breath in the sunny wind. It is small and ineffectual.

It is Angelica's fault. She was born mean, a breech birth, and now she is a child filled with Godless ideas, too old for her age. They will have to move now, somewhere else, San Diego or Bakersfield. Somewhere where there are no movie stars, no graves, no whores.

Delilah knows they have gone through the hole, and bends down ungracefully to see if she can get through it. The hem of her dress catches on the century plant, and the tip of one of the juicy, sharp leaves runs down her leg, causing a long line of blood to trickle down to her ankles. She barely fits, and as she pulls herself through, she is covered with garden dirt and bits of crushed fern and mint.

'Children!' As she walks into the Hollywood Memorial Cemetery, the sound of her gospel program becomes dimmer.

'Children!' Delilah staggers across the in-ground markers, looking as though she were pulled out of the earth. One of her favorite earrings has fallen off and she touches her ear as she walks, promising not to cry, not to be frightened. She only knows she has a few more hours until the girls get back, and that the children must be napped and fed and ready to go home. They will have one more drink for the road, even though they all live on the same two blocks of shade and chain link fence.

As she walks through the silent land of mausoleums and monuments to studio heads, she crosses herself, thinking there is nothing more horrifying than a graveyard in a high wind, when bouquets tip over and spirits dance. She looks for cars on the twisting, narrow lanes that cut through flat, grubby orchards of palms and stone but everyone is home today. Home.

Delilah sees statues of women who died too young and they are made to look like angels, but Delilah knows they weren't, their eyes white stone balls eaten away by car fumes and rain full of sand. She walks past chipped stone doves and marble roses, long sleek sarcophaguses of famous men that keep the heat of the sun and rot the bodies inside. And everywhere wind carries voices, beating against her ears.

She sees the children in the distance and walks rapidly towards them, furious, her right shoe of purple leather now wet with blood. Again she crosses herself, her lips tightening. As she nears them, she realizes they are playing on top of a movie star's tomb. She reads 'Tyrone Power' and repeats his name over and over and stops walking. I shall remember you in my prayers, Tyrone Power. She remembers seeing Tyrone Power in *Captain From Castile* in the Dominican Republic, the film already ten years old by the time it played there, scratchy with age and dubbed into Spanish. She remembers she let a boy put his finger in her, and she let him, grinding down on it because it felt good, and how it came back to her with whispers behind the aloof face of her mother. She remembers her living room of red and gold, and its lizards swept out daily. She remembers the shame; that movies made boys do this. She remembers being beaten, and how it didn't hurt.

She watches the children, transfixed and suspended by a barrier she does not comprehend. She sees that Angelica and Little Howie are naked, and the other girls are laughing and watching them as they continue a charade. Delilah begins to cry, large moaning, shaking sobs that force her to her knees and blind her. She will pray for their souls. She will pray for her own soul.

The children suddenly become quiet when they hear the sobbing, turning around to see where it is coming from and see Delilah on her bloody knees, with her hair in cobwebs.

Mary Francis screams, but one of the other girls nudges her in the ribs, telling her to shut up. Slowly Angelica and Little Howie hop down from the top of the tomb and find their wind-scattered clothes, putting them on, embarrassed and flushed.

Delilah can feel the Scotch coming up on her breath and she can't stop crying. She can't see the children, but she can feel her nose running down to her lip. Everything in her mind moves rapidly, drunkenly to a finish and she is crying because she does not know what it is. Angelica circles her mother, terrified. The children run back to the wall, to the hole, and climb through it, resuming their party. Delilah stays alone on her knees for quite some time, crying because there is nothing left for her to do on this day, because Jesus does not walk through Hollywood Memorial, and Delilah must have him with her at all times.

When the girls return they wink and sip another drink with Delilah, who has come back and put on a fresh dress and cleaned her leg. In May, Coco will have her turn with the children, and Delilah will go to an upholstered bar on Venice Boulevard where the men speak Spanish and palm trees are painted on the walls. Coco will take the children to the beach and Delilah will close her eyes on another man's bed.

Coco wants to make sure Little Howie has behaved himself and Delilah says he was an angel, a little angel, and that the children have had a grand time. She shakes her head and lisps in a Castilian tongue that Angelica was punished, that she is in her room without cookies and cake.

Delilah is humming to herself as the women and their children leave, words galloping over her starched tongue, a song her mother taught her. How you don't give bread to wolves, because they will spirit your children away, to a place where even the strongest men don't go. Angelica is screaming behind her locked door, and Delilah takes out her crucifix and a piece of lace from the linen drawer, touching it to her face, running it over her eyes so the light around her becomes flowers of ivory and white.

shalimar

WHEN THE ROLLS-ROYCE broke the white wooden barrier off La Cuesta Drive, it shot out at such speed and angle that it appeared to float, briefly, without moving. However, no one could see it in the clear, crescent moon night; perhaps the headlights of the car appeared briefly to houses perched on cliffs, and the inhabitants peering through their picture windows assumed the shooting lights were part of the same asphyxiating glitter of the city beneath the trees. But then, no one with a view of Los Angeles looks at it long.

The screams from inside the car were quite loud, but people are used to screams in the hills; couples fighting on balconies and coyotes marking territory and hunting household pets, lovemaking and overdoses on Mulholland Drive, police helicopters with search lights and the sirens that follow them like hunting dogs. The screams of people about to die are also quite misleading, sometimes coming off as hysteria or the high-pitched laughter of an amusement park thrill.

And it was late, around three a.m. Very little sound was made in the actual forming of the accident. The wooden barrier was rotted and soft as a new sweater. La Cuesta Drive was above Mulholland, a private drive without streetlights, one narrow lane that carved the entire part of a hill like a punk haircut, and a drop of four hundred feet into a rich, hidden canyon of highly-prized homes.

As the Rolls began to dip down, its heavy engine and chrome

angel pointing to a black earth, it did not twist or roll, but went down swiftly, perfectly, the engine still purring and the tires lazily spinning as though they were pulling up to a première.

Falling exactly four hundred and eighty-seven feet, the car smashed into the shallow end of a swimming pool of an estate called 'Shalimar', built by a maharaja in the fifties, who pawned his mother's jewels to build the tasteless and extravagant replica of an Indian temple, down to reflecting pools and stone replicas of goddesses with a hundred arms.

The sedan hit with such force that the front end of the automobile broke through the Gunite and concrete on the swimming pool and wedged itself a full five feet into the earth. At this moment the four doors were torn off by gravity; one flew and skidded across the back lawn and one disappeared into the reflecting pool. Another toppled a plaster urn and the fourth cut through a grapefruit tree.

There were two passengers. The driver was a Latin male of about sixteen, and the passenger was, from what can be gathered, his girlfriend, a blonde fourteen-year-old girl. The male was decapitated by a shard of glass from the windshield and his head fell into the deep end of the pool. The rest of his body was crushed under the steering wheel and dash.

The girl was thrown out of the car upon impact and tossed about twenty feet onto a barbecue grill, in which her ribs, kidneys, thighs and vagina were punctured severely. Still, possibly in a state of shock, she managed to pry herself loose from the grill. Losing an enormous amount of blood, she managed to crawl with her arms across the patio by the pool, away from the car, leaving a blanket of blood across the yellow and white tiles. From there she tried to climb up the hill, across jagged granite and ice plants. Perhaps an instinct had taken over and she had truly believed that if she went back to the scene of the accident it would have never happened. The climb was straight up, and she continually slipped on the syrup of the ice plants until she landed into a untended bath of mustard weed. There she died from loss of blood, choking on her tongue in a paralysis brought on by severe shock.

The entire accident took place with almost no sound, as the pool muffled much of the impact and the September night beetles and crickets had had an exceptionally prolific year. Before dawn the pool had filled and absorbed the young boy's fluids, and with the pool light on, it almost shined a pigeon's blood ruby red. After twenty minutes the automatic sprinklers came on, and much of the young girl's blood became mixed with garden run-off.

It was determined by the police that both the boy and the girl were loaded on a Hawaiian cocaine called 'ice', and that they had the markings of long-time drug addiction. This explains how the girl was able to keep going up the hill while the blood poured out of her. She didn't feel a thing. Apparently, between the two, they had ingested enough to kill up to five people.

The current owner of Shalimar had put the house up for sale and was living in San Diego. For two days and nights neither the two teenagers, or the Rolls-Royce, or the elderly couple they had beaten and killed to get the car, were reported missing. By the end of the second day, the young girl had begun to attract wasps and blackbirds had begun to gather on top of the half-submerged automobile. Dogs began to bark on neighboring estates, hidden by long drives and eucalyptus. People assumed it was the heat.

*　　　*　　　*

Only red flowers grow in the gardens of Shalimar; American Beauty Roses, scarlet geraniums, sunset carnations and chrysanthemums in a simmer of burnt sienna. Red hibiscus grow wild as borders to the hills. This is what attracted Pamela to the house, why she bought it a year after the accident. So much was attached to the house. There was death and royalty, too many owners who tried to change the house but couldn't, and through the decades the statues of Indian goddesses stayed in the garden, as did the carved elephant front doors, mirror-chipped halls and tiled ceilings.

She had always wanted to live in an exalted state, tied in with something larger than herself, and she knew that the last romantic palaces were being built here, in Los Angeles, and nowhere else. It was here at Shalimar that she could create her costumes for films and store her enormous wardrobes.

She remembered how the real estate agent stared at her as she walked around the swimming pool, looking out at the city and smiling. The man couldn't believe she wanted to buy this house. He said she was the only person who had shown interest. She merely smiled, touched the stone goddesses rising from the sago palms, and wrote out a check.

Pamela considered herself a gentle, honest person, but admitted to herself that the sheer cruelty of the accident a year before had transfixed her. The idea that she had bought the place where the two psychopathic children had landed out of the sky fascinated her. Its morbidity was sexual and mythic, and she wanted to know much much more. Her life was now in this house and her life was feeling history pulse in her fingers. She was analytical and enthusiastic about legend and image; how glamour is pulled from thin air.

Pamela liked being alone because she was easy to hurt. At thirty-three she stood five foot and had a dowager's hump which the doctor said was incurable, and would worsen into severe debilitation as she approached her fifties. Her sweet Irish face strained out from her calcimined shoulders that made her look, in her eyes, like a turtle. It was so much just to peer up at the sky.

She wished she could see everything in black and white, like a cat. How beautiful everything must be when shadows take over and form their own flesh on the floor and walls; how light becomes more than shine but something alive, beckoning. Her inspiration for her costumes came from old films on AMC, like *Moontide* where Jean Gabin kissed Ida Lupino with such force it looked like he cracked her neck. She kept her eyes for classics that no one ever saw, that hadn't been on release for years. Those were the ones where she'd seen a hat, or a neckline that would work. Or shoes and flower brooches that consumed a woman's shoulder.

Pamela had been nominated for an Oscar but she was glad she didn't win, as she didn't attend for fear of others, not so much pointing and whispering, but others in Hollywood who frightened her with faces so blank they must be dead. She worked hard and kept to herself, but had friends, close friends, with whom she spent her time. She read voraciously, everything about women in Los Angeles from the twenties to the present and tried to see if she fit their mold, if there was some common link of heart, but there was none.

She loved her clothes and the clothes she created more than anything else, more than the men who never entered her world, and she wanted them to. She wanted a man to sit in a chair and let her spread herself over his groin and chest, but she knew the act of her making love to a beautiful man would be hideous as a praying mantis and it made her cry. It was an impossibility as real as her mornings, which she wrote every day as poetry. She had ten small books of mornings carefully described; the quality of light and the change in her thoughts were dutifully set down and immaculate as her collection of clothes, all the clothes of Hollywood she bought and tagged and indexed. There were gowns and swimsuits from MGM musicals, Hedda Hopper's hats and the minks Bette Davis would toss on a chair. They were hers and she sincerely believed that they had the power to transform, as this house did, a channel to a world of images that kept her strong.

Pamela wore certain clothes and never tried to be naked if possible. Even in the heat of September, the air conditioner would be turned on and she would wear one of Joan Crawford's suits from *The Women*. She owned Jean Harlow's ostrich feather peignoir from *Dinner At Eight* and would wear it with marabou puff high-heels when she got up to make coffee promptly at six. It made her walk different. When she was sketching she wore a white suit Garbo had worn in *The Painted Veil*, a favorite, and dressed her thinning red hair in a tight white turban that pulled her face up till she could feel her lips against her teeth.

Each piece of clothing she pulled apart and restitched herself to fit her back. They were her jewels and dressing was a precise, exhilarating experience. She did not want to be a hag. Anything but a hag. She wore red lipstick, a blue red that would catch arc lighting and came from setting the garden flowers on the kitchen table and looking inside the bloom, to where the color pulsed. That was her shade. Her nails were long and thick with polish, and she liked the sound of them tapping the paper as she sketched.

In this devout limp of solitude she watched as the news opened and closed on the children. She believed them to be only children, and deeply in love.

Pamela believed that this was an extraordinary destiny; that she was tied to ghosts and they spoke through her. It was hers and hers alone, and in her dreams she had seen the children walking towards her with flowers in their palms. They repeated with words soft and slick as birds' bellies 'You will understand.'

She knew houses are named for a reason; that Shalimar was the garden of love where lovers came to rest, that the loveless become loved in the garden; that she would find the flowers and discover answers. That a love would happen to her.

There were many things said about them she refused to believe. By this time it was common knowledge that the names of the boy and girl were Raven and Veronica. They were drifters, or runaways, and their families came from Omaha, Nebraska. According to the coroner, they were malnourished and had been addicted to cocaine for about three years each, which would have put the beginning of their addiction at thirteen and eleven respectively.

It was also known that the two had been in Los Angeles only one month before their deaths. In that period they had dealt drugs out of a crack house in the San Gabriel Valley and had been responsible for a robbery on Ventura Boulevard. It was also discovered they had performed in two pornographic films. The filmmakers were later arrested for making and distributing child pornography, and the tapes had become an underground cult item on Melrose Avenue. Hardline rock and rollers had turned them into heroes. Several had knocked on the front door and asked to see the pool, but she wouldn't open it.

Raven and Veronica had stolen the Rolls from an elderly couple in a hidden ranch house on La Cuesta Drive, but before they did, they had tortured the couple for a period of hours. The wife had Raven's semen stains on her face and her eyes had been used as an ashtray for his cigarettes. There were traces of her husband's tongue in the garbage disposal. The kids had been looking for jewelry but all she had was costume.

Of particular interest was magic paraphernalia left on the couple's dining room table, in front of the bound and gagged corpses. Regular playing cards were shuffled and mixed with the Tarot, and balls of string and tied scarves were found in the dead girl's pockets.

Pamela did not believe the children had committed an atrocity. Even in their state, they must have a sacrifice, an innocence. They probably stumbled upon the couple, but she realized that couldn't have been true. She chose to believe her own truth; that nothing is completely evil, that circumstance and the new world they lived in, without laws, allowed their love a savagery. For she knew they were in love. It could be the only complete answer. And writing this morning into her book, looking at the still, renovated pool and early sun, she thought today is the anniversary of their death, and that later she will go into her closet and bring out pieces she bought from the police after the case was closed; a black leather jacket with 'Raven' spelled out in studs and Veronica's cloth coat with swastikas painted in white and pink, so quickly and crudely done they looked like open, dying flowers.

Her friend Charmaine was expected at six. Charmaine had stopped her career as an actress in the early sixties, when her brand of glamour had become dated. She had starred with Burt Lancaster and Richard Widmark in many film noir thrillers as a husky-voiced blonde who was bad, always very bad. Charmaine never married, and it was the general consensus that she was a lesbian, which was untrue, as Charmaine was exactly like Pamela.

Charmaine always believed she was ugly, that someday she would be destroyed like a piece of paper because she was no longer the image the studios had fabricated; this constant distrust of herself had led her to retreat into a smoky, luxurious world that reeked of 1955. She was precise as Pamela with clothing and make-up. Sometimes she would be seen at old Hollywood restaurants like Musso and Frank and Nickodell; the staff knew to put her in the darkest booth by the bar. She dined alone on steak and sliced tomatoes, had a double vodka martini and smoked two cigarettes. Then she was gone. No one bothered to whisper any more.

Charmaine was a creaky blonde with a stiff pageboy and a too-tanned face. She had the capability of seeing people she wanted to, and generally walked right through rooms in total disdain of others until she reached an old friend. Pamela was her only new friend, and they were fairly close, speaking in a Hollywood language. Things were implied but seldom discussed, and pleasantries were brittle as candy. Pamela had many of Chairmaine's old gowns from RKO and Paramount, and many times Charmaine would walk through Pamela's closet and finger her old dresses, telling stories. The two women dressed up for each other and spent evenings alone at their houses, watching old films. They were never without conversation.

Charmaine considered Pamela a romantic and never discussed her deformity. In her eyes, Pamela's belief in love was a purifier, like music, and must be treated with respect. When Pamela opened the elephant front doors, she was wearing a gold bugle-beaded gown that Rita Hayworth wore in *Gilda*, and its exaggerated shoulders made her look like a dictator, but Charmaine only smiled. She always smiled for Pamela. It was a powdered world that was safe, glamorous and utterly without consequence, and both women protected it fiercely. What Charmaine did not believe in was Pamela's attachment to this horrifying, déclassé house and the idea that torture was acceptable, and she was determined to change Pamela's ideas about the two children.

'You look beautiful tonight. It's *Gilda*, isn't it?' Pamela nodded her head.

'Please come in, Charmaine. I invited you over because tonight is their anniversary.' Charmaine blanched.

'Yes, I know. I cannot see why this is a cause for celebration. However, I decided to join in the festivities, and I went out in disguise and bought the tape of those two so we could finally see it, instead of talk about it.'

Pamela hated it when Charmaine became arch, waving her hand. She shuffled over to the bar and poured Charmaine her evening cocktail, iced vodka and three baby onions.

Disguise indeed. Charmaine wasn't recognized anywhere. Pamela neatly handed her her drink and looked into Charmaine's black-rimmed eyes. How could she? She admitted to herself the thought of seeing the two angels making love excited her.

'Charmaine, there's a movie I wanted to see tonight. *This Gun for Hire*. With Alan Ladd.'

'And Veronica Lake. I was too young then. Still in high school.'

'Of course. And I have baby chicken later, with roast potatoes.'

'How lovely.' Charmaine swept into Pamela's studio, where she kept her sketch easel and stacks of drawings and her television. She could tell Pamela had been drinking. She could hear Pamela pouring a big tumbler of brandy in the next room. Then the fizz of the ginger ale. And the ice dropped in, one at a time.

Charmaine was constantly astonished at Pamela's exceptional talent and wanted to protect her. Pursing her lips, she squinted at the VCR and slid the tape in. As Pamela came into the room she looked at Charmaine, then at the television.

'You really aren't going to put that tape on?'

'Hush. You haven't seen it, have you?' Pamela shook her head and her eyes were beginning to tear.

'Well then, you might as well.' Charmaine went to the couch and sat down on the edge, lighting a cigarette, staring at the screen. Pamela stood, refusing to sit down, clinking the ice in her glass. As she drank the brandy, she could feel the cool fog from the glass hit her nose.

The two women sat in silence, as they often did, watching the screen. As Raven came on in the gaudy video color, he stood in the middle of a small motel room with orange and pale green walls. He grinned at that camera and swayed. Pamela watched, entranced. He was higher than she'd ever be. And thin, with a sweet face, like the young Cuban boys she'd seen on Santa Monica and running errands at the studio. He began to strip, and she could see he was listening to someone off camera. It was clumsy and his wiry, mocha body was bruised. When she saw his penis flop out of his briefs it was dark, like a black man's, and she felt herself get dizzy. He began masturbating, keeping his eyes closed. Once he stumbled and fell, then picked himself up and started over, grinning at the camera. Very shortly he came, and Pamela watched, mesmerized, as she realized she'd never seen a man have an orgasm. She flushed. She reminded herself that at thirty-three, she was still a virgin. So this is how blood is attained. How simple and pathetic.

'Wait. This is just for openers.' Charmaine stubbed her cigarette out in the marble ashtray.

'You mean you've already seen it?'

'Yes.' Pamela said nothing. Briefly the two women looked at each other.

When Veronica came on Pamela gasped, then took a slow gulp of the warm September air. She was nothing more than a tiny girl, with nipples beginning to swell, and needle marks on her freckled, stringy arms. She had no pubic hair yet, and Pamela watched with increasing terror as the two began to make love, the camera closing in on their genitals, surrounded by bruises and cigarette burns. She was getting drunk as she watched, and felt herself weave in the lilting breeze of the hills.

'They loved each other. They were young. They didn't know what they were doing.'

Charmaine turned around and snapped at her.

'The hell they didn't. Those little bastards are disgusting

fucks if you ask me. They were deranged garbage. Just look at them. I'm glad they died. Stop believing in the devil, Pamela.'

She had never heard Charmaine swear, much less hear her voice turn dark and guttural, but she realized this is how Charmaine survived all her years of fear and solitude.

Pamela suddenly saw how Charmaine's fingers were withered and yellow from cigarettes. She saw them touching men with boxer shorts and sharkskin suits, men whose skin was sore and cold as January. She saw Charmaine at thirty, touching her face in the mirror with a cigarette in her hand, the smoke running through her hair like the first minute of a rape. Then Charmaine at sixty, smoking in the sun, rubbing creme on her knees, her eyes foreign and dying.

She couldn't be in the room any longer. She knew madness comes in rooms, and there was a time to walk through a garden, a night, a wind. She lurched past Charmaine, through the open sliding glass doors, out to the lit pool. She could hear Charmaine turn the tape off and follow her. Suddenly the stillness was a menace, leaving her too alone, and she was always alone, and she began to cry.

She felt Charmaine's hand on her shoulder. Charmaine had never touched her or anyone she knew. She was surprised at how light and bony it was. Pamela suddenly found herself talking about everything, about why she bought the house.

'This is the pool where they died.' She turned and looked at Charmaine.

'It's just a pool. Babies drown in pools. Dogs and people who can't swim. It means nothing.'

'This is where she crawled, trying to get up the hill. See?'

'She died. She wasn't a god, or a movie star, or anyone to believe in. She was worthless.'

'No!' Pamela sunk to her knees on the grass. She could hear bugle beads snap around her shoulders.

Charmaine helped her get up, and began slowly walking her to the house. She could hear Charmaine whisper in her ear, as though she was in a crowd of people. The trees above them gaped and swayed.

'There is no myth. It is this simple, Pamela. We are two women who prefer to be alone, sometimes with each other, but we are always alone. We were born that way, and that's the way we die. No one dead will make our lives any different. We are capable of perfecting our own private world and we are capable of surviving. No one will ever love us, but we can survive. We're not beautiful. We don't have the white light, Pamela. But we are not cruel. And we cannot believe in cruelty. It'll destroy. I've seen it.'

Nothing more was said. Pamela went into the kitchen and prepared dinner. The two women spoke little, letting the summer air rinse their thoughts. Pamela asked Charmaine if she would like to stay and watch *This Gun for Hire*, but she smiled graciously and declined.

'No, darling, it's a little before my time.'

As Charmaine got into her black Mercedes, Pamela realized they had become too close, and this was the end of their friendship. She knew Charmaine cut relationships off when they became too close, and she understood.

She began turning the lights off in the house and sat down in front of the television with another brandy. The breeze had become a wind, and the heat it brought into the house was from deserts and small towns she would never discover. As *This Gun for Hire* came on she realized, with a slight shock, that Alan Ladd was playing a killer named Raven. She leaned over, studying the television, her eyes widening. The open doors let in gusts of perfumed Indian summer air, and her sketches began floating through the room and the floor, the drawings done on tissue paper flying up and circling like cigarette smoke. She did not care, in fact; was enjoying the disarray, her sketches of dresses flying by her as though they were alive. When Veronica Lake came on, she was singing in a shimmering gown and as she was walking through a cheap nightclub, she performed magic tricks that went along with the song. She was making fish appear in water, pulling scarves from the back of necks and smiling at all the older men, her hair covering one eye.

Pamela felt her skin chill white and dampen. Now she knew who Raven and Veronica were, and that they were still children who discovered how to fly. Slowly she pulled herself up from the couch and watched Alan Ladd in the shadows, the drawings flying around her. Her silence became a wall, like the hand-built mud walls in Mexico that dry in a day. When the film was over she turned the set off and stood in the complete night of her room, the city lights an ember from a much larger fire.

Rita Hayworth's gown was glistening in the black like a stagnant pond, and Pamela walked like a child through the tiled halls, where she came to her bedroom and the two coats of the children laid down on the bed. She bent down and picked up Raven's coat and put it on, with some difficulty, around her shoulders, and walked outside towards the pool, where she sat for the remainder of the night, letting the wind toss her thinning red mane, taken down and covering her hump with a soft breath.

It was on this anniversary evening that she realized she

would always be alone and never know what it meant to find a destroying passion, a passion that disfigures flowers and children and flies in silence on summer nights. She smiled, thinking to herself that in the morning she would write again of light and sounds and color, and never try to cry again for night, or the shell between her legs and the shame she carried with strong, long hands.

the fire of bells

THE RESTAURANT IS a purple black fuzz, its shadows out-lined by pulsing red candles in jars that dot the room like fireflies. Angie feels she has fallen here, from a discreet plateau that might be a heaven. She is aware of air-conditioning and a heat that ebbed with the padded leather door. Her little boy is fat and killing her right arm. He is dazed by the sullen, dry wind. He's all she's got.

She's been here once before and she likes this place. Its smoked air paints itself over throughout the afternoon, like clouds seen by plane that become faces or animals running. Signs from God if you know how to read them, Angie thinks. Even in this place, if you look hard enough, you'll tell your future.

Angie nods to a center red leather booth under an oil of a nude woman swathed in bells and diaphanous sheets.

'That'll do just fine,' she remarks under her breath to the hostess as if they are old friends, which they aren't.

Angie's proud of the way everyone in the booths stop and stare at her with her baby son. She bounces him on her right arm and smiles to no one in particular. Women who become mothers command respect, she thinks to herself. We become another breed and we rule. We can get anything we want.

'You got a high-chair? I want it sturdy. Something for Tony. He's special, you know.' Angie kisses Tony on the cheek and bounces him. He loves it.

The hostess doesn't care. She brings over a heavy, 1960's high-chair that looks like a space ship, with a glitter laminate tray. She grunts when she puts Tony in it, snapping the tray into place around him. Tony gurgles and opens his eyes to the room, bending his head and reaching for the stale, oily air.

Already he's learning how to grab, Angie thinks. And people notice her little boy. Tony has a way of smiling at everyone around him that Angie knows is the sign of a don, of an important man.

She is still seeing a white snow from the sewer like heat and blinks twice, knowing this should get rid of the dots. The Santa Anas in the San Fernando Valley have made her tight curly bangs turn sloppy with sweat, and she dabs them with a napkin then gives her head a good shake. Tony laughs.

'So you think your mom's funny, do you?' Angie's voice booms. She has never been able to tame it, nor understand why people feel they have to talk in hushed tones just because a place is dark. She doesn't care. She's always been the center of attention wherever she goes. She expects it.

An elderly couple in the next booth smile. They are dressed in golf outfits and the wife's face is thick as a dessert and heavily lined. The old man's face is a dirty milk chocolate. There is a melanoma on his neck which he touches constantly as though he were in communication with it.

'Where the hell is my waitress?' Angie puts her elbows on the table and stares across at the couple. She smiles. She knows her face is too large. Her teeth are too large. Back in New York no one cared. But here in Los Angeles you've got to fade to beige. You have to be perfect. Like at Tony's commercial audition. All the perfect babies.

'You guys been playing golf? My dad used to love golf, but in New York it rains so much he didn't get much time on the course. But I know it's a great way to exercise. All that walking. My dad never used a cart. He said they looked dumb.'

She stares at them like food, wondering if they could ever be her friends. Six months in Los Angeles and not one friend. Not even a girlfriend to yak with. Her husband Sal said they had to keep a low profile; they were playing straight and new people would get in the way. So she stayed home with Tony, and watched the birds of paradise by the drained pool go brown.

She is going to make small talk and she knows the entire room will listen. It's part of my life, Angie thinks. I got to talk to a person. Strangers in restaurants will do just fine. She looks at the two. She can see they obviously don't want to be bothered. The wife decides to speak first.

'What an adorable little boy. How old is he?'

'He's fourteen months. A twin you know. He's my boy Tony. Is that a face or what?' Angie smiles a certain malicious, voluptuous smile that startles the old woman.

'A twin? My goodness. Where is the other —'

'He's dead.' Funny how words sometimes cross into an existence she can't control. Angie's eyes frost and the old woman looks down at her tablecloth.

Angie looks at Tony and reasons that animals discard the weak and eat their dead. Perfectly pure an act, death. She understands now, after those months in drape-drawn rooms and the hiss of sedatives in her blood, that maybe one is better than two. She remembers hospital white and blindness, trying to stare into the face of Tony's exact other and seeing stone, marbles, sand. Spring disappeared, then summer. Now it's the beginning of September, and she still walks with liquid legs and a drowned, slow heartbeat. She decides not to talk, not just yet, not until the waitress comes.

She looks around her. The restaurant is an old blood red tinged with gold fleur-de-lis and mahogany that's never been polished, just run over with a damp cloth, and is now cracked and buckling. This is a good place, Angie thinks. Someday it'll be mine. With small cash and big tactics I could have this place. Angie knows how to get things. Jewelry, money, men. Other things come more difficult.

Their Italian food is cooked New York style, just like on the Island where the boys hung out and there was a party every Sunday for the wives, no charge for anything on the menu. And a party every Thursday for girls like Angie, who graduated into being wives, but first had to learn how to have a good time with the lower mob, spit-clean white-skinned boys with one dollar wallets and dumb stud charm. Angie learned how to fill a place with heat and sass, keep her nose clean in the toilet and make sure she got something every time she went out.

She first came to this restaurant with her husband Sal and decided then this place would be hers. Soon as she saw it she knew it was plenty dark, oozing martinis and mink coats, the kind of place her parents would go to and bring home tinfoil birds of manicotti and ravioli. Her mother and father always had a good time. She wishes it would be the same with Sal.

Places like this never change, thinks Angie. Full of businessmen in their fifties and their heavily eyelashed, silent wives heaving in half whispers. Women chagrined into a ten-year muteness that makes Angie think of her aunts in

New York, of all women she promises to herself never to become.

I will die if I stay in Los Angeles, Angie thinks. I can't breathe the river or the snow, and I will wind up making telephone calls in air-conditioned rooms as dark as this to people I no longer know. I can make Tony a famous baby. That I know I can do. The rest is up to the smoke in this room and what appears immediately before me.

Angie remembers as much as she can. Of the middle of every night when Sal rolled off her and she could hear babies crying all over Brooklyn, from the bottom of rivers and windows and in half kept parks. Here babies don't cry. They are kept hidden in tract houses and condominiums with stucco walls and circular drives.

It pleases her that her entrance causes so much attention. She and Tony are going to be noticed for the rest of their lives. That's a sure fact. Angie is still in awe at how quiet it is. Because of her voice. A huge voice, something she has lived with all her life. It is a dangerous grasp; uncompromising and deep as a violent man's. The steady menace of someone who knows how to kill. Angie likes her voice. It gives her respect. She knows she's smart, that she thinks higher than what comes out of her mouth.

She realizes everyone in the restaurant is curious of what she will say next. She can hear buzzers in the kitchen ringing up a new order of lasagne. Angie has the room. The old couple are back in focus. They avoid her eyes and she decides to continue.

'Tony's twin was named Christopher, like Saint Christopher, my family's patron saint. It happened six months ago. We took the baby boys in to the doctor to be checked up, you know, just shots and stuff. Chris gets four shots for flu, like a baby flu, and some other stuff, chicken pox I think, and suddenly he dies, in a matter of minutes, just like that, in front of my eyes. The other one, Tony, he's fine. Can you believe it? I was pretty shook up. This is my first lunch out with my family.'

The old woman's eyes become bright.

'Did you sue?'

'WHAT?'

Angie realizes she is talking into shadows. Two old nothings.

'What did you say to me?'

Silence. That didn't happen where she came from. Too much to think about. She was taught to avoid court, lawyers, judges. A matter of pride, of family.

'Where the hell is my waitress? Enough already.'

Angie's hair is black as her grandmother's from Naples, and she has let it grow into an immense, permed tangle because it reminds her of Maria Schneider in *Last Tango in Paris*. She shakes her hair and tries to fluff it, sticking her long pink nails in it like a fork. She's proud of her breasts. They're a double D cup and men like that. She keeps them up and out, with her lace blouse open to the brassiere so everyone can get a load of her line. She thought they might shrink after nursing the twins but no such luck. Still, they look great above a white tablecloth in a big red leather booth like this.

Tony looks at his mother and chews out several mono-syllables, then begins to cry, banging the sides of his high chair. Slowly Angie turns her head and glares at the child. He becomes still.

'I'm hungry too, and I don't want any crap from you, you

hear?' Angie quietly strokes his forehead. The old couple leave without saying goodbye. She hates them.

It has been like this ever since she came to this cruddy town. People ignoring her, even in the hospital. She remembered screaming at the nurses, the doctor. How they put a restraining device on her and she broke out of it. How all she heard were the palms blowing outside and the ding-dong of the intercom.

Angie becomes reluctant and soft. As soft as she knows.

'That's my boy. You were a good boy today. You're going to get that commercial, Tony my boy, and we're going to be rich.'

Suddenly their waitress is everywhere, hovering over them. Her name card reads Nina and she is a fat thing with pink orange hair and mosquito bites.

'I wondered when you were coming. I'm starved. And I have a hungry baby, too. Do you want him to start crying again?'

'Please ma'am. I have to ask you to keep your voice down. I'm sorry.'

'You're sorry? Listen honey, I've had this voice all my life, and when I whisper it gets even louder. You got it?' Angie hears giggles from another booth, and laughter from a drunk sitting at the bar. She decides to continue, addressing the room, banging a knife against her water glass.

'Attention! Sorry everybody, but you'll have to put up with my voice. It's the only one I got.' Angie hears scattered applause. The waitress purses her lips, pretending to write something, anything, down on her pad. Angie thinks to herself, when I take over this place, I'll fire her fat ass.

'Will there be two?'

'No, three. I'm waiting for my husband.'

Nina seems to be relieved. Angie realizes this woman is frightened, but she doesn't see why. What is so frightening about a young mother with a big voice and a cute baby boy? She taps her nails on the table and stares up at the waitress.

'Finally some service.'

'Our kitchen is understaffed today.'

'Well. Okay. I turned twenty-one last week. You got any house cocktails? Something fun?'

'No. Just regular drinks.'

Biting her upper lip until there is lipstick on her teeth, Angie tosses her driver's license on the table and orders a bottle of red wine. Two glasses. A child's plate of spaghetti, tossed and chopped, a glass of Seven-Up and a large pepperoni pizza and have the chef shave some salami on it too. Like New York.

She glances around the restaurant. People are beginning to leave and soon it looks like she'll have the place to herself. She got here late, because she had to sit for four hours waiting for Tony's commercial audition to come up. Some cruddy little dance studio near Warner Brothers. All he had to do was sit and smile and clap his hands in front of the camera. All the other babies were so exact she wanted to kill them. And their mothers! Whispery little broads in aerobics outfits drinking Evian out of the bottle with brisk little feminine motions. Tony was damn good when he got out there. She was proud.

The bartender turns on a football game, staring at Angie as he stubs out his cigarette and uncorks a bottle of red wine. You like girls like me, Angie thinks to herself as she lights a cigarette and blows smoke to the bar, flicking her pink nails.

You'll never get me, buddy, so go back to cleaning glasses. It's all you're good for.

Angie studies the heavy gold bangles on her arm, six on her right and six on her left. Her grandmother had told her when she got seven on each arm things would happen, things she wouldn't be able to control. It was the spirits, she said. They'll come to you in a fire, and you'll hear them walking on bells. Angie didn't believe her but the old lady seems to be right on everything. Like when the Del Rubios were shot a block away from the police station in Queens and no one found their bodies for a month; her grandmother knew they were dead. Told everyone so. But Angie's grandmother was old and didn't speak English. No one cared.

Tony is waving his tiny hands at the light attached to the oil painting. Maybe he thinks the broad with the big tits and bells is me, Angie reasons. Staring unfocused at her child, she wonders what her grandmother is doing right now. If it's cold and she's wearing the white rabbit fur coat her father bought her. If she is sitting on her bed in the basement, reading Italian newspapers and comic books and tarot cards, talking in a low, serious voice with the Puerto Rican woman who brings her candles with Jesus on the cellophane and perfume bottles full of green water with herbs. She thinks of her grandmother's perfume and her knotted, twisted hair; a lilac stayed around her that Angie could never find in department stores, an intense lilac, or more a trace of something abandoned, like incense at funerals.

Sometimes her grandmother's voice comes to her. She heard it constantly when she was on her medication. Other voices too, occasional voices from her childhood and her party years. Voices that had spoken to her once and she had recorded. Voices that yelled to her from ripe, outdoor markets pulsing in a spring steam, or from the back of local bars. They came together like pearls to wear around her neck, each sentence a puzzle. And then Christopher's voice, wordless and a caress; as soft and distant as a vacation. She still hears the voices. They come, float away. They mean her no harm.

She thinks of Sal and his beautiful, stupid face. How during the months they were trying to conceive his face was above her, sweat dripping off his chin and she had come to feel sore as earth that had been turned over. His mouth was always open and his eyes were always closed, as though he didn't want to see where his semen went. She was always sure there was someone else but she was not allowed to question. It's just the way it was.

Together they stayed wet as sap on summer trees. Then suddenly she was pregnant in an autumn that was bitter as it was dry.

Angie thinks of snow, of Italian restaurants like this, smelling good a mile away. Of the Hudson frozen over, fish in blocks of ice hanging on tongs. Some slipped off and flew like silver cars on glass streets, followed by giggling girls with coarse black hair, their breath settling above them in the frigid air. Animals, faces, flowers rising and dissolving. It is the same snow that covered her eyes when she walked in here. Only now it is from the sun, and Angie gestures toward no one, closes her eyes and takes a deep drag on her cigarette.

Angie hates California. She hates the crappy little blondes with hundred dollar hair and husbands who stink up a room. She hates being separate, alone, disavowed. There is nowhere to go, no place to walk that is not a struggle.

Back east her husband Sal had made a pretty good living in petty theft and jewelry store jobs. Angie always had first pick of the take. She had even bought a magnifying glass to check whether the goods were 14K or 18K. One time Sal had brought home some goods from the neighborhood, which was dumb, because they were just gold filled, and she made him return the stuff to the people's doorstep that same night. People in her neighborhood had to look out for each other. Here there are no neighborhoods, only cul-de-sacs and areas they call estates, even though the houses aren't too big.

Sal was rising in the family and she was livid when he decided to move to Los Angeles and play it straight. They could have had some real power if they had waited and Sal stayed alive; maybe in fifteen years or so the right slots would have opened.

His face was a yellow ash one night when he came home. He pulled down the blinds and locked the door. Angie had never locked a door in her life. The cocaine went down the toilet and he flushed it twice, telling her they were leaving in the morning and to pack up. Tell her sister to take everything of theirs. Call no one except her. She understood.

She also had two screaming twin boys. And party dresses and a make-up case full of jewelry and cash. She wanted to speak to her grandmother, but didn't. Asleep on the plane, a boy on each side and Sal in the seat behind her, she dreamed of women traveling, of blood and men, how they slip so easily inside a woman and then bury them. How there are junctures that spell out new emotions like paint on a billboard. She had kept her bracelets and she would keep her traditions like the women before her and she decided to take everything out of life she could get.

When Christopher died Sal didn't speak for a week and she couldn't stop screaming in the morning. In the evening as well, when light vanished in slow, uneven steps that distracted her. She was in exile, she was touched by plague and bad air. Sal never looked at her again, in the eyes. She decided Tony would be her eyes. The world was his, after all. He was male.

Sal was doing as he was told, working as a security guard and now she lived in a tract house in Panorama City with overgrown banana plants and birds of paradise, sharp ugly flowers that could do a girl damage. She refused to water anything, or fill the pool. They needed more money, always more money, and good furniture, something with a little class, like back home. Sal started doing small jewelry jobs and Angie got more gold bangles for her arm, cash, appliances, rugs, reproduction oil paintings in fancy frames. They were always left with a note, sometimes no note. She kept everything and said little. Her son Tony would be in movies and commercials and make her rich. Her husband Sal was the greatest lover in Brooklyn. Her husband Sal was expendable.

Angie realizes that she is talking to herself and the restaurant is empty. The waitress has finally arrived. Angie closes her mouth and gazes at Nina, who puts Tony's cut spaghetti and Seven-Up on his tray. She pours Angie's red wine.

'I'm kind of tired. My son Tony went on his first baby commercial, like an audition, and he wowed them.'

'That's nice. I hope he gets it.' A kind face after all. Angie figures the waitress doesn't care anymore. Everybody's gone.

'Is your husband coming?'

'Oh sure. He'll be here.' Angie looks around the restaurant and decides this will be a wonderful place when she gets it.

Movie people will come here. They could launder some big money through this place. Important people would know her name. Angie sips her wine and thinks about decisions. That women make decisions and men only follow. Think only of the future. Make it a bible. Her grandmother would have flipped a tarot card on her TV tray and nodded her head.

The voices come back and Angie is not in the mood. She can hear the hospital voices, the radio in the next room, the nurse clicking her tongue against the roof of her mouth. Her fury is beginning to make her hands shake, her bracelets are clanging, and she can feel her own blood. She knows she could have killed any one of those doctors, followed them home and shot them and their families. And she knows that after the act she would feel exhilarated and completely unafraid. It was her religion. But the voices stuck a needle in her and she woke up staring at a drained pool and a black and white television.

Men and women can be cruel in groups. She sips her wine and looks at the paintings on the wall. She's seen them before, back east. Women barely covered, with perfect pointed breasts, dressed as gypsies or peasant girls, all looking with flat eyes out at the room. Their nipples are rouged and there are flowers, red and magenta, behind them. When she was a child she thought all women looked like this for their men, behind locked doors, but they changed form when they came out, molding their skin into mothers and older sisters. She believed women were magical and when she became a woman she would hold all the magic. She reasons now it is just cigarette smoke, air, the right light.

Little Tony is a smart eater. She watches him handle his chopped spaghetti with pointed fists that he sucks on, then dips again into his bowl. He always watches her and she turns her attention from the inside of her head to him. Angie smiles and blows smoke rings in the still air, popping her eyes. He laughs.

'That is one ugly baby. Another fat wop.'

Angie looks around. Who would say such a thing?

'Who said my baby is ugly?' She realizes she is shouting. She stretches her arms against the tablecloth. Her lips curl down.

'Who the fuck said my baby is ugly?'

Angie realizes the restaurant is empty. Even the bartender is in the kitchen on a break. She realizes it must be the voices, and that even now, she's talking to herself. She is suddenly aware of her last statement, a wail, something recorded for her pearl necklace. No echoes here. Her voice sinks into the wallpaper, the low piped-in music, the whirr of the air-conditioner.

'My little boy is going to be a stud, just like his father. He's going to be famous. He's going to be respected. So don't tell me lies. I can cut through a lie.'

'Are you all right?' The waitress is standing over Angie and Tony with a pizza.

'You were talking —' Angie stiffens.

'I know what I was doing. Thanks.'

The waitress puts the pizza down on a candle stand and cuts it quickly. She looks at Angie and wants to say something. Angie sees it on her face, the way her chin is crinkling.

'Is that your husband?'

Angie peers through the smoke and yellow electric wall candles. She smiles.

'Yes, that's him.'

'Ma'am. He's been here for over twenty minutes. Just standing there by the door. Didn't you see him?' Angie's palms begin to sweat. She looks up at the waitress and for a cold moment they judge one another, seeing each other's silhouettes.

'No I didn't.'

Angie watches the waitress bring Sal over. She doesn't have to. He knows where she is. Angie suddenly reasons this is a pity gesture. Sal has been watching her talk to herself for twenty minutes. So has the waitress. Perhaps they were making signals with their eyes and hands across the room, above the dim, crappy fog biting through the carpet. Perhaps they were laughing. A woman's allowed to talk to herself, out loud or even shout to herself in an empty restaurant, Angie thinks. As long as the bill is paid.

Sal stands in front of the table and rubs the top of Tony's head.

'That was quite a show you were putting on, Ange. I could sell tickets.' His voice is soft and cruel, slithering around her.

'Nice to see you, Sal.'

Sal slowly smiles. Angie looks up at his sable brown Roman hair and his blue eyes, the bluest in the world. Little Tony is laughing and forming the dada word. Angie lights another cigarette and blows towards the ceiling.

'Sit down, Sal. Have some pizza. I had them shave salami on it, just like New York. Take a load off, honey. Sit. Sit.'

As Sal sits down Angie studies her beautiful man. He is the same age I am, she thinks, and he is already old, with gray hair on his chest and on his temples. He is the tallest, meanest, stupidest and most beautiful man to come out of Brooklyn and now we're sitting in an empty restaurant in the

Valley and I chose him to be the father of my sons. My son. We are barely living together in the wrong city; hot and foreign and near dead. In this life I will pick up my own consequences, she thinks, but not always pick them well. And if I have to, I can kill, reinvent and never mourn.

Since Christopher exhaled and turned gray, Sal journeys in a different geography, weather and time of day. He is only a traveler and this could be an airport lounge, and I am part of some layover or city he tries to avoid. Angie considers. She leans back.

But certain things are good. Sal has gone back into the business and she is more than glad. She is exhilarated. She is gathering her power again because she knows what to expect.

Angie doesn't know why, but her gestures become exaggerated when Sal is around her. Teasing and coy. His eyes are staring just beyond her, in an ice, and she knows something has happened. He makes her feel like a tart when she looks into those blue eyes. Their perfection immobilizes her. She knows she can step into them at any time and not return.

'You look real nice, Angie.'

'Thanks. I put on my special blouse.' Sal takes a piece of pizza and eats, watching Angie with a full mouth. Swallowing, he grins at her, a bit of pizza on his front teeth.

'You taking the pills like the doctor said?'

'Yes, Sal.' Angie still enjoys the occasional lie.

'Good, good.' Sal keeps his eye on the bartender, who has returned to his place near the beer signs.

'I got a present for you.'

'Thanks, Sal. Really, you shouldn't.' Angie tries to inject a prettiness in her voice but fails. Sal reaches into the pocket of his maroon leather jacket and hands Angie a small satin pouch. She looks at him, then opens the pouch and laughs.

'Keep it low, Angie, I mean it.'

On her palm are two exquisite bracelets. She can tell even in this low light they are a good 18K. One is thick with diamond chips and opals, and the other is a charm bracelet with twelve gold bells smothered with baby rubies. They glitter like the real thing because they are. Angie smiles. She loves anything that can sparkle in the dark.

'These are nice.'

'Don't wear them for a couple of months.' He bends his neck and reaches over to her. Angie studies them briefly, then puts them in her purse before the waitress walks by. Sal touches her hand. It is the first time he has touched her in three weeks. The last time was when they made love, or had sex, for no other reason than old time's sake and because they had nothing to say to one another. She could see then that touch would become an infrequent gesture, one meant for signaling a new pattern to their lives, or to smooth the rocks.

'How do you feel, baby? You sure you're okay?'

'I'm fine. The doctor said I can go out now.' Angie knows she's a cool liar. It is how she will survive. This is good practice.

'I still think it's too soon. And this stuff with Tony. C'mon Angie. Stop dreaming.' Sal takes the shaved salami off his pizza.

'Tony's going to work in show business. That's the only reason I'm staying in this town.'

'What about me?'

'What about you, Sal?'

There is a compromising silence that slaps against the table. Angie decides to speak first.

'What's the matter? All of a sudden you don't like shaved salami anymore?'

'It gives me heartburn.'

'Sal, you're twenty-one years old. Already an old man.'

Sal stares at her with such viciousness Angie gasps. He begins to say something to her but stops. We live hard, Angie thinks. We got a lot on our minds. We'll forget this afternoon. Sal taps his nails on the table. Angie knows this sign. Good news. Bad news.

'I want the best for our boy. Tony's special, Sal. He's a twin.' Angie feels her voice break and her eyes sting. Little Tony has fallen asleep. She takes her compact out of her purse and lights another cigarette. She watches her husband as she powders her face. His eyes, as always, are blank. Devoid of combustion, consequence.

'I got good news, Angie. I've been in touch with some people and we're moving. Into town. Guess where?'

Angie knows that in a half hour Tony's diaper will have to be changed.

'Where?' She knows her voice sounds unreasonably flat.

'We're moving to Beverly Hills, Angie. Rent free, like we owned the place. You don't look so happy.'

Angie does not have time to assess what is happening. She knows Sal is going to deal. That is obvious. Big shipments from the south. Big risks.

Sal always loved his coke. In Brooklyn the lines never stopped. Angie understands this is what will happen and she approves. It is what they are best at. This is how they climb the ladder.

'No, Sal. I'm pleased. Are you kidding? Beverly Hills beats Panorama City. The schools are good. Tony'll know the best kids . . . I'm just kind of tired. It's my first day out, and that audition. Jesus.' Sal is oblivious. Angie knows he is not listening.

'I'm going to be gone a lot. I expect you to behave yourself. Make me proud. Make the house pretty. You'll feel better in a big pretty house. I'll see you when I'm in town.'

'Angie this, Angie that. What do you mean, when you're in town?' Angie feels her bracelets burning, writhing in her purse. Sal becomes very cold.

'What I said. Once a month, maybe. When I'm in town. For a while. Then it'll get easier.'

'Alright, Sal.'

The air is fetid, full of tomato sauce and age. Sal and Angie pause to study one another.

'Sal, why did you stand there for twenty minutes and watch me?'

'I don't know. You were like a picture. I just wanted to make sure you were okay.' Angie knows Sal speaks the words of a man who will die young. He is already memorizing indistinct moments of his life to keep himself brave. Men are fools. Men do not see fate as a woman.

Sal sighs. He digs into a pocket for a cigarette, and pulls out a tiny bottle of coke. He offers some to Angie, who declines. He makes sure no one is paying attention and takes two perfect snorts. Back into the pocket. Fool.

'You know how things are done, Angie. I can't tell you any more.'

'Just like New York.'

'Yeah, just like New York.'

All she can do is think of New York. Of Brooklyn and the river and the children, the lights and the smell of their bed where Christopher and Tony were made. And she remembers the rules.

'Good. I'm pleased. We should be back in business.'

Sal laughs and bites into a floppy piece of pizza.

'Sal?'

'Yes, sweetheart?'

'I want this restaurant. Someday.'

'What do you want a hole like this for? What the hell?'

'Just think about it. It's legal. We need something legal.' Sal looks around, and confident the bartender is not listening, smiles. It is a big smile, and he rubs his neck.

'You're always planning ahead, Angie.'

'Just like my grandmother.'

'I guess.' Sal stares at his sleeping son.

'You've got to be careful about going out, Angie. With this new place you'll never have to go out. They have servants and stuff. You get upset so quick. I saw you in here. Now you won't –'

'Now I won't . . . what?' Sal takes a breath.

'Now you can get better. You know, after Christopher, I did a lot of thinking. About things.'

'What kind of things, Sal?' Angie stares at Tony, touching his sleeping, clenched fists. Sal doesn't say anything, and when she looks away from Tony into the face of her husband, she sees a man who is leaving forever.

'This is for the best, at least for now. We've still got a boy to think –' Angie watches his eyes glaze over and his lower lip curl down.

This will be a time for gifts, Angie perceives. A season of exile and intention. Sal will be in South America and I will be in Beverly Hills, losing control, just like my grandmother said. I will buy this restaurant with drug money and I will grow old in this restaurant. I will never go back to New York or feel snow seeping through my boots. Sal won't last long. He'll be extinguished by some kid who doesn't speak English. My husband will be left under a thick green mountain full of parrots and coca leaves and I'll remarry someone else in the business because it's the only kind of man I understand. My dead husband's stupid soul will search for his son until it finds this place, old and tainted, a noiseless memory with a spaghetti machine and red gold wallpaper. And I'll be here, remarried, feeling the old air in this booth.

'Eat your pizza, Sal. It's good.' Angie lights another cigarette and watches him. She's not hungry. She hasn't seen him for a week and he looks scrawny. Too much coke. He's with another broad, that's for sure. It is part of tradition. It is everything they have been groomed for. Angie thinks of peering inside the chrysalis to see who formed them. Who tells women like her to wear gold bangles sliding up their arms and purchase memory by them, or associate their lives by something with a clasp that glitters and scrapes in the right light.

'So where are the keys?'

Sal tosses a set of freshly made, bright copper keys across the table at her.

'You can move any time. Tonight if you want. The address is on the keychain.' Angie rubs the keys between her fingers.

'Whatever you say, honey. Tony'll wake up in about ten, fifteen minutes.' Sal knows his cue. He rises and goes over to Angie, kissing her on the cheek, very formal, then on the lips. She has it memorized. She touches her arms. She runs one finger along her long, sharp pink nails and watches Sal walk out into the withered white of Ventura Boulevard.

Angie notices the waitress has been watching them from the shadows, her check in hand. She signals her to come to the table.

'Good looking man, isn't he, Nina. His son's going to be even better looking. A real stud.' The waitress blushes and begins to say something, but changes her mind.

'What time is it?' Angie lays down her cash and Nina glances at her watch as she picks the cash up.

'About four o'clock. We start the early bird dinners about four-thirty. Should be a lot of people in shortly.' The waitress pauses.

'You don't plan on staying, do you?'

Angie ignores her and looks once more around the room.

'What kind of dinner trade you get in here?'

Nina seems taken. She almost smiles.

'Mostly retired folks. On a budget.'

Nina leaves. Angie sees the bartender is asleep to the hum of the football game. He will wake up and I'll be gone. He won't care.

Angie can feel the air-conditioning directly on her face and it has a mesmerized, comforting feel. She goes into her purse and puts on her new bracelets. Screw Sal. What has been given to me no one can take away. Or become suspicious of.

The bells on the charm bracelet go with this place, Angie thinks. Their rubies are dull as any fire seen from a great distance; a point of heat that glows and warns. She shakes her arm and the bells lightly jingle. She hears the church where she was born, where the twins should have been christened. She hears the bells of river-front schools with tangled weeds where little girls become Angies and are toxic to everything they touch; little girls who wind up with everything because they have to have it, or die.

Her thoughts splash in air. Angie says to herself, clenching the tablecloth; I am twenty-one and I have a dead son, a dead husband and seven bracelets on each arm. I come from a nest of women to whom such numbers and facts are prophecies. My son will be a killer like his father and I will struggle to keep from flying apart. I will go anywhere I can hide, and today, in this dark place, I can plot how to do it, because it is written on my arm like a fire of bells, the lips of an old woman and a snow that won't leave me, intense as whatever is outside and waiting in the heat.

Tony is still asleep. Angie carries him, nestled against her breasts, to the front door. As she opens it, she staggers, then convulses from the laundered, liquid hot air, murmuring rotten, rotten, and spits into the smell of palm blossoms and auto exhaust. I will pray tonight, she murmurs, I will pray tonight in my new house, and she walks out, absorbed into the haze like any smart animal who is running from the brush.

casa alegre

IT IS LABOR DAY, September 5, 1921, and Fatty Arbuckle is drunk. He does not realize that Virginia Rappe, who he has just screwed with the end of a bottle and a chunk of ice, is dying in front of him of peritonitis. Fatty, being a real card, just laughs it away in his suite at the St Francis Hotel in San Francisco.

The news hits Hollywood overnight and Happy Sams, who worked with Fatty on many a Mack Sennett comedy before Fatty became a star, has his eyes on a piece of property Fatty owns just south of the Beverly Hills Hotel. Once Arbuckle is conveniently behind bars, Happy contacts Fatty's lawyer, and with his trademark laugh, a high squeak like a cat having its tail yanked, Happy Sams buys Fatty's one and only piece of California for less than it would cost to stay at the Astor Hotel in New York for one night. Happy is pleased with himself. He thinks, you dumb fat son of a bitch with no prick, you did the same thing I woulda done, only you got caught.

Happy Sams will build his legendary home here, calling it 'Casa Alegre'. Happy will build many office buildings, a synagogue on Wilshire Boulevard, half of Warner Brothers Studio, and a casino just outside Palm Springs that will be raided and closed in 1931. Arbuckle will die broke and in obscurity, but Happy Sams will make eighty-seven pictures, be awarded an Honorary Oscar in the early seventies, and secretly kill two seventeen-year-old girls he had in 1927. They, along with several other unknowns, and the worst thing to be in Hollywood is to be completely unknown when you die, will be buried in the monastery-like garden of Casa Alegre, on a succession of hot July evenings, and will not be found until 1991, weeks after Eve has visited this immense ruin and claimed it for her own.

Who is Eve? She is completely unknown. She is young, only just thirty, with extremely blonde hair and a tanned, childlike face. Her lipstick is a dusty silver-pink. She wears heavy gold jewelry, white linen, and sandals. She is an alcoholic.

Eve is married to a much older man, who is also an alcoholic. He is rich, kind, and very relaxed. Other women whisper about Eve. They say she married for money. They are wrong.

At night Eve dreams in color as the Bombay Sapphire Gin constricts her veins. She sees a beautiful house; old, with history, heavy stone and a tangle of vines. The house on the top of the hill; the house on a cliff by a sea; any sea, with turrets and incredible sky.

Eve loves to dream of this house, which changes its walls and windows nightly. In this house she does not see her husband, or the family she walked away from, or the lovers she's had. She cannot see herself, either, but she knows she is there – like a caretaker. Unseen, but committed to perfection.

Scandal will break again, and Eve will read about Casa Alegre and its landmark status. The City of Beverly Hills will try and hush the whole thing up, so the City can get back to doing what it does best; the quiet handling and shuffling of the fortunes of the world. But Eve won't forget.

For two hours Casa Alegre was hers. Eve owned it without paper and the house knew she was there. The house was both obscene and obsolete, abandoned and hissing with charm. No one cared if a lonely young woman walked through it and tried to breathe in all parts of its being. Or that precisely at this point of her life, alcoholic and lurching through canyon afternoons and hushed, rich homes of other alcoholics, she would suddenly be in an empty house with an absolute power to absorb and dismiss someone else's life.

Two weeks after Eve walks out of Casa Alegre with her treasures, a munitions dealer from the Mediterranean will buy it at full price for his daughter, who doesn't like the house anyway, having seen a picture of it at her home in the South of France. Staying within boating distance of the Casino at Monte Carlo, she will fax plans to a Beverly Hills based design firm to begin renovations, which will finally unearth many skeletons in the garden. Altogether five, but there is speculation that there may be more under the house itself which, unfortunately, is not being torn down. His daughter will have the house painted titty pink and plant a fortune in Egyptian reeds on the front lawn. She will never bother to fly to LA to see the house or live there.

Eve will no longer use the street as a shortcut, because she hates seeing how people destroy her favorite houses.

Eve's husband Wayne tells her to stay away from the house, that it carries a lot of bad stories and scandal.

'Some houses are like that, you know. Just bad news.'

He goes on about what this area was like in the fifties, with cocktail parties and shootings and women in taffeta who dressed three and four times a day. How the DeSotos and

Cadillacs were huge and polished and hot, and the flower gardens were magnificent.

They are passing Casa Alegre on their way to a party on Elevado, near Whittier Drive, at the house where Bugsy Siegel was murdered. It is another December of warm, calculated air. Roads and front lawns are slippery with moist, fallen jacaranda blossoms and their syrup.

'It's a beautiful old Spanish house, Wayne, and it's a fixer. Everything's possible in life. You always said that.' Eve had wandered through empty houses for months, in contaminated iris yellow afternoons when the city rolls with the ease of someone bedridden and alert. In her frantic imaginations, maybe they could afford Casa Alegre, and she says so.

'Dream on. That house is millions of dollars. And that kind of money we don't have.'

Eve lights a cigarette and studies the invitation. Glittery stars fall out of it on the seat and Wayne curses.

'I am so damnably tired of these theme parties.'

Suddenly Eve feels the last of these old houses in this pretentious, scalped-clean street. They still hold the echoes of the women who married their men for money and walked through halls in an icy execution of not being. Their footsteps had the same rhythm of the fountains and the Eucalyptus shielding the golf courses from view. A rhythm of quiet control.

'Besides, certain houses in life are simply not meant to be lived in. Not because they are haunted or any of that rubbish, but because the ego that built them takes over and poisons any and everything around it. Now you don't want that, do you? You are trying to be far more sophisticated than that, I do hope.'

'Of course. I suppose I am.' Eve stubs her cigarette out and lets it rest. It is another party with the same group, and they will both smile when they walk through the front door. Eve will test that same smile in thirty more houses over the next six months, some empty and waiting for me to deliver my own particular brand of artifice to their barren light, saying buy me, I will be your life. I will let you live the way you've always wanted to. Buy me.

Happy Sams is a happy kind of guy. Nothing bothers him too much. He does his schtick at the studio and gets paid well. He's no Chaplin, but the public likes the way he mugs and does all the Keystone stunts. Happy's worked with Swanson, Mabel Normand, and Mary Pickford. Mary was the one who told him to buy up land in Beverly Hills and he has, figuring the way things are going he'll unload in a year or two for a tidy profit.

Happy loves women, loves the way they smile when he pokes them good and hard in his big, draped bed. Even though he's only five feet they all tell him he knows what to do, that he's a giant. He's also found he likes to see a little pain, that it gets him hot.

At the end of 1921 he decides to marry Constance Mac-Murray, who's making it big as a protégé of D.W. Griffith's and dumb as a cow, but pretty, with an angelic smile and a tiny voice that smells of Iowa. Happy doesn't like D.W. or any of his arty, what price is entertainment, crowd, and does not invite them to the wedding. Only the Hearst syndicate is allowed and, of course, the family, and Happy gets some serious publicity and a $500 a week raise.

Six months into their marriage Happy takes Connie over

to see this lot he stole from that dumb fuck Arbuckle, pointing to their future in a lot full of high grass and sunflowers. Connie just wrinkles her nose and takes out her compact.

'So, whaddya think, Connie? I'm going to build us a palace right here. Whaddya say to ten thousand feet of bedrooms and onyx bathrooms with gold faucets? The works. Whaddya say?'

'Fine with me, Mr H. But why do we have to live so far west? No one lives out here.'

Happy slaps Connie so hard she lands on her side and breaks three ribs.

'I'm doin' this for you, Connie. Now get up.'

Nothing is said. Constance loses a diamond bracelet in the fall, and it stays lost in the wild, high grass for six months until one of the construction workers finds it on his shovel. Happy, ever shrewd in matters of money, quickly thanks the man and pockets it, giving him a dollar tip.

Happy is pleased, as it won't be going back to Connie. She is dying at the Angels of Mercy Hospital; her broken ribs, undetected and ignored by both of them, have become infected and there is internal bleeding, now causing a painful and bitter death. Happy chuckles to himself, thinking this little bracelet is going to buy him some pretty pussy indeed.

When Connie dies, Happy is adamant that her face, and particularly her bee-stung lips, be perfectly made for the photographers, with himself bereft at the foot of the bed. Connie's bronze casket is adorned with one silver-mauve rose, courtesy of Happy. As he collapses at the stairs of the Hollywood mausoleum, the fans and the newspapers go insane. Happy's salary is raised to $5,000 a week.

It takes two years for Casa Alegre to be completed. When Happy takes up residence, the living room has vaulted ceilings with frescoes, a hidden pipe organ, walk-in fireplaces at each end of the room with Florentine mantels, cedar closets, and in the back of the house there is an earthquake proof vault, lined in iron, with a bronze door made especially for Happy by the Wells Fargo Company.

The house itself is patterned after a monastery, with a three tier fountain in the central garden, and a lush, tiled loggia with marble columns on all four sides. In the back of the house is a blue tiled swimming pool, a badminton court, a pool house with four bedrooms, men's and women's locker rooms, and a small theatre, where Happy shows his highly prized collection of stag films to studio heads and investors; friends one and all.

At the party Eve is talking to Moira, a tiny woman with glittery clothes. 'Men love women who are petite,' is Moira's opening line. Eve has heard it often. Everyone here has an opening line.

'You live on Whittier,' Eve whispers. 'Tell me about that big Spanish place just below Sunset.'

'It's a tear down,' sniffs Moira. 'The bathrooms stink, lousy kitchen. Who needs it?'

'I quite like it.' As Eve says this, Moira turns, putting down her diamanté frog-shaped purse, and smiles.

'Why, Eve darling. I didn't know you were in that kind of bracket.'

'Is it big?'

'Huge.'

Eve smiles and sips her drink. The room is getting a good fuzz to it, like a candle-lit dinner in a movie.

*　　　*　　　*

Happy's second wife is Iris, whom Happy meets at the races in Tijuana. Iris is a showgirl for Ziegfeld. She is no true beauty, but a sexual gymnast *par excellence*, and they stay married two years, until Valentine's Day, 1925, when Iris is found floating in Santa Monica Bay in an evening gown. Happy knows Iris is sleeping around, but he has been filming with Laurel and Hardy in the Arizona desert and, once again, is totally and utterly despondent.

Iris, not being in pictures, is passed over by the press, as Thomas Ince had just been shot by William Randolph Hearst on the yacht *Oneida*, after a tryst with Marion Davies, or so legend attests. Traveling by studio car from Tucson, Happy puts Iris quietly in her crypt, just down the hall from Connie, at Hollywood Memorial. He is relieved not having to worry about family, as Iris was one of those girls who had changed her name many, many times.

Happy never spends money unless it is on himself, and he begins to worry he is not as funny as he should be. W.C. Fields is being lured to pictures from Ziegfeld, and Harold Lloyd and Chaplin make much bigger pictures than he. He decides not to marry until he is completely on top, and that takes time. There are a million whores in town he can hurt for a laugh, so his recreation won't go away, only his possible respectability, but his best friends are the heads, so who gives a damn.

He has also found the younger the flesh the better, and that includes various young girls and the occasional young boy who seem to vanish after visiting Uncle Happy. In 1927 Betty and Cara pose a great problem for Happy. Adorable seventeen-year-old girls, identical twins with carrot red hair and white skin, they threaten to expose, along with their hawk-like mother, Happy's passion for rope ties and the oral arts.

This could be changed with a generous gift, perhaps a quarter of a million dollars, which the girls and their mother know that Happy has. But he pays no attention, immersing himself in his work, grinding out five features in three months, and ignoring Betty and Cara's calls.

When their mother is found gagged and stabbed to death in a boarding house in Culver City, the girls are frantic, and decide to visit Happy on a mild Sunday in July, right after church. Determined to confront him with the murder, they take along a small recorder they steal from a sound studio, the smallest they can find which, in 1927, is difficult. But Happy knows what they are up to, and soon as they close the enormous Philippine mahogany double doors of the front hall, Happy shoots them both in the face with a pearl-handled revolver given to him by Teddy Roosevelt.

One of the girls is still twitching and Happy just laughs, shooting at her some more. At this moment Happy realizes that comedy is cruelty, that this is very funny stuff. Ever practical, Happy sorts through the girls' wallets, cash and jewelry before he buries them that evening in the garden. Above them he will plant two white rose bushes, affectionately called 'The Twins' until his death in 1986.

That very same evening Happy is annoyed because he has to go to their house and eliminate all traces of their existence, and he has a very early call in the morning. What he finds surprises him. The twins, and their mother, had quite a racket going with some very important men in town. Their house is still loaded with cash and jewelry, and Happy, being a shrewd investor, uses this small profit to buy more land on Wilshire Boulevard, which he will later donate to a synagogue.

*   *   *

Eve thinks about what it would be like to be 'in that bracket', and sips her drink on the terrace. She is sitting on a vinyl covered bamboo chair and it makes her dress ride up her thigh and she decides, let it. Perhaps in the right bracket I wouldn't have to count my sins. Perhaps in the right house I would feel clean, do whatever I damn well pleased. There must be a way, Eve thinks, to fall into 'that bracket'. It must be a fall. She can't imagine it being a climb.

Finally, in 1929, Happy has his first international hit, *Doris In Danger*. He is also furious that sound has come in. The Great Depression hasn't fazed him, with his vault and land. What terrifies Happy is sound, and the sound of his own voice, shrill and high and unmanly. Knowing comedy better than his peers, he works hard to create a character that chatters and shrieks like a baboon, dressed in a loud pinstripe suit and bowler hat, and this turn of effects puts Happy in the top ranks, with Garbo and Harlow and the Marx Brothers.

Happy becomes so respected and rich he joins every country club in town, and at the Wilshire Country Club he meets his third wife, Mary Ellen Dodson-Stone, from a *very* founding family. He decides to change his old tricks, at least in front of his wife, and through the thirties all the way into the fifties, the Sams were an ideal movieland couple, until Mary Ellen decides to plant fuchsias in the central garden. Mary Ellen, highly bred with exquisite teeth, was always frail of health. What she finds, in her plaid sun skirt, gardening gloves and large Jamaican sun hat, gives her a stroke so sudden and severe she dies over a large mound of mulch, face down. Happy is still half asleep, waking up late after a roast in his honor at the Friar's Club, and he has to quickly smooth his garden over before the maid comes back from the market.

Happy buries Mary Ellen in a more expensive section of Hollywood Memorial, and goes to visit his wives on a regular basis, chatting on and on about day-to-day things. He always feels so much better after his visits.

In the sixties he still makes movies, although the parts are smaller. Happy Sams still has his sexual wanderings, but now they are less violent and concerned more with aesthetics, like voyeurism. He goes to swing parties and drugged-out fiestas where Happy, now hitting sixty-eight, is the life of the party, standing naked and fat in the middle of the room, doing his old routines until someone remembers him and he can get laid.

Then it is always back to Casa Alegre, dark and simmering, where Happy turns on the sprinklers and smokes a good cigar. He walks through the distilled, fragrant rooms and thinks about what was really funny and what wasn't. Comedians never laugh but they know what is funny, and Happy feels he should write a book, on the art of being funny, how life is valueless, how you can be king.

'Right here. This is where Bugsy was gunned down.'

The hostess of the party guides Eve into a nondescript room. She turns on more lights and continues her tour.

'They say there were bloodstains they couldn't get out, but I don't see a thing. Do you?'

Eve shakes her head. The luxurious murmur of the party comes through the hall. Eve points to a black and white photograph on the wall.

'That's him,' her hostess says in a breathy, reverent voice.

'How many bullets?'

267

'Maybe a hundred. It was a machine gun.'

Eve smiles.

'He wasn't bad looking.'

'Are you kidding? He was utterly *divine*.' The hostess sighs and turns off the lights.

In 1975 Happy receives an Honorary Oscar, and does the old baboon schtick before a wildly appreciative industry crowd. Watching him and smiling is his new wife, Yvonne, twenty-nine and beautiful. To Happy, it felt like he had finally met a wife he could trust and enjoy, and even though an operation for cancer of the prostate had left him impotent, he truly cared for Yvonne, who, at six feet tall, was a dream Amazon. By 1986, Happy is confined to a wheelchair, suffering from severe emphysema. Yvonne, knowing she has spent ten of the happiest years of her life with Happy, throws him in his own walk-in Wells Fargo safe, closes and locks it, and tapes the sides of the doors.

The next week the newspapers run a lovely, full picture obituary of Happy Sams, who died in his sleep of the complications of emphysema and old age. That he was an endearing Hollywood star is irrefutable and, of course, his civic and charitable contributions to modern day Los Angeles are well documented. But more importantly, he left Yvonne close to a hundred million dollars.

And it is here, at the end of his life, sprawled and gasping for air, that Happy thinks about sitting at the club, playing cards with other men who look into his eyes and know he is the same monster as they, psychopaths who kill their wives and destroy their children, and yet have built this city, glittering like cutlery and floating in Hibiscus and steam. And Happy

Sams is a rich man with a rich history who has given more than most. Where would Wilshire Boulevard be without him? Or Warner Brothers and NBC? We owe him the way we think.

Eve often wonders if there is something wrong with her. How vacant houses, still possessing the grime and perfume of another life, reach out to her and beg for something she cannot decipher. Wayne has always told her she sees everything in beautiful terms. That she leads a charmed life.

Perhaps. After seeing Casa Alegre the night before, with its sign half fallen in a gardenia bush, she is determined to see it today. Eve remembers dragging Wayne, seven years before, to the old Norma Talmadge mansion in Los Feliz that Norma and her husband, Joe Schenck, built as a tribute to their happiness. MGM lions were poised against walls of grimacing, stained plaster, and they guarded with one foot up the base of travertine stairs. They were eight feet high and snarled like watchdogs at an Abyssinian tomb.

It was the same thing then, and she was just twenty-three. *I want this. This is where we should move to.* Wayne sneered and rolled his eyes, saying it's garish and huge and all this stone is cold in the winter. It's not made for refined living but for people who cannot live with themselves; their spirits will hover over us and bitch. We would be miserable here.

Eve thought, not me. She wanted the tarnish to rub off like a suntan. She wanted to wear a caftan and walk up those immense stone stairs and feel the breeze of two-story windows, secular and grandiose and full of religion. She wanted to hear her footsteps echo and see the city light up every night like a whore in a safe bar. She wanted it all and knew she could mold herself.

The first thing Eve realizes as she walks into Casa Alegre is that no one gives a damn. Not the stockholders next door who would have torn it down if they could have afforded it, and built something white and laden with steel. Wayne told her she was a fool, that she could be arrested for trespassing. Eve said, nonsense; there's a sign in the front and that's the invitation.

The front doors are left open by painters, with paints and buckets everywhere, but the silence is sullen, open, and juvenile. A test. No one is here. In the enormous living room there is a sofa from the twenties that looks like it was sawed in half, and the sheets covering windows have tiny lace birds sewn on, so, when the wind moves, they fly.

This is a house of long hallways and closed doors, only now everything is open and flies are hovering around bathrooms where the toilets have been ripped out, the precious onyx toilets, and moist holes in the floor beckon. Eve walks through every room, deciding how she would paint them in brilliant colors to catch the heat of the afternoon sun; Chinese red, amethyst, candlelight yellow.

The inner courtyard overflows with roses that have become trees, and Japanese Magnolias. She sees two exquisite white rose bushes and looks around for some garden scissors, thinking she will cut them and put them in a bag to take up to the house, but when she gets closer, Eve sees they are covered in ants and lice.

The fountain is all stone angels and fish, black with dried algae, and Eve makes mental notes on how it should be cleaned; on the parties Wayne and she could throw in the garden, with pink tablecloths and hurricane lamps and tinseled mariachis playing something slow into the dusk.

Happy Sams and his wives threw many beautiful parties here, where the men patted each other on the back, and their women traded secrets on men and jewelry and hot, hot places where they went to rest. There was laughter and film stars moving around delicately hushed, relaxed, and impeccable.

Eve walks slowly through the house and speaks to it as though it is hers. She wants to pet it and soothe it with words meant for tiny animals who have taken a fall, or become blind in old age and do not understand.

She finds the pool house and the screening room and it frightens her. Someone homeless may be living here, as homeless as she sometimes feels, and she doesn't want to interrupt them. If they live here it is their house too, and she would be intruding. No one is here. No one wants this place.

The screening room has one window, blacked out and covered by heavy drapes. Everything is ruby red velvet. There are ten rows of seats, eight seats each, with elaborately carved backs that spell out the letterhead of the Orpheum Circuit. Silence. Eve can hear flies. She walks with a quiet delirium through each row, running her hands over the tops of the seats, until she sees the front row center seat, with 'Happy Sams' spelled out in gold letters, and the masks of comedy and tragedy underneath. There is a telephone attached to the seat, connected by a padded, thick black wire that disappears into the wall.

Eve picks up the receiver. The line still works, and she starts laughing. Then she calls Wayne.

'You will never believe where I am.'

'Oh Christ. God only knows.'

'I'm sitting at Casa Alegre, the Happy Sams place. And I'm sitting in his private screening room, in his own chair, talking on his own private phone. What do you think of THAT?'

'Get out of that house.'

'It is so beautiful here. We could live here. I know we could.'

'Forget it.'

'No one is here. The phone still works. Can you believe it?'

'Get out of that house. You know the police in Beverly Hills. How they get.'

Eve is having a lot of fun. She is suddenly important.

'The phone must be connected for the caretaker or the painters or something.'

'You're going to get arrested.'

'Look. There's a "For Rent" sign and the doors are open.'

If the police arrested her, she would be famous.

'Get out of that house.'

His voice becomes steely and he hangs up the phone. Eve slowly puts the polished black receiver back in its place, and smiles to herself.

She walks through this church of wasps, honeybees, and shadows. Eve doesn't realize she has been walking over graves and dreaming in the air of a killer. In the main house she finds Happy Sams' safe, the door held open by an onyx toilet, and she walks inside, running her hands over the carvings on the bronze door. When her grandmother died, Eve had dreams of doors like this; of pink marble mausoleums and women who came up from the earth with heavy steps that made her heart flutter and her feet twitch.

Now, in Happy Sams' safe, surrounded by boxes full of

photographs from the twenties and mildewed correspondence, Eve grabs with lazy, carpetbagger's arms through mementos the last Mrs Sams did not feel were important. She reads Happy's love letters to Connie and Iris and Mary Ellen, and to other women where he included crude pornographic drawings. She finds matches from 'The Stork Club', 'Ciro's', and 'LaRue' with numbers written and then crossed out. She finds pictures of women being tied up, dressed in expensive black negligées and wearing thick, 1940s high heels. Every woman was blind-folded, and her lips gashed with liver red lipstick. Eve finds cheery notes from Gable and Darryl F. Zanuck thanking the Sams for another happy party, and then notes that Happy wrote to himself about comedy. How to make people laugh. He wrote: 'It's all in the way you walk out and let them know. The audience is one person and that one person is a stupid son of a bitch. He'll laugh at anything as long as you let him know it is supposed to be funny. If you can do that, then everything is funny, and you get away with murder.'

Eve runs her hands over the photographs. She looks closely. One of these women was her. She knows it.

She doesn't know if she was a hooker in lingerie with a gag in her mouth. Or if she was one of the wives, fresh from Two Bunch Palms, sitting next to Clark Gable, wearing a ruby brooch, a beige silk turban and a constant blank, surprised expression.

Eve realizes each of these women was just as nameless as the next, vultures hiding as orchids, as much of a nobody as her, only there to serve someone else's purpose. She begins to want to cry, and suddenly wants a drink. A big one with a lot of ice.

Then Eve finds something at the bottom of the box, velvety and soft. She pulls it out and papers flutter and disintegrate as though they are burnt. It is a casket-shaped, very deco, black velvet jewelry box with the initials 'CS', for Connie Sams. Inside there are pictures of her with D.W. Griffith on the Babylon set of *Intolerance*, with Lillian and Dorothy Gish, and a picture of Connie and Gloria Swanson posing with a sea lion on the beach. She was beautiful.

Eve takes everything. Death certificates, pictures, matches, letters, and pornography, shoving them into that black velvet jewelry box, and walks again through the house, knowing no one is coming today, the casket under her arm.

It is now she realizes, as she walks out into the Beverly Hills haze, that you can own whatever you want; that it's yours to be taken. You can own it for two hours or for fifty years, and take someone else's life home in a jewelry box on a languid afternoon of no motives, and no one will care. And there will always be one last person who will know more about you than you ever thought possible, and you will have never met. But they will know everything.